LEGEND OF THE BLUE OWL

LEGEND OF THE BLUE OWL

❁

Wayne Parrish

Morro Press
Cayucos

Legend of the Blue Owl
All Rights Reserved by Wayne Parrish

Morro Press

Cover Design by
Rocki de Llamas

Front cover painting by Ted De Grazia
Courtesy of De Grazia Gallery in the Sun

ISBN 0-972-5000-4-9

Printed in the United States of America

PROLOGUE

Night came and with it a cold wind. I'itoi sat in the entrance of the cave and warmed his gnarled hands over a small bed of glowing mesquite coals. Earlier he had smoked the strong tobacco that made him listless. He watched the bright warriors and the winter moon move across the sky. All the signs and omens told him that the bad times had come again.

I'itoi held up a fiery ember and stared owlishly at the figures the cave guardians had drawn over the millennia on the smoke-blackened walls. A horny toad, beads of water pecked on its back, marked the departure of the Old People. They left after the Great River had run too low to feed their canals and the lakes had turned into salt marshes.

Pale half-men, half-animals, carrying sticks that belched fire and thunder had appeared in the south searching for yellow stones and slaves. These fearsome monster-men had put their marks over those of the Wanderers and the Old People who were there before them on the sacred boulder that stood beside the marshy lake. A spotted lizard symbolized the plague that had struck down the Wanderers. Their young had died clutching their groins, fire arrows protruded from their bellies. The carved faces expressed shock and horror.

The rock drawings told I'itoi many things: of a man struck by lightning; of a child killed by a rattlesnake; of eclipses, floods, droughts, earthquakes, and meteor showers. In the moon following the meteor shower, the Yumans had attacked and stolen the harvest. In the spring, the floods came and destroyed the fields.

Much later, the brown-robes had ventured as far north as the earth dwelling of the powerful shaman-chieftain, Morning Blue, which sat some distance from the wide bend of the river. They begged for food and the people had given them baskets of corn, pumpkins, mesquite beans and the agave fruit. The brown-robes had gone away, but they left behind a coughing sickness that killed young and old alike. Even Curing Woman's skills could not prevent the deaths.

Morning Blue blamed the disaster on HA-AK, the evil giant girl-child of his unmarried daughter, Woman-Who-Makes-Sleeping-Mats. Morning Blue told I'itoi to inscribe these tragic events so that the rocks would speak of them forever.

I'itoi prepared for the arduous work by fasting and smoking strong tobacco. He had let his heart tell his hands what to do. First he selected large rocks in the right shapes from the holy mountain on the east end of the vast valley and had them carried to his cave on the lone butte that overlooked the marshy lake.

Using a hammer and an awl made from the sacred stone that fell from the sky, he inscribed a different figure on each rock. He scraped the soft metal from the yellow cross and the other foreign objects that the brown-robes had left in the pit they had dug near I'itoi's home in the earth. He hammered the filings into the eye sockets of the blue owl that he had inscribed so carefully.

After finishing this task, I'itoi had prayed to the Earth Mother and the Sky Father for a vision, and the Earth Mother had blessed him. Once again, he would be a savior to his people. According to his vision, the people must break up into clans and scatter in the directions of the four winds. He told the people they must collect their shields, leave their houses, and each clan should separate. One to the east; another to the west; the third to the north; and I'itoi's clan to the south.

The Earth Mother told I'itoi that the clans should not return to this place, the center of everything sacred, until she sent them a sign. They must leave behind the objects that once belonged to the Old People. All the rag-dolls and kick-balls must be placed in the cave along with the glass beads and bells the brown-robes had given them.

All this I'itoi devotedly inscribed on the chosen rocks and boulders inside the cave. Only in this way will the clans be forgiven for burning HA-AK. The Earth Mother had told I'itoi that he must remain there forever and guard the rocks that speak.

The sun came up sluggishly. The first rays cast a reddish glow on the lone butte, dispersing a false gray dawn, changing into paler hues of bluish-gray. A velvety shadow at the cave entrance contrasted with the brilliant incandescent light as the sun climbed higher.

Overhead an eagle soared across the cobalt sky, creating a dark shadow that sliced across the yellow ochre earth below. A green-gold eyed lizard slithered inside, and after a brief halt, sped swiftly past I'itoi into the darkened interior and perched beside a small pool of water that had seeped down from a crevice above its head.

Outside the cave a drum began to beat. A singer's song lifted in the air:

> *"Hear I'itoi our prayer, purify the land, water,*
> *and air.*
> *Protect us on our journeys to the four directions.*
> *Spare us from enemies, sickness, and witches."*

At the beat of the drum, the men smartly raised their shields and pounded the ground. The dancers had wood coverings on their heads, woven bands on their arms, and rabbit fur bodices and kit-foxtails on their rumps. The deer bones on their ankles jangled as they imitated the movements of the deer and other creatures. Their bare arms and breasts were painted with red ochre from the canyon walls, with black mud from shale, with white made from pale clay, with brown from the sandstone, and with yellow and violet made from cactus flowers.

I'itoi tasted the sacred pollen made from the blue corn flowers and blew a handful into the air. He tossed his prayer bundle made from owl feathers onto the fire. The blue smoke drifted upward through the spirit chimney as he began his song:

> *"Tcutcunoni ko'kovoli sis'vunuka-a*
> *Apu tuvavki wunanita.*
> *Apu tuvavki wunanita.*

The Blue Owl is bright
And happy when we leave her home alone.
And happy when we leave her home alone."

The first baskets full of stones that would forever separate I'itoi from his world tumbled down and blocked the cave entrance. Morning Blue's voice rang out and echoed in the chamber: "Farewell I'itoi. You are no more, but you will be remembered... forever."

CHAPTER 1

A cloud of caliche dust floated behind the 1936 Ford pick-up, obscuring the overpass where Ocotillo Road crossed over Interstate 10. Jack Reed centered the truck on the washboard road and tried to avoid the deeper ruts. He dodged a pothole and the back axle shuddered as the rear wheels scrambled for a grip on the shale surface.

A cattle pen, with a stack of dog-eared straw bales, cow piles and human detritus bordered the left side of the track. On the right, a ragged curtain fluttered out of a paneless window of a demolished Airstream trailer. Rusted bedsprings and a rotted mattress rested under a palo verde tree. Dashing out from under a tractor tire, half buried in the sandy wash, a roadrunner outpaced the truck and veered into the brush.

The road dropped down into a gully, crossed a cow-guard and climbed straight up the face of a second ridge. A twelve-foot wide, brightly painted white gate blocked the road. The truck skidded to a halt in front of a large sign that was riddled with bullet holes:

> Ocotillo Ranch
> No Trespassing
> No Hunting
> No Shooters
> No Motorcycles
> No Off-Road Vehicles

"Someone doesn't believe in signs," Jack said. He reached out the window, pulled a bar and swung the gate open. He drove through the wide gap and stopped the truck. The door creaked when he pushed it open with his shoulder. As Jack stepped out, a puff of powdery silt covered his boots. He put a foot on the bottom rail and rode the gate while it swung backwards and slammed into the support post.

"Damn," Jack said, rubbing his shinbone and focusing his eyes on the crude drawings etched on a huge half-domed boulder that sat at the base of the ridge. A pair of incised eyes stared owlishly back at him. An arrow pointed to a double spiral higher up the face of the rock. Shotgun pellets had blasted a stick-figure man, drawn by some ancient hand. Bullet scars also marred the other figures on the rock. "Jerks, mindless macho jerks. Hurray for the NRA!" Jack shouted. He reached into the truck, grabbed a bottle of spring water, and swallowed deeply, clearing the dust from his throat.

Jack crossed a narrow gully and climbed to the top of the ridge. The desert flattened to the south, forming a basin that lowered gradually to the well house and beyond to Mollie Gentry's dairy farm where a laborer was tossing bales of hay off the top of a massive haystack to the cattle milling below.

Beyond the dairy, white-topped cotton fields stretched for another five miles before the land turned brown and barren, marking the beginning of the Indian Reservation. The San Tans stretched in a long line eastward towards the Superstitions; all but the tips were lost in a cloud of dust and brown haze. On the other side of the freeway, an endless sea of pink tiled roofs marched westward. "The Californians are coming," Jack said. The South Mountain range ran from east to west for twenty miles, cutting off any view of Phoenix.

A dust devil swirled across the alkali sand in the lakebed where the ancient HoHoKam canals ended their journey. To the west, broken glass glazed purple by the searing desert sun glittered in the graveled shards. Two gigantic eucalyptus trees towered over the adobe ranch house, stable, tool shed, ramada, and orchard. Terraced cactus gardens surrounded the buildings, the verdant blue-green contrasting vividly with the whitewashed adobe walls and rock buildings. A bent figure of a man was raking the gravel yard.

"Old Ruiz!" Jack almost shouted. The roadrunner approached the top of the ridge, eyed Jack warily with one eye, and turned the other towards a blue-green lizard with golden eyes. "What will I tell the old man?" Jack asked the roadrunner. "This place is mine now, Ruiz. The entire 160 acres. Mine to live in, mine to sell, and mine to pay the taxes. Why did they build here? They might as well have built a ramada on the rim of Popocatepetl."

The roadrunner rushed the lizard and dashed off into the brush holding a quivering blue-green tail proudly in its mouth. The tailless lizard scrambled under a rock. "Everybody's a winner," Jack said. "God, how I hate this place!"

Paco, Ruiz's dog, part Aussie and part coyote, raced out of the yard barking furiously. Jack parked the truck under a rustic ramada. Aged ironwood posts supported a roof of ocotillo branches, covered with long palm fronds that offered some protection from the blistering summer sun. Sunbeams filtered through and danced across a perfectly stacked cord of wood.

Jack stepped out of the truck and dropped one knee to the ground, "Come here, boy." Paco hesitated for a moment and then rushed forward, nearly bowling him over. Jack wrapped his arms around the dog and hugged him as Paco affectionately licked his face.

Ruiz was waiting for him, his straw cowboy hat crossed over his chest. "Buenos dias, Jefe," he said solemnly, his eyes twinkling.

"Buenos dias, Ruiz," Jack replied and the two men hugged each other.

"It has been too long, Jack."

"Nearly three years this time."

"You have filled out even more," Ruiz said stepping back and sizing him up. "You are a jefe now, but there is still a little jefito in you. Only a jefito would swing on a gate. I used to tell you that often when you were a boy, but you were so like your grandfather, El Jefe. He was stubborn. He was muy hombre. Your

7

grandmother was even more stubborn. We called you Jefito –
Little Boss."

Jack laughed. "How do you know I swung on the front
gate?"

"Some things never change, Jefe, but I heard the gate slam
shut. Then I heard the truck. I knew you would be coming soon."

"I saw the sign at the gate when I drove in. Looks like
we've had visitors."

"That is not all, Jefe. Last week someone shot some milk
cows the Gentrys were drying out in the pen by the big haystack.
They set fire to it and tore down a mile of fence."

"Who would do that?"

Ruiz hesitated, "Someone who wants to make life hard for
you and Mollie. Making it easier for you to sell your land. Are
you going to sell the ranch, Jefe?" Ruiz asked softly.

The question floated in the air. "I may have to, Ruiz. My
mother left a warehouse full of antiques to my stepsister. She gave
me the ranch but no cash, so I'm up to my ears in taxes and debts. I
may have to sell, unless I find water, a lot of water, Ruiz. Even
then I need financing to develop the ranch. You see, I've left the
university, and I don't know what an oceanologist can do in the
middle of the desert."

"When the time comes, you will know what to do. It is
good that you are here. Someone wrecked the pump house, Jefe,
and they shot up the water tank."

"The water tank? When?"

"Sunday, Jefe. Maria and I went to mass in Guadalupe. I
was not here. I could not fix it. Too much damage," he said
shaking his head sadly. "But I cleared out the old tank and started
the pump in the orchard. There is enough water for the trees and
the house if you are careful."

"Let's take a look," Jack followed Ruiz down an irrigation
ditch on the backside of the citrus grove.

"Careful, Jefe, that old grandfather rattler still lives under
the tool shed. Someday I'll catch him."

"You've been saying that for ten years," Jack said as he made a wide circle around the shed. "I saw him once, Ruiz. He was sunning himself on that flat rock. I went after a shotgun, but when I came back he was gone. He must have been five feet long."

"Maybe seven feet now, Jefe. I caught him one day. I grabbed him by the tail and pulled him out from under the shed. The devil turned on me and chased me all the way to the stables. Your grandfather thought that was very funny. Every year he would ask me 'Have you caught any snakes by the tail lately?' and he would laugh. It wasn't funny. I can tell you that much."

The two men entered the clearing where a large steel water tank lay on its side. The supports had been chopped through with an ax, and several large holes perforated the sides.

"Someone used a howitzer on that tank. From the size of the holes maybe a .458 Winchester or a 45-70," Jack said. Ruiz nodded.

"They smashed the batteries and poured acid on the generator. It will cost a lot to fix."

"We won't fix it, at least not soon. We'll use the back up. I can carry in bottled drinking water. I'll survive." Jack listened to the pump on the back up tank; it ran smoothly. "You've done a good job, Ruiz."

Ruiz smiled. "Gracias, Jefe."

"If we drill for water, I think we should try somewhere else."

"Where will you look, Jefe?"

"I think there might be an aquifer under the old lakebed. There should be a lot of water trapped there."

"I think you're right, Jefe. I dug the first well here behind the stable. We found water at twenty-five feet and this well was only eighty feet down. When it dried up, your mother brought in a rig. They had to go to 600 feet. I told them not to drill there, but no one listened. That is the way to go," Ruiz finished and pointed at the dry lake. "No need to pump uphill from there either."

"I'll get some hydrographic maps; maybe they can tell us where to look."

"A willow wand is better," Ruiz said, but Jack didn't reply. "I really hate to see you sell this place, Jefe. Your mother wanted you to have it someday. So did your grandmother." Ruiz made the sign of the cross. "They were good women. Sometimes a little loco." Ruiz grinned at Jack. "Your grandmother made me plant the orchard and the bushes and those eucalyptus trees. Then your mother brought this cactus. It comes from all over the world, from Africa and Baja, California, even some from Asia. 'Ruiz,' she would say, 'I'm going to have the best damn cactus garden in the world.'"

"It must have been a lot of work."

"A lot of work, Jefe. It's been the work of my whole life. But it is done, and it is the best damn cactus garden in Arizona, if not the world," he said proudly. "It will be here when both of us are gone."

"You're right, Ruiz. If I do sell the ranch, we'll save this piece. Make it into a public park. Whoever buys the ranch won't miss a few acres. Tell you what, we'll call it the Vargas Cactus Gardens or Ruiz's Arboretum."

"Thank you, Jefe," Ruiz said quietly and put on his hat. Jack could see the old man was moved by his spur-of-the-moment gesture. "I will tell Maria. She will be happy to know this thing. Adios."

"Adios, Ruiz." Jack carried the groceries into the house through the back door and waited while his eyes adjusted to the darkened interior. After popping open a can of beer and swallowing deeply, he turned on the oven and opened the door. The oven coughed, and he opened a side oven door, hoping to find a plate or a pan to heat a burrito. He bent over and looked inside.

"Keerist," he yelled and jumped backwards, his can of beer sailed upward dousing the ceiling. A spotted skunk was staring directly at him and sitting in the middle of a round copper bowl surrounded by her litter of black-and-white kits. Jack kicked the door shut, but it was too late!

10

Jack retreated into the dining room and put the burrito on the table. He raced back into the kitchen and opened the dutch door and windows. The skunk odor quickly permeated the entire house, forcing him outside.

The evening star followed a blazing sunset as the sky turned pink, purple, blue, and then black. Jack lay in a hammock swung between the two heavy posts at the end of the front porch, taking advantage of a slight westerly breeze. It was a warm July night, too hot to sleep outside, but inside, the cool adobe still reeked of skunk. He watched Altair, followed by Vega, and then the Pleiades, as they marched across the sky.

CHAPTER 2

Jack awoke with a start. Something or someone was moving about in the gravel yard. Quietly easing himself out of the hammock, he crept stealthily to the edge of the porch. The first gray-blue hue of pre-dawn lightened the yard.

Jack ducked under an oleander bush and crept up the stairs to the cupola above the stable. A pair of wild burros was nibbling at the edges of the giant prickly pear cactus just inside the fence line. He watched for a full minute before the male burro spotted him and with a quick leap, cleared the fence line. The mare followed. They raced across the raised gravel mound and disappeared behind a clump of creosote bushes, startling an antelope jackrabbit. It began to lope up the ridge, then stopped, tilted one long ear and stood up, paws in the air, nose twitching and surveyed the terrain. A desert cottontail moved out from under a tall saguaro and cautiously hopped closer to the well house. Beyond the orchard, a band of javelinas was moving through the creosote bushes. Mesquite, cats claw, and huckleberries sprang up in the sandy patches between the granite hillocks. Ironwood, sapote, and white-flowered plumbago were scattered along the wash. A Gila woodpecker, its red head flashing, sat half-hidden behind one of the limbs of the eucalyptus.

A white-necked raven landed on top of the scarecrow, made from saguaro cactus ribs and clothed in Ruiz's faded jeans and flannel shirt, cocked its head and surveyed the bean patch. The colors of dawn luminated the peaks of the far-away Superstition Mountains, lighting the blue-gray mists that floated across the Salt River Valley. The first pinks turned to electric orange and finally to a searing white slash that streaked across the cobalt sky.

The air, which had been somewhat cool thirty minutes before, warmed quickly as the sun reflected off the sand and shale of the desert floor. A heat haze began dancing and shimmering and a dust devil whirled across the dry lakebed throwing up sand and dry debris.

A low hum broke the silence as the rush-hour traffic increased on the distant freeway, muffling the chattering and chirping of the Gila woodpeckers, cactus wrens, thrashers, and quail. A big horned owl swooped across the yard. Its powerful wings carried it westward directly into a man-sized opening high up the face of Lone Butte. "So that's where you live," Jack said. He began humming a long -forgotten aria. Taking a deep breath, he sang, "My desert is calling. Calling to me!"

A coyote yipped loudly, crossed the wash and looked back over its shoulder at Jack. The two stared at each other silently for a couple of minutes. The coyote started to trot off, then stopped, tilted his head back, and howled.

The magic spell was broken by a sharp whiz that sounded like an angry bee. Jack sensed more than heard a thud as a roof shingle ripped apart and sailed in the air. He dove inside the cupola as a second round struck the iron weather vane on the roof. The only thing he could hear was his own heart pounding. He remained motionless for two more minutes, then he slipped down the stairs and moved to the edge of the porch. From his new position, protected by thick post, his eyes quartered the high ridge behind the house, searching for movement.

A shadow moved beyond a boulder. Jack moved down the porch and peered through the thick leaves of an agave cactus. He backed into the sunroom and pulled a pair of binoculars off a tall shelf. He searched the ridge again. Nothing – just a shimmering morning haze.

Jack slid into the house, crawled under a window and opened the antique family gun case. He grabbed a Colt .45 revolver, checked it for cartridges, and stuck it in his belt. He pulled out a Remington .243 rifle with a scope and grabbed two clips of shells. He jammed a clip into the rifle, put the other in his shirt pocket, eased a side window open, crawled over the window box, and slid into the yard.

Jack dodged behind a palo verde tree and then ducked into a run-off trench that led down the hill to the backside of the ridge. He moved cautiously from one boulder to the next, taking advantage of all the cover, and never going in a straight line. In five minutes, he had worked up a good sweat and had reached the end of the ridge.

To the north, a cloud of dust moved down the line of power poles obscuring a gray or white van that was speeding away from the base of the ridge. Jack checked the area and crossed over the ridge and dropped behind the huge boulder where he thought he had seen the shadow.

"Bingo," Jack said. "X marks the spot." There were some boot prints, a stoved-in cigar and a couple of matches. He looked for shell casings. "Nothing." Then he picked up the cigar butt and put it in his shirt pocket. "Well, maybe something."

Jack returned the same way that he came, staying low and dodging behind boulders just in case the sniper was still hiding somewhere above. Jack shoved the .243 into the gun rack behind the seat and slid into the truck.

He drove behind the well house and followed an old trail to the power lines. Turning on to the Salt River Project service road, he scanned the tire tracks, but couldn't distinguish one set from another in the soft sand. Giving up, he turned at the nearest crossroad and followed it to the overpass.

On the other side of the freeway, a long yellow trailer sat on a cleared patch in the middle of several acres of tumbleweeds. A four-wheel drive dun-colored Bronco was parked at the side. A "Maricopa County Sheriff Department Substation" placard was tacked to the end of the trailer.

Jack parked beside the ramp that led to the front entrance. He took a deep breath and slowly cleared his mind as he exhaled. Feeling calmer, he turned off the engine, slid out of the truck, and walked up the ramp. He opened the patio-style door and closed it quietly behind him. A tall black deputy sheriff was standing at the counter filling out a form. Deputy Smith glanced at Jack, briefly sizing him up, nodded, and continued writing.

"Can I help you?" a soft musical voice drew his attention to a raven-haired, olive-skinned woman seated at a computer console. She stood and approached the counter. She was well proportioned, tall and lithe. Jack sensed something familiar about her, but he couldn't make an immediate connection.

He read the nametag above her badge. "Good morning, Deputy Alcaraz," looking into her startling cobalt blue eyes. "I want to report a sniper. Someone fired some shots at my house or me. I'm not sure which."

"And where and when might that have been?" Deputy Smith asked.

"This morning, about 30 minutes ago. I live at the end of Ocotillo Road." Jack looked at the deputy and turned back to Deputy Alcaraz.
"I spotted a gray or white van. We've been having some trouble with shooters out there."

"You live in that adobe north of the dairy?" Deputy Smith asked.

"That's right."

"We've had a report on some milk cows being shot, a fence torn down, and an arson," Deputy Alcaraz said to Smith.

"My well house was shot up last Sunday and someone has been using the gate sign for target practice."

Deputy Smith looked at Alcaraz. "You want to check this one out? The shooter is probably long gone by now, but keep your eyes peeled anyway. Better keep me informed of your location."

Deputy Alcaraz turned to Jack. "I'll meet you at the end of the ridge."

Jack opened the sliding glass door for her. "I'll follow you."

Deputy Alcaraz started down the ramp. The holstered, heavy-framed, round-butted, Smith and Wesson .357 magnum pistol bounced in rhythm with her rapid gait. A broad black leather belt accentuated her narrow waistline and round hips.

"I'll bet," Deputy Smith said and gave Jack a knowing grin. Deputy Alcaraz appeared not to hear the exchange.

Deputy Alcaraz drove slowly, her hair blowing as she stuck her head out the window to scan the shoulder of the road. She stopped the Bronco at the edge of a wash, stepped out and squatted for a moment beside a rut. Apparently satisfied, she got back in the vehicle and renewed her search.

Parking the Bronco halfway up the side of the ridge, she waited as Jack parked his truck and got out. "I found these about here," he said as he handed her the shredded remains of the cigar butt and pointed out the heel marks.

"You shouldn't have picked up the butt. You've contaminated the evidence," she frowned. Deputy Alcaraz sniffed the cigar butt and stared at the ranch house. "From here all you can see is the roof and that cupola. Not much of a target unless he was sitting up there." She moved fifteen feet to her right and studied the rock ledge. She stooped, picked up a twig, inserted it into the mouth of a brass shell, and slipped it into a small clear plastic envelope. She turned sideways. "Here's another one," she said and put it in the envelope also. "They're bagged!" she smiled.

"I missed them, but I'm guessing it was a .458. Something like that was used to punch holes in the water tank."

"You're close. It's a 45-70."

"A buffalo gun, right out of the Old West?"

"You'll find a lot of collector pieces at gun shows. But since they've started manufacturing them again several years ago, they're regaining their popularity. The bullet has the same diameter as a .458. It all adds up, doesn't it? A tall heavyset man, wearing a Stetson and snakeskin boots took a pot shot at you."

"I'm impressed. How do you know all that?"

"Easy," she replied. "He rested his rifle on that ledge, so he has to be tall. Staring into the sun at that angle, he would be wearing a Stetson. He smokes Cuban cigars, drives an older van with Dick Cepik tires and owns a .458. Those shells and tires aren't cheap, so of course, he can afford snakeskin boots." She pointed to a shred of molted snakeskin under a creosote bush. "I watched *Dragnet* when I was a kid. That's why I became a cop. It's my job," she said with a straight face, but her eyes smiled.

Jack laughed, "You got me."

"Well, I don't know anything about cigars. Whatever it was, it couldn't be Cuban; it smells like a dead rat," Alcaraz responded. "Everybody and his brother who goes off-road have Dick Cepik tires or Big O's, including the sheriff department and the SRP service trucks. I have a set on my own rig. Our shooter would've had to have caught a live rattlesnake, skinned and tanned it, before making a pair of boots. But I do know something."

"What's that?"

"You sure took a risk going after the guy." Before he could reply, Alcaraz said, "Let's check the yard and the house." As they walked the crest of the ridge, Jack pointed out the ditch and the boulders that he had used for cover.

"Better a moving target than a sitting duck."

"You still took a risk."

"What should I have done? Called 911? And wait forty-five minutes for a sheriff's posse to show up? No thanks, ma'am," Jack said defensively. "If someone shoots at me or my place, I'll handle it myself. Anyway, the phone isn't connected yet."

"You sound like all the old timers," she said. "But the city is coming this way and help is closer than it used to be. The ranchers out here are going to have to change their attitude about taking things into their own hands. If a neighbor's dog comes on your property and chases your lambs or calves, you just can't shoot it like Shorty Rogers did last month when Jim Warner's dog wandered onto his land. That started a ruckus and Warner took a shot at Shorty. The days of friendly feuds are over. That's why there's a substation here."

"You may be right about the feuds. However, the only person I'm interested in who has an attitude is the shooter." Deputy Alcaraz shrugged her shoulders and ignored the firm set of Jack's jaw as they moved into the yard.

They spent the better part of the next thirty minutes examining the cupola and the roof, searching for a spent bullet. "I don't think we're going to find anything here," Alcaraz said. "That bullet could have landed anywhere out there." Ruiz was standing by the rear gate with a .410 shotgun in his hand when they rounded the cactus garden. "Buenos dias, Ruiz."

"Buenos dias, Cierra Rose, " Ruiz touched the brim of his hat. "I heard the shots, Jefe. I started up the hill, and saw a white van drive down the power lines. I've seen it before out on the flats. Then I saw you go after it. I yelled, but you drove off and left me. I went back to tell Maria. I saw someone on the hill and had to walk all the way here again," Ruiz said accusingly.

"I'm sorry, Ruiz. I didn't hear you."

"Everything is all right, Tio Ruiz. No one has been harmed," Cierra said.

Jack looked at Ruiz and the Deputy and asked, "Are you two related?"

"Oh, yes. Ruiz is my great uncle. His sister married my grandfather, Jaime Alcaraz."

"I knew you looked familiar! You're that Cierra! You and your older brother Angel came up a couple of times with your mother Patricia to help Maria when my parents were putting on a party. You used to make faces at me out the kitchen window."

"And you used to make them back," Cierra said, "and not very good ones, either."

A pathetic mewling came from inside the stable. Paco charged through the door, barking furiously. Jack followed him inside. A scrawny orange kitten, its back arched, was spitting and hissing at the dog. "Easy, Paco," Jack said and walked between the dog and the kitten. As he approached, the kitten tottered on its unsteady legs, tried to scoot under a stack of lumber and fell on its side.

Jack scooped it up gently and walked outside into the sunlight. The kitten spit and scratched him. "What have we here? Where's your mother?"

"I think she go finish," Ruiz said. "I saw her down at the canal three days ago. Maybe a coyote took her."

"Poor thing. It needs water," Cierra said.

Jack carried the weak kitten across the yard, with Paco circling his legs excitedly. "Back off, Paco," he said and went up the steps and entered the kitchen. He wrapped the kitten gently in a dishcloth and laid it in the sink. "You're damn near a goner. There's an eye dropper in the first aid chest…on the wall."

"Whew! You must have been skunked last night. Is there one under the house?" Cierra asked as she opened the chest and located the eyedropper.

"Closer than that," Jack said and filled a bowl with some warm tap water, stirred in some salt, and filled the eyedropper. "I'll hold him while you feed him, okay?"

Cierra forced several drops down the kitten's throat before he stirred and began spitting. "Good boy. You're going to make it."

Ruiz stood in the kitchen doorway watching Jack and Cierra feed the kitten. "Enough for now," Jack said and laid the kitten gently into a box. The kitten leaped for the top scratching and clawing the sides as soon as he let go. The box was too tall and it fell to the bottom. "He's damn near dead one minute and roaring to go the next," Jack said.

"Who's going to feed that thing when you are gone?" Ruiz challenged.

"I'm not going anywhere," Jack said. "Not soon anyway."

"Good," Ruiz said. "I found two others. They are finished. I think for sure a coyote got the mother cat. You'll need milk. You can get some at Tina's and you'd better get some mothballs, too," Ruiz said.

"Mothballs? What for?" Cierra asked.

"To run that damn skunk out of the stove," Ruiz laughed and held his nose. "If I was the kitten, I would be jumping out of the box, too."

"The skunk's in the stove?" Cierra asked and quickly stepped away from the stove.

Jack smiled. "She lives there. We share the kitchen." The kitten tugged the dishcloth into a corner, laid down, and promptly fell asleep.

"It's exhausted," Cierra said softly and stroked the kitten gently. "I need to go. Smith will be wondering." They all tiptoed out of the kitchen, and Jack gently closed the screen door.

Jack and Paco walked with Cierra down the rutted track to her Bronco. "You only visited here a couple of times when we were kids. Were you raised near here?"

"I was born in Yaqui Town, on the edge of Guadalupe. Ruiz and my grandmother came here from a small Yaqui village in the mountains south of Guaymas. They walked all the way from there to here. After the Mexican Revolution, the new government tried to starve out the Yaquis, even though there were Yaquis who fought with them. My great-great grandfather was a Yaqui General," Cierra said proudly. "My father was Yaqui. He gave me this pistol and holster when I became a deputy." She touched her holster and continued, "My mother's Irish-Mexican. Since my father died, I've lived with her in Guadalupe," she said tilting her head upward and staring directly into Jack's eyes.

"We have something in common, I guess," Jack said. "My grandfather was Irish. After graduating from Michigan State University, he worked as geologist for one of the Arizona copper mining companies. He met my grandmother in Globe; she was part Mexican and part Pima. During a fight on their wedding night, she threw a kerosene lamp at him. The old ranch house burned to the ground."

"I know the story," Cierra replied. "Not a great beginning was it?"

"Maybe not, but when I knew them, they were good friends and, I think, still lovers. A very passionate pair."

Cierra didn't reply. "Thanks for coming," Jack said as she climbed into the Bronco.

"I need to take the shell casings to the sheriff's lab in Phoenix. I'll see if they can come up with anything on the cigar butts. This stuff will get a low priority. There's a huge backlog of cases. The department doesn't have money to throw around unless it's murder one or a high profile robbery. The Sheriff has to fight the county supervisors every year for adequate salaries and equipment. We even have to purchase our own guns and ammunition."

"That surprises me. I didn't know that deputies had to do that."

"We have a long list of weapons to choose from, but most deputies prefer the magnum revolvers because they're more accurate. But no matter what weapon we carry, we have to re-qualify every year. I'm scheduled for next month. I have a day off coming up. I'd like to do some target practice in the back canyon, if that's okay?"

"Sure," Jack said. "Anytime."

"I'll drive through the Gentry's and Evans' on my way in. It might give the shooter something to think about."

"Sounds good to me."

"By the way, what will you call the kitten?"

"Orange Cat, O.C. for short."

"That's cute, but wouldn't O.K. for Orange Kitten be better?"

Jack rubbed the scratches on his hand. "Well, he'll grow into an orange cat pretty fast, but it's still not as pretty a name as Cierra Rose." Cierra rolled her eyes and arched her eyebrows. Jack stroked Paco's head fondly as she started the Bronco and drove off.

"She's smart, complicated, and stands on her own two feet. That spells trouble. All cats are not alike in the dark, Paco, no matter what Ben Franklin said. That feline has claws."

CHAPTER 3

A decrepit school bus was parked at the side of Tina's Mercado. Campesinos were shuffling in and out of a side door, trading hard-earned wages for beer, soda pop, tacos, burritos and cigarettes. The excited laughter and chatter quieted as Jack approached a group of men loitering near the door.

"Buenas tardes," Jack said and touched the brim of his hat.

"Buenas tardes," the men answered politely, but their faces were guarded behind narrow mask-like smiles. Jack stepped inside the restaurant. Two field bosses were playing a game of pool. The shooter paused and looked Jack over, a suspicious frown on his face. Few gringos ever stopped at Tina's, a hangout for Latinos and illegals several miles south of Guadalupe.

"Jack!" Tina shouted and handed one of the men a carefully wrapped burrito. She wiped her hands on a clean towel and stepped around the counter and hugged him. "It's good to see you. Ruiz told me you were back. I was afraid you'd leave again before I saw you." The laborers and bosses relaxed and the chatter picked up. If Jack was a friend of Tina's, he wasn't a border patrol agent in plain clothes.

"Sit down," Tina said and ordered him to a table. "Let me bring you something. I have fresh green corn tamales." She was gone before Jack could reply and she came back quickly with two steaming tamales and a side dish of rice. "I have beef burros and enchiladas."

"No thanks. I'll do well to handle this, but I could use a Pepsi."

Tina returned with a cold Pepsi, sat down and smiled. "It's good you are back. Your mother was a good woman; I liked her very much."

"Thanks, Tina. My mother liked you, too. She often spoke of you in her letters." Tina smiled and her eyes sparkled. "You look busy today."

"Anymore we are always busy, day and night. It's not like the old days when just a few campesinos came across the border to work the melon fields. Thousands are coming north looking for work. They come up from Altar, pass through the Estrella Valley, and find their way here at night." Jack remembered his mother had often handed out water and food to dehydrated and starved young and old men who had come to the door, hat in hand, asking politely for something to drink. They were poor souls who had gotten lost in the desert.

"The Border Patrol is everywhere. Patrol planes fly over day and night. Their trucks and four-wheel drive vehicles are all over the Valley. They even stop people who were born in Guadalupe and demand proof of citizenship or a green card. I was stopped myself only yesterday." Tina looked indignant.

"That seems a bit extreme. What can be done?"

"Nothing. There are a thousand agents in Nogales alone, and still the coyotes bring them by the truckload. They dump families on the desert at night without food or water. They walk the El Camino del Muerte. The coyotes use them as mules to bring drugs in for the dopers. If they arrest a hundred, a thousand get past the cordon. There is no time to educate them."

"Why are they coming, Tina?"

She laughed, "The same as always… for food and work. Most of all, to be free, to be able to live like human beings -- the American Way," Tina said and crossed her arms. "I guess, there's some coyote in all of us, after all I'm making a profit off them, too. Jack, but I'm no banma, no greedy two-legged coyote."

"I know you're not. Everyone knows that. What can I do?"

"The coyotes bring families into the Valley at night. Don't go out there if you see lights. Don't let Ruiz go either. Those men are dangerous. They carry guns and they won't hesitate to shoot.

The dopers are worse. Time has changed, Jack." Tina left and
went back to wait on some late arrivals from the fields.

Jack finished his meal and went up to the counter to pay.
"Next time, Jack," she waved him away.

"Thanks, Tina."

"You take care, Jack, and take care of Ruiz."

"I will. I promise."

Jack rolled the truck to a slow stop a hundred yards outside
the front gate. Dave Gentry paused, stuck his shovel in a pile of
dirt and grinned. His mother Mollie, her floppy straw hat perched
above her brown, weathered face, was standing by a 6-foot-deep
trench Dave had dug beneath an ironwood tree.

"How are you, Jack?" Mollie asked.

"Fine. What are you doing?"

"Looking for the Yaqui gold."

"That's an old wives' tale, Mollie."

"No, it's not. My grandfather was in the posse that caught
the three robbers who killed the Yaqui miners out there on the
flats. The thieves didn't even bury them. They rode to Phoenix
and cashed some gold dust. The sheriff called them out in front of
the old Adams Hotel where they were drinking. They shot him
and ran for it. The posse killed all three men, but before one of
them died, he claimed they buried the gold on the north side of an
ironwood tree somewhere around here!"

Jack looked around the flats. "There are 5,000 ironwood
trees around here, Mollie."

"Not many as old as this," Mollie said defending her
choice.

"Yeah, the roots are six feet deep," Dave laughed.

"You hear about the commotion here last week?"

"Ruiz told me a little, Mollie, but not much. What
happened?"

"Rustlers," Dave said.

"Rustlers? Here?"

"Yeah, must have been two trucks. They came down the power line road. We were drying out some cows in the old feedlot. They shot six cows. Two died. If Pete hadn't waked up, the carcasses would have been hanging in Yaqui town by morning. Sure a lot of strange happenings here lately, Jack. Hal saw a low flying plane out over the flats twice this year. Hal thinks maybe it was a drop. He thinks the dopers shot the cows and tore up our back fence."

"Why would dopers shoot a cow?" Dave yelled at his mother, "Or burn a haystack?"

"I don't know. The city is getting too close, Jack. On the weekends, dirt bikers run up and down the hills. Wherever they go, nothing grows again. I'm thinking of selling out to that land broker in Phoenix."

"You mean Carpet Bagger Carver, Mom."

"You don't know that he's a Carpet Bagger."

"All developers are carpet baggers as far as I'm concerned. They don't know a damn thing about land, and couldn't care less, period." Dave said. "If they keep paving over cropland, how are we going to feed people? They ruined California; we're next. They call it progress, but it's just greed, Mom. Big time greed." Dave shouted, his face red.

"Be still, Dave. We're out here digging for gold, aren't we? Gold from someone who stole it from someone else who probably stole it from someone else… there's no end to it."

"There is if we find some," Dave said, getting in the last word.

"Where would you go, Mollie?" Jack asked.

"Me and the boys? Prescott, maybe. We could move our milk base and ship to Arizona Dairy from there. Price of feed is too high here. What about the Ocotillo Ranch? Are you going to sell?" Mollie asked.

"Not unless I get my price. Mollie, you said your grandfather picked up some pots and a couple of rocks with petroglyphs on them from the ranch. Could I bring someone by to look at them?"

"The pots, what's left of them, are all in the floor of the old barn. They broke up when Papa hauled them in his wagon. He scattered the pieces on the barn floor. It was dirt then. The last time I saw the rocks, they were covered with weeds behind the old barn. You're welcome to look. You can have them if you want; after all they came from your place, except it was Doc Chandler's land then."

"You keep the glyphs. I just want to look at them. I may give mine to the Desert Museum in Mesa."

"Well, they can have mine too. No good to anyone covered up on the back lot."

"Mollie, my granddad moved the glyphs up to the house years ago. Someone swiped a few when they were building the new ranch house."

"I was just a girl then. There weren't many people out here in those days. It must have been someone local." Mollie brightened. "We're having a reunion next week at Hudson Park, all us old timers. Why don't you come by? I might have a surprise for you. Chance Clark will be there. He is the son of your granddad's foreman. He might know something."

"Thanks, Mollie. When?"

"We're meeting at Hudson Park next Saturday afternoon." She laughed. "You can be my beau."

Jack laughed. "Proud to be, Mollie. Don't get a sun stroke, Dave."

Taking the long way to the ranch house, Jack passed the well and rounded the curve, prepared to slip his way through the sand trap in front of the giant saguaro. To his surprise, the track had been smoothed down to the caliche surface. He rounded the curve. The sand was neatly banked along the side, creating a gentle embankment. The potholes and jeep ruts were gone. Up ahead a road grader was clearing a smooth track towards the ranch house.

He pulled up alongside the rig. "What are you doing?" Jack asked the driver.

"Clearing your driveway," he said with a grin.

"Don't remember asking anyone to clear the road."

"I guess you didn't, but it sure needed some help! Carver's idea. He's up at the house waiting for you."

"I hope he plans on paying you."

"He does. He will," the driver laughed and moved the grader forward.

Jack stopped the truck beside a white Cadillac stretch-limousine that was parked under the shade of the ramada. A swarthy-faced man wearing a straw Stetson slouched behind the wheel.

"Are you Carver?"

"He's inside," the man replied without shifting his position. He spat out the window. "Waiting for you, dude."

Jack opened the door of the truck, got out and slammed it behind him. As he walked into the yard, a small cloud passed overhead. A tall, thin, cadaverous-looking man in a black suit, black string tie, and a white Stetson rose slowly out of a chair, moved down the porch steps, and approached Jack. He extended his hand.

"I'm Charlie Carver." Jack took his hand reluctantly. "We're grading the flats. I'm putting in a temporary airstrip. Couldn't get the big machinery in until the back road was improved. We were on our way out there, and I saw your road was in pretty rough shape. Seemed the neighborly thing to do."

Jack didn't respond, so Carver went on. "I wrote you and tried to call, but apparently you don't have a phone. No one seems to know where to reach you."

"Sorry. The phone's been disconnected since my mother's funeral. I've been busy and it takes awhile to get it turned back on. Anyway, I was going to call you after I checked things out here."

"Always a good idea to check things out," Carver conceded, slapping Jack on the shoulder. "Let's go to the car. I have something to show you." Jack reluctantly let Carver lead him to the limo.

"Rudy, hand me that map." Carver unrolled the map, laid it on the hood of the limo, picked up a rock, and pinned down the upper edge. He shifted his weight, peered at the map, and stabbed at a point with a bony index finger.

"That dot, Jack, is Lone Butte. Your property line runs due east from there. My property extends all the way from the foothills to the Proving Grounds. I intend to build 60,000 homes on this side of the mountains, Californian style. Big houses, small lots, all stucco with pretty pink and gray Spanish tiles, not clay of course, but some rubberized crap I pay a fortune for. Add a couple golf courses and a dozen puny ponds, we'll call them lakes, of course. Throw in a greenbelt, a senior citizens center, and the finest medical complex this state has ever seen. You get the picture. Surround the whole place with shopping malls, office complexes, and a couple of movie houses. Then I'll wrap the whole damn mess with condos, villas, and apartment buildings. Sell the whole works and move on before the good people of Phoenix realize they've been had. That's Cowboy Capitalism, Jack. More roads, more psychiatrists, more jobs. But what it really amounts to is more debt, more traffic, and more smog. I didn't invent this, Jack; I'm just riding the wave. It's a dirty job, but as they say, somebody has to do it," Carver snickered.

"The problem, Jack, is that to pull all of this off, I need water and it has to come all the way around South Mountain. I also need pump stations to get the water in and the sewage out. The pumping station has to go up your ridge. Can't afford to move the water in and sludge out any other way. I needed permits from every regulatory body you can think of. The Economic Development Plan has been approved. It took some doing. I greased every palm from the environmental office to the Governor. I need your acreage, Jack. Do we have a done deal?"

"Mr. Carver, I tried to tell your people that there is water. My dad sunk three wells and I have a hunch there's an aquifer out there. Maybe under that dry lake bed..." Jack pointed to the alluvial fan below the South Mountain Park. "You don't need the ranch house." He pointed to three black squares beneath Lone Butte. "The ranch part of the property could become a desert arboretum site or a public park. You spread some good will around. You could get some positive press."

"Jack, there's no way I can afford to let you keep Lone Butte or twenty acres for an arboretum, whatever you call it. I've been through this with everyone, top to bottom. You're talking garden hose water. I'm talking gray water, black water. Two hundred and forty thousand toilet flushes daily. I can't afford to make a gesture. I offered you $2200 an acre; twice what I paid anyone else for their property. Your land barely sustains some cholla and prickly pear cactus. Add a few saguaros for the woodpeckers and that's all you've got. No water, nothing."

He paused. "Twenty-five hundred. That's top dollar, Jack." He scratched the numbers onto a contract and initialed it on the side. "Take it or leave it!" He held up the pen for Jack. "I'll be creating thousands of jobs and millions in tax revenue. You can't stand in the way of progress. If you hold out, Jack, the Governor will have the state claim your property, eminent domain, you see? If I build up this whole area, they can grab your land for a city park, or something like that. There're ways. You won't even get $1000 an acre; I promise you that."

"Sorry, Carver. I'm not ready to sell. Thanks for the economics lesson." Jack smiled. "I'm sure you can find your way out on my new road."

"The clock is running for you. I know your situation, Jack, you just got a divorce, you quit your job, and you have taxes to pay. I can give you twenty days, after that…" Carver rolled up the map and slid into the limo.

"See you, dude," the driver said, spat on the ground and rolled the window shut. The limo peeled out leaving a trail of dust.

Ruiz materialized out of the side door of the stable, "Those two are coyotes, Jefe; they cannot be trusted. I think they are behind the trouble here."

"Why do you say that, Ruiz?"

"The man in the black suit has the Ojo de Diablo, the evil eye. The driver, the one called Rudy, dumped his ashtray on the ground. I had to clean it up." Jack smiled at Ruiz.

"I can't call the Sheriff with that."

"No, but I will tell Cierra Rose," and Ruiz winked at Jack. "Adios, Jefe."

"Adios, Ruiz."

Jack sat on the porch steps. The twilight sky cast deep purple shadows across the yard. He watched a black tarantula amble slowly up the side of the stable wall. Somehow, it was a somber reminder of the conversations with Tina and Carver. "Vandals, drug runners, illegals, and now, a developer who wants to run me out of here," Jack said to Orange Cat. "I don't like being pushed."

A desert tortoise clacked across the darkened porch, tottered on the edge of a board and skidded over the side. Orange Cat sank into a crouch and watched. The tortoise stretched out a long wrinkled neck, reaching for some dried yellow flower stems. The kitten launched his tiny body off the porch. The tortoise drew back into its shell and Orange Cat approached tentatively, tapping the outer shell with one paw. The tortoise peered cautiously from under the lid of its shell, and waited patiently for the potential predator to go about its business. Orange Cat yawned and began grooming his fur, pretending to ignore the visitor.

"Stalemate," Jack said. "The irresistible force meets the barely moveable object."

CHAPTER 4

Tourists and holiday shoppers jammed the barricaded streets at the Desert Museum's annual Native American arts and crafts show in Mesa. Makeshift booths and tables filled the museum parking lot and spilled over onto the sidewalk and grass border. Traders were selling their wares from the tailgates of pickup trucks that lined the street.

Inside the museum, tables were piled high with concho belts, bracelets, beaded purses, scabbards, holsters and cigarette cases. Opulent squash blossom necklaces, silver bracelets and turquoise rings were spread across Navajo blankets. The shoppers scratched and clawed their way from table to table, frantically searching for bargains.

Making his way past display cases filled with pots, shards, arrowheads and axes, Jack crossed into an anteroom that housed the administration offices. Two telephones on the vacant reception desk were ringing. A brass placard reading "Curator" hung on a door that was slightly ajar. Inside a slight, fortyish man with silvered-streaked black hair, olive skin, and round brown eyes was hunched over a desk and speaking into a telephone cradled under his chin while writing vigorously on a pad. He glanced at Jack, and without hesitating, waved him into the office.

Jack entered the semi-darkness, illuminated only by a brass desk lamp with a green glass shade. The curator pointed to a brown leather wingback chair placed directly in front of the desk and spoke in soft, gentle tones directly into the phone. Now and then a grin or a frown crossed his face. He ended the conversation abruptly, without saying good-bye.

"I'm Mike Chernov." He extended Jack a limp handshake. "Another irate dealer. They blame me for forcing rug prices down.

What can I do? Donors drop off hundreds of rugs they no longer want. Trade rugs mostly, rarely anything of museum quality. Once in awhile we get the odd German Town or Two Grey Hills. We're up to our ears in no time. No place to store them, so I have a little sale. I invite Hopi, Navajo and Zuni craftsmen and lease out space to traders. Everyone makes money. I pay the utility bills, fill a few more display cases, and empty the storage rooms. Everybody's happy, especially the Friends of the Museum. If you value your freedom, don't ever become a curator of a museum, especially a special interest museum."

The curator paused and rolled his eyes upward toward a row of gilt framed portraits behind his desk. "The Board. They represent the industries that helped steal the Native American land and artifacts. Now they want to ease their consciences by collecting every tangible object and housing it here to preserve and honor the very cultures they destroyed. Oh, well, the Board's my problem, what's yours? Oh dear, I hope you're not here to donate some rugs, are you?"

Jack couldn't help smiling. "No, not rugs. I called regarding some petroglyph rocks and fetishes that I inherited. You asked me to drop by whenever it was convenient." Jack handed the curator a packet of photographs.

Chernov opened it and deftly flipped through the photographs, pausing only once briefly before handing them over to Jack. "What do you think they are?"

"I don't know," Jack shrugged. "I was hoping you might have some ideas."

"Jack, I'm a curator, basically an administrator and caretaker of the museum. I'm not an archeologist, but I've picked up some knowledge about Indian artifacts along the way. Part of my 'on the job training," Chernov smiled slightly. "Well, what you have here aren't really petroglyphs in the strictest sense of the word, except for that odd one with three circles. They're more like pictographs, as if the artist were telling a story. The distinction between the two is often blurred. These are highly symbolic and definitely very interesting. They appear to be more modern than, say, the HoHoKam or Anasazi periods."

"How about the fetishes?"

"The animal fetishes could be anything, but they have a definite HoHoKam ring to them. You might have uncovered a mixed site. Where did you find them?"

The curator's eyes caught and held Jack's, no smile this time. Jack explained the circumstances and the location of the ranch. "Perhaps you could visit the site and give me an appraisal."

"I see," Chernov replied. "Well, I am curious. I'd like to see the site, but I cannot give you an appraisal. It is not in my province as a curator to give appraisals for items for sale or for donation to the museum, especially if a tax write-off is envisioned. Conflict of interest, the IRS would say, but I do know some people who can. I could bring them with me if you are interested. We don't have funds even for interesting pieces such as these ... but I can help you obtain a substantial tax write-off."

"Write-offs are not my problem this year," Jack said.

"There is another possibility. If I find something interesting, I can sometimes persuade a private benefactor or a corporation to purchase material from an individual, then donate it to us, taking a substantial write-off -- that sort of thing. Let me show you something."

Chernov led Jack to the other side of the room and opened a pair of wooden shutters. "My ambition. Chernov's Folly, the staff calls it." A ping-pong table held a scale model set of buildings, painted sidewalks and artificial trees. The curator beamed.

"Air conditioning, security systems, basement storage room, restoration rooms, a wood shop, an art studio -- a modern museum." He pointed to the front entrance. "I've been searching for something for the foyer, an indoor-outdoor arrangement. Your petroglyph rocks could be perfect."

"My glyphs in the entrance of the new wing of the Desert Museum? Yes, I would be delighted. Why not?"

The curator flipped through his desk calendar. "Say, next Saturday morning about nine?"

"That's okay," Jack agreed quickly.

The phone began to ring, Chernov excused himself, picked it up and said to Jack, "Leave a map and directions with the receptionist, would you? She should be back from her break by now. Thank you. See you Saturday." He waved as Jack made his way out of the office.

Jack drove to Arizona State University, parked at the Visitors Center, and walked the short distance across an empty sizzling sidewalk to the Hayden Library. He entered a cool spacious subterranean mall, where a handful of students sat, staring wistfully at a sterile concrete fountain.

"All day I face the barren waste without a drink of water, clear, cool water," Jack hummed to himself and scanned a directory. He jabbed a button and the elevator door slid open. A swift lift and Jack stepped out of the door. Directly in front of him was a reception desk. A sprightly man in his late sixties, blue-eyed, fair-skinned with a shock of white hair greeted him. A silver-plated nametag shaped like a sheriff's badge proclaimed him to be "Patrick Garrett, Hayden Library Docent".

"Can I help you?" the man said genially.

Jack handed him the packet of photographs. "I'm looking for collections that might be similar to these or any information about artifacts of this kind."

Garrett looked through the packet for a moment. "Come with me. We'll have a look." He led Jack down a hall and through a doorway into a large area stacked with books, some in locked cages. "The Arizona Room. Take a seat," as he nodded towards a desk. "I'll see what I can find."

In the next hour Garrett buried Jack in monographs, manuscripts, and publications containing detailed reports of recovered pots, fetishes, petroglyphs, and human remains from the Salt River Valley. In a tome on the Snaketown Archeological site, he found photographs of recovered material similar to his petroglyphs. Back in 1946, Dr. Ryder had published a book of maps and photographs of petroglyph sites in South Mountain Park. A monograph recording petroglyphs marking significant trails leading in and out of South Mountain Park was collaboratively written by Dr. Tracy of the Arizona Museum in Tucson and Susan Schaffer. Two items in a *Desert Trails* magazine caught Jacks' attention: one covered the opening of a Cultural Center near the Snaketown site and the second documented several searches for missing gold. Mollie might be interested in this, Jack thought.

The docent came to the edge of the desk and studied the materials. "Anything useful?" he asked.

"It's a start," Jack said. "These researchers seem familiar with the region my artifacts come from, but there's nothing here on the Ocotillo Ranch."

"All the more reason that your materials could be of value," Garrett said. "I'll be right back."

Jack made copies of the pertinent information and then stared out a window. The sun was dropping behind a fan of swaying palm fronds. Nothing else moved on the sidewalk below him.

Garrett was back in a few minutes. "You're in luck. Dr. Ryder is in his office packing. He's retiring and moving to someplace in Utah. Dr. Draper has office hours at four o'clock and would be pleased to see your photos. And Dr. Tracy's secretary gave me his home phone number. He's visiting a site, but he'll be back this evening. I let her know to expect a call."

"Thank you! I hadn't expected this kind of help. You've given me a windfall."

Garrett beamed. "We do what we can," he said and disappeared into the stacks.

Jack left the library, crossed the mall and stopped momentarily to admire an older Arizona Territorial building. A neatly lettered sign by the entrance informed the visitor that Old Main was the original administration building of Arizona Normal School, an institution dedicated to training teachers. The mall surrounding Old Main included a vast complex of structures that encompassed a dozen architectural styles. Tall towering structures of steel and glass contrasted with the squat windowless territorial buildings. At the end of the mall, the Gammage Auditorium designed by Frank Lloyd Wright was a jewel set in a surround of palm trees. Pink and white oleander bushes, rows of sour orange and olive trees showcased the main entrance to the university.

A portly man wearing a white shirt with no tie was sitting on a slab cement bench under the sparse shade of a palo verde tree smoking a cigarette. "The campus is a tribute to modern man's ingenuity," he said. "A miracle in the desert. Just add water and a barren wasteland is suddenly filled with people. I remember when this campus had no more than 1200 students. I liked it better then. I knew everyone by first names. Now I don't even know half the faculty in my own college. Can I help you? Are you looking for someone?"

"I'm looking for Dr. Ryder or his office."

"Well, you found him. I'm Dr. Ryder," he said and ground his cigarette out in a sand-filled receptacle. "Let's go inside. Too damned hot to stay out here for long." He led Jack into a darkened hallway. "Have to let my eyes adjust." They waited a few moments and then Ryder led the way down the hall and through the open door at the end.

Jack stood in the doorway of a large workroom stacked to the ceiling with cardboard boxes. An assistant was busy filling the boxes with books and manuscripts and marking obscure symbols on the boxes with a black felt pen.

"A fine mess," Ryder said. " I'm moving it all into storage. A lifetime's work. Someday, someone will find it, but they'll have a hell of a time sorting it out. I'm headed for Utah," he said with a happy grin. "Maybe I'll get five or six years of peace and quiet before it's discovered. Kanab. Ever hear of it?"

Jack said he hadn't. "Good! It's God's country. Now that you know, keep it to yourself. What did you bring me?"

Jack handed him the packet. Dr. Ryder sat down on a stack of books and shuffled through the photos. He handed them back to Jack. "They don't mean a thing to me. Not the same stuff I found in South Mountain, but I never did get beyond the park. I can't help you. I don't know much about petroglyphs, really. I picked up a grant from the government. They gave me a surplus jeep and the art department lent me a camera. I took a sabbatical and spent a year crawling around those hills. I can tell you how many glyphs were there in 1946, how tall they were, and how wide. I chalked them in, you see, and took a picture. Chalking petroglyphs is a serious offense in the eyes of the petro-hounds, but I didn't know any better then, you see?"

Dr. Ryder handed Jack his book of photographs. Jack leafed through it, slowly studying the pictures of a wild turkey, a parrot, and a humming bird incised on rock panels. "These are interesting."

"Lucky I got there when I did. I went back last year and followed the trails. Most of the glyphs have been destroyed. Some are shot up and louts have vandalized the rest. You name it. Graffiti artists with spray paint. Souvenir hunters rip off whole panels with a chisel, but they break the rock before they get it off. Morons. Well, I'm out of here. I've seen enough crime, grime, traffic, pollution, and graffiti. Try your luck with Draper. He has an office in the basement. Call Tom Tracy at the Arizona Museum. He knows more about the Southwest than most people. Native American artifacts, burial grounds, prehistoric cultures, myths and legends are his sort of thing. He probably won't tell you much unless you ask the right questions. Take the book; I've got a couple of hundred extras," he laughed sardonically. "Sorry, I couldn't be of more help."

Dr. Draper was a musty, tired-looking older man, a real contrast to the energetic, bustling Ryder. He stared at the photos with blank, watery blue eyes and then at the puffs of smoke from his pipe that drifted up towards the cracked and peeling paint of the storage room. Jack looked down the aisles of marked and unmarked boxes. Fragments, shards, baskets, the detritus of several civilizations were casually strewn about on workbenches. An aesthetic-appearing, pale young man with large owl-like eyes with thick glasses was busy pulling cartons off the shelf. He opened a lid, examined the contents, and moved to the next carton.

"They must be here, Dr. Draper. I saw something like that last week," he said.

"Ask Trisha in the morning, Tom. They'll turn up." Draper swung his swivel chair around and spread the photos out on his desk. "These three are probably from the Pacific Northwest," he said authoritatively. "These three are definitely HoHoKam, and the last three are later, probably Pima or Papago."

"Are you sure?" Jack asked.

"Pretty sure. Those arches over the eyes aren't from here. More like the stuff on Northwest totems. The owl is definitely northwest. Those circles are a HoHoKam design. You might send them to Susan Schaffer for a second opinion. Rock art is a special interest of hers. She's done a lot of work in the Mimbres area."

"Mimbres?" Jack asked.

"New Mexico, Rio Grande Valley. Far more advanced than anything we have over here, including the HoHoKam."

"They all look alike to me," Jack ventured. "They appear to be done by the same hand."

Draper's assistant peered over their shoulders. "Could be fakes," he said. "Used to be a man who made glyphs to sell to the tourists back in the 1950s. He has a shop full of that sort of stuff on Indian School Road. Right next to the map shop."

"I'll check it out. I need to pick up some maps anyway," Jack replied. Draper gave him a quizzical look. "Thanks for your help, Doctor."

"I'm not certain that I've been much help," Draper replied. "Good luck."

Jack took the scenic route to Indian School Road, passing by the Hole in the Rock in Papago Park and the Phoenix Botanical Gardens. He parked at the side of an imitation Southwest Indian pueblo. The owner was sitting on a bench in front of his shop. Jack showed him the photographs of the petroglyphs.

"No, I never did any work like that," the heavyset man said, his lips stained brown by an ever-present dead stogie he rolled around his mouth. The owner pointed to some ten-inch square pieces of sandstone in the window display. "Just a few spirals, and maybe a lizard or two. I did do a few designs on flagstone slabs for tabletops, but nothing like that. You've got the real McCoy there. If you want, I could make you a coffee table from that big one. It would be impressive as hell."

"No, thanks," Jack said and went next door to the map shop which catered to outdoorsmen, treasure hunters and rock hounds. The manager wasn't very encouraging.

"There's no water between your place and the St. John's Indian Reservation. The Proving Grounds sank a dozen wells out there," he said jamming his finger on a grid to make his point. "They ended up tanking in water from Laveen. The Army tried in '42 when Patton set it up to test his tanks. They came up dry, too."

"How about city water?"

"If you want city water, you'll have to pipe it in from Chandler. The right of way will cost you a pretty penny, and Chandler will charge you an arm and a leg for every drop. They want it for their own expansion. Phoenix? Forget it. You're on the wrong side of the mountains. No way to get across unless you tunneled through the gap. What you need is a dousing rod and a lot of luck. Just happen to have one for sale, if you're interested."

"How much for that metal detector?"

"Five hundred. It's a White and I retuned it myself."

"Throw in the dowsing rod, and you've got a deal."

"Hell, I'll throw in the maps and the aerial photos, too."

"I'll take them." Jack said as he began writing a check.

"Well, you've got a better chance at finding gold out there than water, my friend."

"Maybe I'll get lucky and find both!"

When Jack returned home, he opened the oven's storage door. The mother skunk was not there, but her five kits were.

"You're not going to like this." He started to drop in a few mothballs, but changed his mind. "Oh, live and let live," he muttered and shut the door.

He opened a can of tuna. "Feel well enough for some solid food? You don't want any mayonnaise, do you? Probably not," he said to Orange Cat and sat half the tin down on the floor. The kitten shoved his nose into the tin and ate furiously.

Jack made himself a sandwich, picked up the aerial photos of the area, and went out to the porch. Orange Cat followed and rubbed up against Jack's leg purring softly. Jack scratched the kitten's ear absentmindedly while he studied the photos. He located the ranch house and the outbuildings. A curious elongated X pattern marred the gravel at the head of the ridge. North of the ridge was a mound of gravel that didn't match the other strata. Jack used a magnifying glass to study the mound. There was an odd depression in the almost circular mound, as if someone had dug out a hole deliberately. He drew a circle around the mound with his pencil.

Jack stood up and switched on the railroad lantern that served as a porch light. Orange Cat stuck his head over the edge of the roof and looked down curiously at Jack. With one paw, he began toying with the rope sling that held an old olla. "Get away from there," Jack said to Orange Cat. As he moved towards the pot, something soft brushed his neck and shoulders. Jack ducked instinctively as a large blue owl landed momentarily on the rim of the olla. Orange Cat screeched and leaped onto Jack's shoulder, sinking his claws into Jack's skin. He yelled and the blue owl pushed off its perch and swooped into the darkness.

The rope holding the olla snapped and the pot crashed onto the ground, causing Orange Cat to dig deeper. Jack pulled the kitten off his shoulder, removing one claw at a time, and set him gently on the deck. Orange Cat immediately scrambled for cover under a wicker chair.

Jack picked up the faded red, green, and white sash that had been wrapped through the olla's handles. He rolled it up and put it in his shirt pocket. He found a wicker basket on the porch and carefully picked up the scattered potshards. "Maria gave my mother this olla and sash as a wedding present for good luck," he told Orange Cat, who was watching from his hiding place.

The kitten's tail began swinging. "The pot's damaged, but it can mended. We need to keep our luck. Keerist! What's next? God, I hate this place. Skunks, snakes, and now it's owls."

CHAPTER 5

Jack entered through the main entrance of the Arizona Museum, a sprawling three-storied windowless territorial brick edifice. On the ground floor, glass offices opened onto an inviting, open-aired plaza. A perforated copper ring squirted plumes of water skyward from the center of a fountain decorated with colorful Mexican tiles. Jack sat down on a bench and watched the water play tricks with the sunlight while he waited for Dr. Tracy.

Twenty minutes passed before a tall dark-haired man in a Hawaiian shirt and light blue slacks stepped out of an elevator, trailed by a flock of chattering students. He smiled and waved at the entourage, turned and walked directly to Jack, and offered his hand. "I'm Tom Tracy. Sorry I'm late. It's difficult to break off when your students are enthusiastic."

"I know the feeling. Sometimes, I really miss teaching. I didn't mind waiting in such a nice spot. Thanks for agreeing to look at my photographs." Jack handed them over. "I'm a bit confused. It appears to me that the same hand did the glyphs, but Draper says that three different groups probably created them at different times in different places. He suggested that these three," Jack pointed at the photographs, "were probably done somewhere in the northwest."

"Where were they found?"

"The human icons were found in a cave on my property. The animal fetishes and the petroglyph rocks were out in the open. Some were stolen, so they were moved to the ranch house for protection. I wish these rocks could talk; I think they would tell us that Draper is wrong."

"Why do you say that?"

"Well, as I said, it looks to me like the same person did them. If three different groups in different locations make them, how did they end up at my ranch? It seems logical since they are so similar in appearance that they were done at the same place. Even though the smaller ones could be easily transported, the northwest is a long way from Tempe, even if they brought them by truck," Jack laughed.

Tom smiled. "I understand what you're saying." He studied the photographs for a few minutes and handed them back. "Where petroglyphs are concerned, we're all guilty of doing a lot of guesswork, Jack. Someone develops a theory, but sometimes, I'm afraid, we make the facts, or the lack of them, fit our preconceived notions. Draper believes in the Bering Strait theory, that is, that Asians crossed the straits several millennia ago. The immigrants came in waves – the first groups settled in the northwest and later ones moved southward. That includes the ancestors of the Incas, the Toltecs, the HoHoKam and the Anasazi, to say nothing of Algonquins and others who spread eastward."

"That's what I was taught in college."

"Doesn't hold water in my book." Tom continued, "According to Draper's way of thinking, your glyphs were carried south and in one way, and I can see what makes him think that. Some of the markings are similar to the designs found on northwestern totems. For example, these arched eyebrows," he said and pointed at the picture, "are not commonly found on southwestern petroglyph panels. However, I've seen a few, and you do find glyphs incised on small rocks, such as the ones in your photographs. Whoever made these took painstaking care to create them."

"Why did these require such special care as opposed to the symbols found on huge slabs and mountainsides?"

"They probably had a spiritual significance or are related to significant events. Draper doesn't specialize in glyphs and neither do I, although I know a few people who have devoted their entire lives to studying and preserving petroglyphic sites. It's not mainstream archeology. It's only become a concern to university archeologists because the 'amateurs' began publishing their findings and some tribes are declaring a cultural affinity with petroglyph artifacts and demanding that sites be protected."

"Do the symbols or pictures on the rocks have any meaning?"

"Dr. Carros over at New Mexico State doesn't believe the prehistoric, or even historic, tribes were leaving messages on rocks. His interpretation is that the petroglyphs are just an art form. He suggests that many of the glyph sites are filled with prehistoric doodles. At the most, they say, 'I came this way' or 'Kilroy was here' --- that sort of thing. In fact, his interpretation couldn't be farther from the truth."

"Let me show you something." Tom pulled out a large map from his briefcase and spread it out on the bench. "Those students in my seminar come here from the three state universities. We are re-examining the pioneering work done in the '30s at the Snaketown and Colorado River sites. A highly developed and complex society built Snake Town. They had observatories, elaborate irrigation systems that stretched from the Gila and the Salt River all the way to the Colorado." He pulled out an aerial photograph and said, "This figure here is an intaglio, a giant stick figure, taken while we were working at the Yuma site. It's a depiction of the Fisherman, who was the Creator of all things, according to the legend. There are over 300 such figures stretching from Yuma to the massive concentration around Blythe and continuing as far north as Lake Havasu, where some are under water, of course."

"That's incredible! I never know they were there, and I've driven through the region quite a lot going from California to Arizona."

Tom pointed to dozens of site indictors that dotted the map. "The prehistoric and historic tribes traded for shells from California to the Gulf of Mexico. We've found Anasazi pots as far south as Mexico City and as far east as the Great Plains. The prehistoric peoples of the Southwest cultivated beans and maize and other products. Some created magnificent polychrome pottery.

Hard to imagine that they were only capable of mere doodling on rocks. They were a sophisticated people with complex social and religious infrastructures."

"I have always thought so, too."

"All these diverse peoples had to communicate in some way with one another and the basis of that communication was sign language. Whether we are aware of it or not, all humans hand sign everyday and hand signs played a major role in the origin of written language. So, hand signs are the "Great Mother" of communication." Tom laughed.

"Is there a connection between symbols and pictures on glyphs and sign language?" Jack asked.

"Good question. Yes, there are definitely many connections. The word *manography* means drawing a hand sign. The Mayans perfected hand signing." Tom continued, "Designs on the walls in Mayan temples in the Yucatan are similar to hand signs used by contemporary Maya. One of the wall pictures even shows a group of Mayan deities hand signing in unison."

"Gives a new meaning to hand jive, doesn't it?"

"It sure does," Tom laughed. "One of the keys to understanding the Mayan hieroglyphs was studying the intact language system of the Plains Indians." Tom closed his hands together and pulled them apart. "It's the sign for break," he explained. "Hands open," and he made a v-shape with his palms raised outward, "means daybreak. Knowledge of the meaning of hand signs provides insight into hundreds of works of Meso-American art."

"Really? How does that help?"

"Well, most hand signs move. Writing is simply the frozen form of a hand sign. In other words, the writer transforms a moving sign into a static visible contraction. We find evidence of these contractions on stela, wampum, effigies, icons, talismans, bark calendars, and petroglyphs. There is a remarkable similarity between some of the symbols found all over the world." Tom paused and leaned back.

"You mentioned pictographs, what are they?" Jack asked.

Tom took a deep breath. "The term covers a lot of ground. The scholars in the 1800s like Powell, Mallery, and Clark studied sign language and the rock writings in the Southwest. Pictographs was then the term used to describe picture writing, such as depictions of a battle scene, a sacred ceremony, or the arrival of the white men on horses. Quite often, symbols were added to the story. Sometimes simple hand signs or highly stylized depictions like the Zuni rain cloud were used. The term *petroglyph* for rock writing evolved and later was broken into categories. Today *pictograph* refers most often to painted picture writing. Sometimes, the words are used interchangeably which infuriates the purists, but it's the only way to describe a particular object."

"You said those figures are intaglios. What exactly are they?"

"Well, it's a giant morphic form usually created by brushing aside whole rocks, exposing the bare ground beneath, or turning up the gray-tan underside off the surface rocks. Some are trampled into the ground, usually by dancers, we think. But a raised surface feature such as the HA-AK Laying form was hand built by carrying in loads of gravel. The serpent mound in Ohio was created this way. It's called a cameo. But the Fisherman figure I told you about has characteristics of both. So is it an intaglio or a cameo? To complicate it further, some people call them earthmorphs or geomorphs."

Tom paused and looked at Jack. "You know, the intaglio HA-AK Laying is on your way home if you want to see one for yourself. It's behind Indian Joe's Trading Post in Sacaton just off the old Arizona Highway."

Tom examined the photos again. "Some of the effigies or animal fetishes, appear to be HoHoKam and others have a different appearance, possibly historic or pre-historic Papago or Pima. I can't say for sure. Something went wrong in the Gila and the Salt River Valleys around 1150 to 1350. There are several educated guesses, of course, a prolonged drought, or an epidemic, or an invasion. We don't know what happened to the HoHoKam people, but for some reason, their culture and infrastructure collapsed. And sometime after that, the Pimas and the Papagos moved into the Valley. It's hard to tell when one group disappeared and the other arrived. It's always that way with mixed sites."

Tom paused and stared thoughtfully at the fountain. Then he turned to Jack. "I'd like to visit your place if that's all right with you? But first I'd like to have Susan Schaffer look the place over and make some sketches. It's rare to find an untouched location so close to Salt River. We're fortunate your grandparents, in a sense, roped off a section"

"Well, the site won't be safe much longer. I'm thinking about selling the ranch."

"At least we have a chance to do some work before the bulldozers arrive. Susan works for the State Historical and Archeological Site Preservation Department. They have an office here and one in Phoenix. At the present, there're not enough funds to go around, so she works half-time for the preservation office and part-time here. The rest of the time, she is working on her Ph.D. degree in museumlogy. She's taken some courses in archeology and anthropology in the degree program and she and I worked together recording some petroglyphs on South Mountain Parks trails."

"Sounds like a busy woman and perfect for this job."

"She is that, and then some," Tom looked at his pocket calendar. "I have some helicopter time tomorrow. Susan and I are visiting some sites near Phoenix. We could drop by first thing in the morning. Is there some place we could land near your ranch house?"

"Yes, there are some flats about 50 yards from the fence line. It's about 100 acres or so. Is that room enough?" Jack smiled.

"I should think so. Let's go to my office." Tom led Jack across the patio and through a set of glass doors. "Coffee okay with you?" Jack nodded. Tom picked up a telephone off his desk and dialed a number.

"Susan, let's have a cup of coffee. I want you to meet a fellow with an interesting set of rocks… as in fetishes and petroglyphs, yes."

They met Susan in the lounge on the third floor and sat around a circular table. Her blonde hair was pulled back severely, accentuating a pleasant broad face, bright hazel eyes, and just a trace of lipstick. The drawl was southwestern, punctuated with a slight lisp. West Texas? Oklahoma? Jack couldn't tell for sure. Her questions were direct, and her eyes bored into the back of his skull, as if she seemed determined to discover if Jack was deceiving them or possibly running a scam. "I have to run up to Phoenix this afternoon to get an allergy shot." Susan sniffed. "There ought to be law against planting mulberry trees."

"There is," Tom said turning to Jack, "but it's thirty years too late for Tucson. The city will remove them for free, but they're not getting much cooperation from home owners."

Susan wiped her nose with a tissue. "After my appointment, I plan to stop at the Desert Museum briefly. I can come by your place on my way home. Say about four o'clock?"

"Four o'clock? Yes... yes, that will be fine," Jack stammered.

Susan and Tom excused themselves. "Lots to do. The day is still young," Tom said.

"See you later." Susan sent Jack a quick smile, her first.

Jack took the old Arizona Highway and headed west towards Mesa. What used to be a rough wagon track was now a smooth highway. Thirty minutes later, he was traveling through a vast open space halfway between Florence and Coolidge. A huge billboard alongside the highway read:

Indian Joe's Trading Post
Kachina Dolls, Indian Fry Bread, Turquoise,
Jewelry, Baskets
Visit the Sleeping Giant

On an impulse, Jack caught the next exit and followed the frontage road for a mile back to the Trading Post. He parked in front of a wooden two-story building that looked like it came from a frontier town movie set. He entered through a hand-hewn timbered archway.

Papago baskets and Navajo rugs were piled on the ground floor, partially blocking the entrance. Colorful kachina dolls cluttered the shelving along the walls. Rows of silver Zuni trinkets, concho belts, rings and bracelets glittered in brightly lit display cases. Black, brown and red pueblo pottery was intermingled with pastel-hued Navajo wedding pots. Faceless dolls of Indian maidens and children with large black eyes adorned postcards, ashtrays, vases and magnets.

A bald, porcine man watched Jack from behind a partly open venetian blind as he mounted the stairs leading to the manager's office. Jack knocked and waited until the man sluggishly rose from his chair and invited him in.

Crude hand-lettered signs proffering descriptions of the history and origin of the Papago and Pima Indians were stacked around the cluttered workspace. Red-lettered posters illustrated the basics of hut construction, tool making, and pottery throwing.

"For the Native village we're building out back," the man said without being asked. "The slopehead who made these signs can barely read, let alone print. I'm Bob Hirt. I'm the curator, manager, handyman and restaurateur if no one shows up for work, which is every other day."

Curator? Manager? Slopehead? What this? Who is this guy? Jack asked himself.

"I'm out of here next week. Been here three years, but I couldn't make this Chinese Fire Drill work in twenty. The owner wants a first-rate tourist attraction here. He's paying the tribe plenty for the lease, but part of the deal is that he employs Native Americans whenever possible. Worse, he's scared to death that I'll rip him off. What's to steal? Nothing here but tourista junk. To hell with it. One more week on my contract, and I'm out of here."

Hirt stood up, stared out the window at the bored cashier with an Apache headband and feather who pretended to study her nails. He closed the venetian blinds. "Well, what did you bring me?"

Jack reluctantly handed over the photo packet. "Some petroglyphs. I thought maybe you or someone here might be able to identify them."

Hirt shuffled quickly through the photos. "Hmmm. These are story rocks. Could be Pima, but they're probably Papago. I've seen a lot of them. Sometimes a Papago brings one and wants me to sell it. The picture usually has a story that goes with it, if you can believe their stories. The Papagos used to make animal fetishes like that back in the thirties for the dudes over in Chandler." He looked again at the beaver fetish. "Not that good, though. Mostly they made birds and frogs. Don't ask me why. Could be worth a little, could be worth a lot. What do you want for them?"

"They aren't for sale," Jack replied. "I just want to know what they are."

Hirt flipped through his Rolodex, jotted on a notepad and handed it to Jack. "Dr. Felix Hartman. He's with the Pacific Rim Institute in Los Angeles. He wrote a book on artifacts, everything in it from here to Labrador. He's got a monograph on frauds and fake artifacts. You can't fool Felix. He might be too busy to help, but it's worth a call." Hirt scratched another name on the pad.

"James T. Taylor. He's a big buyer, private collector. A real nut case. Whatever he offers you, ask for four or five times as much. He won't blink an eye; you know what I mean? Stay away from the big dealers, especially the Mallory brothers. Robert Arnold at Anasazi Galleria is a scam artist. If you want someone to sell them for you, try Wes Culver over in Scottsdale. I know for a fact you can trust him."

Hirt started to motor mouth more names before Jack could stammer out an objection. "Mr. Hirt, I told you they aren't for sale."

"Sure, sure," the manager said conspiratorially. "I understand your drift. Well, if that's the case, try Mike Chernov at the Desert Museum. They love freebies. You could get a tax write-off. If you want to leave the photos here, I'll ask some of the elders. They wouldn't tell you anything, not much anyway, and they would probably lie to you."

They would probably tell you even less, Jack thought. "Not just yet. I've got a few other sources to check. Let me think on it."

"Want to take a look at the village?" Hirt asked, suddenly cordial. The HA-AK intaglio is out back. It's worth a look. I encourage the tourists to look around. Put a few pennies at her feet or quarters in the palm of her hand if you want to change your luck."

"Where is it?"

"Go out the back. Follow the trail or the signs, if you can read them."

Jack ordered some fry bread and coffee at the restaurant. While it was being prepared, he walked past the ocotillo fence that separated the parking lot from the "authentic" Indian village under construction. A short wooden bridge led across a dry wash. On the other side, a hand-lettered sign pointed the way to the Petroglyph Canyon and to HA-AK, The Sleeping Giant.

Jack followed the path for about 100 yards until it forked again, and he followed the north-pointing arrow. Another 100 yards brought him to the mouth of a narrow arroyo. From there, he could see petroglyph panels on both sides. Jack moved up the path for a closer look.

Some of the panels were scarred. Faces of the ledges appeared to have been deliberately broken off by vandals or souvenir hunters. Others were covered over with recent graffiti. Someone had chiseled his name over a glyph – Jake, Ames, Iowa. There were similar calling cards along both sides. In one place, someone had used black spray paint – Richard, Peoria, Arizona.

"A damn shame," Jack said. "A damn shame." He crawled up a slope and then scrambled to the top of a knob. From this vantage point, he could look down on the intaglio. A head with a large nose tilted southward. An arm and a hand reached out. The left palm was stretched upwards towards the sky. An adobe wall rose twelve feet around the figure and was broken about every ten feet. Thick posts supported the adobe walls and the spaces in between had been covered with two-by-fours laced with ocotillo branches. A collapsed barbwire fence lay just inside the wall.

The intaglio had been created by piling up stones and rocks, creating a cameo effect. A crossed necklace of white quartz rose above the figure's breast. The knees were slightly drawn up and tilted to the south. Beyond the torso and to the left, was a smaller figure. Jack could make out its head, something that could be braids stretched from the sides. The hands appeared to have claws rather than fingers. The child figure, if it was a child, also had claws for feet.

A lot of thought and effort went into this, Jack thought. But what does it mean? He reentered the Trading Post and made his way to the restaurant.

"See enough?" Hirt shouted from his office doorway.

"Yes, I've seen and heard enough," Jack replied and he picked up his take-out order.

Hirt waved. "Come back any time. Spectators are welcome. Work is always in progress." He laughed derisively. "Listen, if you come across any good pots or stone pipes, give me a call."

CHAPTER 6

When Jack returned home, Susan was waiting on the upper terrace. A plastic cup of iced tea rested on the ledge. "No one was home, so I helped myself. Hope you don't mind. Quite an interesting place. The house is made from real adobe bricks."

"My grandparents built it. Actually, my grandfather and Ruiz built it after the original place burned down. They had a fight on their wedding night, and tossed kerosene lamps at each other."

"Fascinating. Who won? Your grandfather or Ruiz?"

Jack laughed. "I meant to say my grandparents had a fight. They were married for 53 years, and then died within six days of each other. Star-crossed lovers, my grandmother used to say."

"This was quite a place in its heyday, I'll bet."

Jack winced. "Yes, you could say that all right." He looked off toward the sea of tract homes on the eastside of the freeway.

Susan changed the subject. "I've been looking around a little. Your glyphs aren't truly petroglyphs. I think your petroglyphs tell a story. I'm almost certain that they came from this region, not the northwest."

"Yeah, Bob Hirt at Indian Joe's Trading Post said they were a lot like storyboards," Jack told Susan about his encounter with Hirt at the Trading Post.

"Bob's not exactly a curator. He's a promoter, actually, a parasite. They're all alike," she miffed. "Guys like him give us honest folks a bad name. You can't blame the tribe. They need all the cash they can get. They own a lot of land, but most of its marginal, and without water; they can't farm it. Did you take a look at the intaglio while you were there?"

"Yes, I did. It's amazing. What's it all about?"

"There's a Pima legend about HA-AK. Frank Russell wrote about it in the 1890s. It's a story about a woman who gave birth to a monster girl-child. When the child grew up, she kidnapped children and took them to her cave where she ground them up with a mortar and pestle before devouring them."

"That's a pleasant bedtime story."

"Many once-upon-a-time stories don't have happy endings, even though we'd like them to. The legend of HA-AK is actually similar to many creation and destruction myths common to most cultures," Susan said. "Anyhow, the Pimas, according to the legend, invited HA-AK to a dance, drugged her with cigarettes made from loco weed and then burned her alive in the cave. She turned into blue smoke and transformed into a blue owl. Even today the Pimas and the Papagos feel that owls are unlucky. There's a lot more to the story and there are different versions. Russell worked closely with the last Pima shaman and recorded the story, prayers and songs related to the HA-AK legend. All living Pimas and Papagos regard the intaglio at Sacaton as being a re-creation of that legend. Russell mentioned that the Pimas placed gifts in the palm of her hand and at her feet. Many still do today."

"Are they propitiating her?"

"Not exactly. Most often they are just hoping to bring luck to their children. In the 30s and 40s late in July, the Pimas used to have a celebration in South Mountain Park. They drank nawait, wine made from fermented saguaro fruit, and they danced in circles and threw straw effigies of HA-AK into a bonfire. The ceremony is performed even today on some remote parts of the reservation. Russell and his contemporaries found other intaglios here on the Salt River and Gila River. There used to be one in Peoria, another in Mesa, and another in Buckeye."

"Used to be? What happened to them?"

"Urban sprawl. The bulldozers scraped them away before anyone realized what was happening. Very few people understood the connection to HA-AK Laying, which has been more or less protected by a fence since 1906. The cave where HA-AK was supposed to have been burned alive is somewhere near here in

South Mountain Park." Susan pointed vaguely at the range of mountains. "The Papago version has her cave in the Baboquiviri Mountains south of Tucson. I know someone who should look at your petroglyph rocks. Lee Begay decodes petroglyphs. He's made the study of rock writing his lifework."

"Susan, I was curious about the glyphs and the more you tell me, the more I want to know." She laughed.

"It's easy to get bit by the glyph bug. It gets under your skin. I've been studying the patterns on yours, and even I can tell the same person made the inscriptions, at least, the ones on the faces and some of the back panels."

"Well, in my opinion that puts you ahead of Dr. Draper."

"How about showing me the cave?"

"It's at the end of the ridge. I'll get the truck."

"I'd rather walk so I can study the ground close up."

They scrambled up the steep incline and picked their way along the crest of the ridge. "Those are cairns," Susan pointed to the mounds of small granite rocks. "My God, there must be fifty to sixty of them. The Old People, the HoHoKam, honored their dead this way. The clans would have added to the piles over the years. The Pimas wouldn't have done that because they avoid the dead. I've never seen so many in one place before, and they haven't been disturbed."

"Would there be bones or relics under the piles?" Jack asked.

"No, they cremated their dead."

"Are you sure?"

"Absolutely." Susan shrugged her shoulders. "They didn't put anything in the cairns that would tempt thieves. The Pimas probably left the kick-balls, the fetishes and the rag-dolls you found. They had high regard for the Vanished Ones. This is definitely a mixed site. Both cultures had some reason to revere this ridge, or maybe that butte." She pointed at Lone Butte, rising up from the foot of the ridge. "Let's take a look."

They followed an ancient path that traversed the backside of the butte and led to a wide ledge a quarter of the way from the crest. "God, you can see the whole East Valley from here! Look, you can see traces of an old HoHoKam canal. It starts at the Salt River and ends there in that salt flat."

"It was a lake once. I hope to find an aquifer underneath it somewhere. If I do, I can sell this place."

"So it can become like the rest of the valley, another tract with a white Camaro in every carport. That's progress." Susan sat down on the ledge and began sketching. Jack watched quietly as she rapidly inked the rows of Xs on her notepad.

"Finished." Susan stood up and closed her sketchpad.

"Are the cairns important?"

"Not really. The people who piled up the rocks are long gone. On the surface or under ground there's no evidence of ruins here of a village or anything like that. But Tom will probably want to look it over."

They worked their way down to the base of Lone Butte. "Careful, it's tricky here." Jack half-walked and half-slid down the slippery incline to the cave entrance. He watched as Susan made her way nimbly down the steep face. "You're as agile as a mountain goat."

"Lots of practice."

Jack carefully removed the wedged-shaped rocks that sealed the top of the entrance and set them to one side. He levered the thin slab of flagstone, pushed it to one side and leaned it against a boulder. "Whew! My grandfather and Ruiz blocked the entrance with this thing. He didn't want me or anyone else to disturb this place." He stuck his head inside the cavern, looked around, and stepped back. "No snakes, but the old man is still there."

Susan peered in, cautiously stepped inside, and squatted in front of a human skeleton. "Wow! The remains are pretty well preserved. His hair is intact and so is much of his facial tissue."

"I used to call him my mummy."

"He's not a Egyptian mummy anyway. The natural process of desiccation causes mummification. In this dry climate and arid soil, this happens. But you're essentially correct. Un-embalmed

Indian remains are properly termed mummies. Your mummy must have been a shaman. That's his medicine bag and those are medicine sticks. I think those are owl feathers. I'd like Tom to see this."

"He'll keep. He's not going anywhere soon." Jack smiled.

Susan frowned, pulled a camera from her pack, and snapped several shots from different angles. When she was through, Jack moved the flagstone boulder back into place, stacked the wedge-shaped rocks and blocked the entrance.

"This is where you found the animal fetishes?"

"No, we found most of the animal fetishes, kick-balls and rag-dolls up on the ridge. A few were at the bottom, along with some pottery shards."

Susan stopped from time to time to make notations as they walked back to the adobe. "Jack, there are some pictographs in the Berber collection that might match your glyphs. The Berbers donated their collection of artifacts in the 1940s. They are stored in the basement of the Desert Museum. Any idea of how the Berbers would have come by them?"

"Someone swiped some of our petroglyph rocks back in the thirties. The others were moved to the house for safekeeping. Tomorrow afternoon I'm going to a reunion of old timers who used to live round here. I'll see if they have any ideas about the missing stones."

Susan got into her state car, a white late-model Ford station wagon. "Let me know if anything turns up. See you tomorrow morning."

"Okay, have a safe trip." Susan waved and drove off. "A shaman, spirals, and petroglyphs: a mystery about to be solved? Semper vigilantes," he said to Orange Cat.

After dark, Jack opened the living room windows. Momma skunk's scent was not as bad as the night before, but it still lingered. "What's next?" Jack asked as he consoled himself with a beer and a cold burrito. He sat in a comfortable chair and scribbled out an inventory of items he intended to sell. Kitchen antiques his mother called them -- a hutch from Monterrey, Mexico, dated 1848; a rustic dining table and buffet; and the wagon wheel chandelier. He added the antique irons that served as doorstops, the soft Navajo rugs that covered the hardwood floors and the majestic red rug that hung like a royal tapestry. On a separate page, he listed the old paintings framed in Saguaro wood: a Burr, an Atwater, and several watercolors by Will Sparks. On the last page, he listed the pots, ollas, axheads, and the fetishes that cluttered the sunroom. Jack checked the yellow pages and noted antiquity dealers and art galleries who might be interested in the odd assortment of antiques, art and artifacts.

"That's enough for tonight." Jack opened a closet door and grabbed a bedroll. He carried it out to the porch and gazed at the brilliant stars overhead. "Come on O.C., let's go topside. It's cooler up there." He spread the bedroll on the stable's roof deck, cradled his head in one arm, and stroked Orange Cat absentmindedly.

"What a collection of oddities my family accumulated," he said to the kitten. Jack let his thoughts drift unchecked. His mother called the ranch their "winter place." The "summer place" was a spacious cabin outside of Vermilion-on-the-Lake in Ohio where Jack learned to sail. Mother was a nudist ... a world-class nudist... a workaholic nudist. Jack smiled inwardly. She and her cohort, Mrs. Freland, published the quarterly *Sun and Health*. Brown-wrapped copies sold from under-the-counter to the drugstore cowboys before *Playboy* appeared on supermarket racks. There was nothing pornographic, or even particularly erotic, in the photos of men, women, couples, and families posing nude at their favorite hideaways. Just nice folks shedding their inhibitions and getting over-all tans to show off their good health to anyone who cared to pay twenty-five cents. One of the preppies at St. Charles had discovered and surreptitiously circulated the magazine. Some bullies called his mother a porno queen and Jack had to defend her honor until they tired of the game and moved on to easier prey.

Jack's mother had coerced Mrs. Freland into buying a quarter section of land to the north of the Ocotillo Ranch. The two ladies occasionally saddled their horses and rode literally bareback and bare-assed into the sunset.

Jack remembered discovering an old photo that had fallen behind a dresser. The photo had been taken after Jack's father had been killed in Korea, at Bloody Nose Ridge, before she married Ned, his stepfather. His mother and Mrs. Freland were wearing boots, chaps, Stetsons, and little else. In the background an ensemble of Mariachi players stood naked, wearing only oversized sombreros. They were the sorriest, raunchiest-looking troupe Jack had ever seen. They looked like deserters from Pancho Villa's army. Each musician had struck a pose, anxiously trying to conceal his genitals with a trumpet or a guitar. Only the bull fiddle player had been completely successful; he was the only one with a smile on his face.

There were no telephones then. According to Ruiz, the two women kept him running back and forth carrying messages between the two ranches. He didn't like it very much, but it improved his English. "The clearer I learned to speak, the fewer trips I had to make," he used to say with a laugh. When the women became aware that Ruiz understood everything they were saying, they passed notes instead, and that's how Ruiz claimed he perfected his reading.

Mrs. Freland sold her spread to his mother when she remarried. Maria reported that she had moved out in a huff. About that time, the two women had mutually agreed to drop the publication. Ned sold the Freland place and bought a marina complex on Lake Meade. An intense summer storm destroyed the marina. As was usual for all his investments, the docks sank to the bottom of the lake along with Captain Ned's "yacht", a converted WWII Higgens motor torpedo boat. They returned to the east where Ned invested more of his mother's inheritance in vapid attempts to recoup their losses.

That had been okay with Jack, for he had hoped his mother's obsession with sun worshiping had come to an end, and with it the "ritual". The ritual consisted of Jack's daily trip to a circular gravel mound that rose from the desert for no apparent reason and was located about two hundred yards from the ranch house. His mother would spread a canvas cot for him to lie on. She would remove his shirt and shorts and take them back to the house along with his shoes, making it impossible for him to pick his way barefooted through "teddy bear" cholla and prickly pear cactus. He spent the afternoons warding off stinging flies and turning constantly to avoid being par-broiled. "That's when I developed a stammer. God, how I hated this place."

A gentle west wind stirred the eucalyptus branches overhead. A meteorite flashed across the sky, split apart, and disappeared over the horizon. An owl hooted in the distance. A coyote barked at the crescent moon that peaked over the San Tans. Jack took a deep breath. The creosote bushes smelled like fresh rain. "Maybe I don't hate this place after all," Jack said to the kitten on his chest, but Orange Cat was sound asleep.

CHAPTER 7

A shotgun blast startled Jack awake and he sat upright. Orange Cat disappeared into the cupola. A Gila woodpecker ducked behind the saguaro and a cottontail scrambled into a thicket. A pall of blue smoke lifted into the pink and blue morning sky.

Ruiz, a shotgun in his hand, stepped out of the citrus grove, "Buenos dias, Jefe."

"Ruiz, what are you doing?" Jack yelled.

"Look what those stupid rabbits did!" Jack came down the stairs to the yard.

"You must be a pretty good shot. You can hit rabbits with your eyes closed."

"I just scare them away, Jefe."

The men laughed. "You are like your mother, Jefe. She wouldn't let me shoot the rabbits or woodpeckers either."

A helicopter, its engine throbbing heavily, broke over the top of Lone Butte and hovered directly overhead. It moved slowly down the ridge and made a return pass and hovered momentarily over the gravel mound outside the fence. Jack cupped his hands over his eyes and stared upward. Someone waved, and he waved back. The helicopter slid to the right, descended slowly and touched down on the gravel flats behind the cactus garden. The blades slowly fluttered to a stop. Tom stepped out, followed by Susan. Paco raced out, barking a challenge.

"Be still, Paco," Jack called. Paco's bark shifted to a low-throated growl as he slunk close to the ground and circled the helicopter warily.

"We filmed the ridge, the cairns, and that gravel mound. Your adobe is sitting on the edge of an intaglio," Susan said as soon as she got out of the helicopter. "From the air, the whole ridge looks like a woman lying on her back with her knees drawn up. You can see all kinds of details from the air that you don't notice on the ground. The knobby ridge at the gate is a head, that rise in the middle is a nose, and below that you can see a criss-crossed necklace, the gravel shards have been turned over. There's definitely different patina. Those two ridges at the base near shaman's cave are feet and..."

Tom stopped her in mid-sentence. "Susan's excited, Jack, and may be jumping to conclusions."

"And that gravel mound...could be a kick-ball. There's a deep impression in the center. A circle with dirt in the middle is a symbol for a kickball. It could be another HA-AK figure!"

Tom smiled. "Okay, Susan. I said it could be, but she's right. The mound is man-made. It's an almost perfect circle. Those gravel shards don't match anything we can see from the air in this area. Whoever made it took advantage of a natural landform to shape the body. All the material around the knob that forms the head and neck and the gravel in the circle mound were carried here, probably in baskets. It's the same technique that was used to build the HA-AK intaglio. There may be a connection."

"Stop hedging, Tom," Susan interrupted. "You know it's an HA-AK intaglio."

"Speaking of intaglios, we want to take a look at a posted site in Peoria. Half of it has been turned into a parking lot, and there's another partially destroyed site near Buckeye. I only have four hours of helicopter time, so we better go. I'd like to come back and take some measurements and do some preliminary investigations from the ground. Jack, with your permission, I'd like to come back and do some preliminary surface work."

"Sure, anytime. Glad to have you."

"I'll be back sooner than that," Susan said. "Can I bring a few friends? They might be able to shed some light..."

"Not the Rat Pack, Susan?" Tom interrupted raising two hands to the sky.

"They are not a Rat Pack. They are my 'A' team."

"They are pack rats," Tom winked at Jack, "to a man."

Susan punched Tom in the shoulder. "Takes one to know one."

They were gone as suddenly as they came with a cloud of dust and a heavy thump-thump-thump as the helicopter accelerated towards the Estrellas. "And a Hi Ho Silver!" Jack muttered. "You can come out now O.C."

Ruiz shut the back gate. "I don't like helicopters, Jefe. They have no wings. What if the engine fails?"

"The same thing that would happen with an airplane. You crash, although sometimes the pilot can control the crash."

"It's no good. The ground is still too hard. What do you want me to do today, Jefe?"

Jack glanced at the high cumulus clouds over the Superstitions. "There's no need to water the citrus grove. There'll be rain this evening. Why don't you close the shutters and tie things down. We'll leave them that way until the monsoons are over."

"I'll throw a cable across the water tank. Those posts are weak; they won't take much wind." Ruiz said and headed for the orchard.

A yellow Land Rover wheeled directly into the graveled yard. The driver turned a tight circle and brought the vehicle to an abrupt stop directly in front of the porch steps. The driver's door swung open and a bulky bear-like man emerged, hitched his pants up over a hefty stomach, and looked around the yard before he turned to Jack and nodded. A bigger man, forty pounds heavier and six inches taller, clambered out the passenger side.

Seconds later, a Morgan two-plus-two roadster with maroon fenders and a cream-colored bonnet pulled in beside the Land Rover, forcing the heavy-set man to jump aside. The driver set the emergency brake and exited over the side without opening the door. He walked across the yard with a decided limp. Orange Cat dove through the agave cactus, raced to the upper terrace and leaped into the lower branches of a palo verde tree.

"What a lovely place," Mike Chernov shouted gaily, "an oasis in the desert, and the view of the South Mountains is spectacular."

The two barrel-chested behemoths followed him up to the porch. "Allow me to present the Mallory Brothers. Doctor Reed, this is Dan Mallory, and this is his brother, Ben." Jack extended his hand, expecting it to be crushed, and he wasn't disappointed. Dan, the eldest, gave a display of power and quickly released his grip. Ben, the younger, held on a few seconds longer, exerting an extra force, and grinned. Jack made no attempt to test his own strong grip as he sized the men up. What a contrast, he thought, two broadswords and a rapier.

"The Mallorys own the Indian Traders Den in Scottsdale. They specialize in artifacts, baskets, and pots, that sort of thing. If you like, they could appraise your materials."

"Yes, thank you. I would appreciate it. Where would you like to begin?"

"Why don't we start with the petroglyph rocks?" Chernov said.

"This way." Jack led the men up to the terrace. Orange Cat crawled higher up the tree as they approached.

Dan Mallory kneeled in front of the glyphs, then walked behind each one and examined the back panels. He nodded at Ben, who stood in the center of the terrace sketching the figures on a notepad.

"This one with the stick figure inside of the larger being is exquisite. Your photos don't reveal their size or proportions," Chernov said. "These are the most perfect specimens I've seen... If they are authentic, which they appear to be, they are quite valuable, don't you agree, gentlemen?" Neither Mallory responded. "Ben, why don't you and Dan appraise the objects inside first." Ben grumbled, snapped his notepad shut, and they all followed Jack into the Arizona sunroom.

"The icons came from the cave; the other artifacts were found on the ridge," Jack said and pointed to the carved stone objects on the shelves beneath the windowsills.

Chernov picked up one of the icons and ran his fingers over the incised reversed swastika on the back. "The sun sign. This is a beautiful piece." He examined the front. "One arm is elongated and appears to be holding a child. The eyebrows have an almost oriental appearance to them."

Ben grunted, picked up a stone kick-ball, looked it over, and handed it to Dan. Jack opened the French doors that led into the living room and switched on the lights. Overhead the western chandelier cast a soft light in the room.

"The rugs on the wall and the floor are for sale. So is that stack piled over there in the alcove; the baskets are on the dining table." Jack motioned toward a doorway at the end of the room. "There's beer and iced tea in the fridge. Help yourself," he said and left to rejoin Chernov.

Chernov put the icon back on the shelf. "It's an anthropomorph, a human effigy. Its eyebrows are very similar to the eyebrows on the glyphs in your yard. It's possible that the same person created both. There seems to be a trace of something that looks like gold leaf on this figure. It makes the eyes stand out. Did anyone alter this piece?"

"Not to my knowledge. I noticed that sheen around the eyes when I took it out to the sunlight."

"I'd like to check out the site? You said the large boulder was nearby?" Chernov said.

"Yes, I'll get my truck."

"No need for that. I can walk it." The two men climbed to the top of the ridge, picking their way warily around the cholla cactus. "Devil's Claw, properly named. Nasty stuff," Chernov said. Jack pointed at the cairns scattered below the crest of the ridge. "HoHoKam," Chernov added matter-of-factly, "nothing in them of value, no bones or fragments. There never is."

"Is that always the case?"

"It's always that way with HoHoKam cairns. And I'm sure that those are HoHoKam. They just piled up the stones and added to them from time to time."

"Tom Tracy and Susan Schaffer flew in here this morning in a helicopter. They feel that this whole ridge and the gravel mound may be an intaglio."

Chernov stopped and surveyed the ridge. "It's hard to tell from this level. But if Tom thinks it's an intaglio, it probably is. In which case, any of the material found on the surface would be of considerable interest to the museum. But this area is solid granite. And I sincerely doubt if there's anything underneath. There might have been a village nearby. One of the HoHoKam irrigation canals ended somewhere near the east end of South Mountain Park. I don't remember seeing a canal this far south."

They walked to the front of a large boulder that sat on the top of the knob. Jack pointed to where the patina on the gravel was lighter than the surrounding material. "Someone drove a truck in here and took some of the smaller petroglyph rocks."

"They would have needed a semi-truck to carry out that large boulder. It's a good thing you grandfather moved the others. He probably saved them from curio seekers and rock hounds. Why don't people realize these artifacts belong in a museum, for everyone to see?"

When they returned to the ranch house, the Mallorys were sitting on a bench, almost as immobile as the petroglyphs in their niches guarding the terrace.

"What's your opinion of the animal fetishes?" the curator challenged. "Special or not?"

"Fairly common," Dan replied. "The large bear and that smaller black bear are excellent pieces, but there's not much of a market."

"We've got a carton full of that museum stuff," Ben blurted.

"Anything interest you?" Chernov asked softly.

"There are some fine blankets and a couple of baskets we could move. The rest is average. If you sell to us, there'll be no charge for the appraisal," Dan offered. "If not, it's $75 for the appraisal and $40 for our trip out here."

"I'd like to have the appraisal, but I'm not ready to sell anything just yet."

"Then why are we here?" Ben growled and glared at the curator. He heaved himself to his feet and walked towards the Land Rover.

Dan forced a smile. "Stop by the Den this afternoon. I'll have an appraisal ready for you by noon." He grabbed the back of the seat and hauled himself into the Land Rover. Even with the seat in the back position, he could barely fit his bulk into the driver's seat. He backed up the car awkwardly, shifted gears, and nearly sideswiped the gatepost on his way out.

Chernov offered a soft handshake and held Jack's arm. "The boys will tell me more than they'll tell you. I have a friend in Washington D.C., Manouch Azad. He's the director of the Antiquities Appraisers Association and also works for the IRS occasionally. He'll be out next week to appraise some museum donations. I'll have him look at the photographs. You're in no hurry to sell are you?"

"No, I'm not. As I said, I'm not sure that I even want to sell. I'm curious, that's all."

"I wouldn't be, if I were you. Well, let's wait for Manny and let's hear what Tom has to say. I do want the glyphs for the museum, safer there than here, I believe, especially if you are away much of the time." The curator lowered his voice, "Thanks for inviting me, Jack. I'll be in touch." He waved as the Morgan pulled out of the yard.

Orange Cat crawled slowly down the tree, stood by Jack and rubbed up against his leg. "Those were the Brothers Grimm," he said to the kitten, "and Dr. Mike Chernov is the nutty curator."

Jack parked across the street from Indian Traders Den, in front of Sally's Rodeo Shop. A banner in the front window read, "Summer Sale. All Western Apparel 40% off." On impulse, Jack went inside.

A stylish fortyish blonde flashed him a friendly gap-toothed smile. "Can I help you?"

"I'm looking for a hat," Jack answered. She led him to an aisle where straw Stetsons were stacked in rows. He searched through a stack until he found a seven and five-eighths.

"You have a big head, honey," she said, "but those straws run large. Try this one." Jack put it on and glanced in the mirror. "That's you."

"I'll take it," he said and waited while she made out a ticket. "What are snakeskin boots going for?"

"Almost as much as you want to pay. The handmade boots can go up to a thousand dollars. We have some hand-lasted Tony Lamas that are on sale for $400. Want to try on a pair?"

"No, thanks. I'll just take the hat."

"The hat is normally $99; you got it for $60 including tax, title, and license fees."

Jack laid his old hat on the counter and started to write a check. "Can you dump that someplace for me?"

"I'll toss it in a dumpster," she replied.

Jack adjusted the brim and set the Stetson on his head. "Thanks," he said and made his way to the exit.

"It's always a pleasure to do business with a man who knows what he likes, Cowboy," she said.

Jack crossed the street and entered the semi-darkened showroom of the Indian Traders Den. Baskets and blankets were stacked on a long row of tables. Locked display cases were cluttered with pawn jewelry. A Porter saddle, mounted on a sawhorse, blocked the middle aisle. Buckskin shirts and moccasins were tacked to the walls. The main room was dark and the goods were badly displayed. The back wall was lined with Civil War muskets, sabers and scabbards. Racks of stuffed antelope heads and Rocky Mountain sheep and a moth-ridden grizzly bear on a wheeled pedestal stood beside the open office. The Mallorys sat on high stools, munching fist-sized deli sandwiches.

Jack stopped by a locked gun case, housing a Sharps repeating rifle, a Henry and three 45-70s. One of them had a vintage look; the other two were newer models. "Do you sell many of these pieces?"

"Those pieces are all sold or spoken for, but to answer your question, the 45-70's are making a comeback. We can't keep the early models or the remakes in stock," Dan said.

"Just curious. I came by for the appraisal, if it is finished."

"Here it is." Jack looked it over and handed him a check. Dan laid it on a desk without even looking at it.

"Thanks. I'll let you know if I want to sell anything."

"That's an appraisal only. That's not what we're offering," Ben said pointedly and stuffed the sandwich into his mouth. Jack touched the brim of his new hat and walked briskly to the front door.

Jack pulled a red flyer out from under his windshield wiper: "Red Opery House, Country music, Line dancing, No cover." A telephone number and brief note had been penciled in at the bottom: "You need to slouch a little when you walk, Cowboy. If you're interested in a little line dancing, give me a call, Sally." Jack turned around and saw Sally dressing a mannequin in the display window. She waved. Jack deliberately sagged his shoulders and waved back before getting into his truck.

CHAPTER 8

Hudson Park was a miniature oasis in the middle of the city. A small lake mirrored the cloudless sky. Mixing with migratory birds, indigenous ducks and geese searched the shoreline for food. Jack crossed the greenbelt to a ramada under the scant shade of a trio of royal palms.

"Jack, you look like a drugstore cowboy. Where did you get that straw?" Mollie asked.

"At K-Mart, Mollie. It was a blue light special."

"Go on, Jack. That straw's straight from Sally's. You going courtin' or just stepping out?"

"Just trying to keep the sun off my face and my head cool, Mollie."

"Sure." Mollie grinned and led him over to a small gathering of men and women sitting at a long table. "These are my high school gal friends, and most of these gentlemen were my beaus," Mollie laughed and the other women snickered.

"They were everybody's beaus, Mollie. Anyone who would have them anyway," Anna said.

"I was never anybody's beau," one of the men said with a smile.

"Chance, no one would have you then or now," Mollie added and the women snickered again.

"Well, I might take a chance," Anna said brightly.

"Be still, Anna, you're embarrassing Chance. We've been talking about the rocks, Jack," Mollie said and handed him some photos. "Each of the girls brought a picture of her rock." Jack looked through the photos.

"We only took the smaller ones, the ones we could lift," Anna said. "The others were too heavy. I brought mine with me today." She pointed to a rock with two circles on it.

"I have one like that," Jack said, "but it has three circles. The ones with circles are different than the other glyphs. These are photos of pictographs or so I'm told. The ones with the circles are petroglyphs."

"Petro or picto, it doesn't matter," Anna said. "We've talked it over and since they came from your place, you can have them back."

"What will you do with them?" Chance asked.

"Well, I'm having people out to the ranch to look them over, some experts who hope that the glyphs may be able to tell us something about the past. I'm not sure, but they should be preserved somewhere, either at the ranch or in a museum."

"You decide, Jack, " Mollie said. "You can have my rocks too."

"Your rocks, Mollie? You're the one who got us in dutch in the first place," Anna said and Mollie reddened.

"Quiet, I haven't told Jack."

"You didn't tell Jack that you wanted to square with Chance for jilting you at the prom?" the women chorused.

"Jilt me?" Mollie shouted. "He jilted all of us. He asked us all to go to the prom."

"I didn't ask you all to the prom," Chance sputtered and his face turned red. "You all asked me. I didn't know how to say no!"

"What else couldn't you say no to, Chance?" Anna said and Chance's face reddened even more deeply.

"Good God, he never could stop blushing," Mollie laughed as Chance stalked off, his hands in his pockets and stood by the lake.

"You embarrassed him, Mollie," Anna said.

"Heaven forbid! He loves the attention, always has. Well, now you have it, Jack. I confess; we took the rocks, but we meant no harm. Things were different back then."

"Funner."

"Safer."

"Happier."

"Times were better. We were all poor, but no one went hungry and no one did drugs. Drugs, heck, we didn't even smoke," Delores said.

"I smoked."

"Well, you always were the wild one, Anna, and you rode horses bareback," Mollie said.

"Still do."

"Anna lives up in Sedona and has a stable of Arabians," Mollie said. "The best in the country."

"Well, the county, at least," Anna smiled. She opened a large bag and handed Jack an old red leather bound book. "It's my grandmother's diary, Virginia Evans. She married a missionary. They lived on the St. Johns Reservation. She mentions Ocotillo Ranch and your rocks. I marked several passages for you."

Jack started to open the book. "Keep it; read it all if you want to. Send it back when you're finished."

"Thank you, Anna," Jack said.

"Time to eat girls," Anna said. "Smelling these beans is giving me an appetite."

"Anna, you were born with an appetite," Delores said, "and not just for beans." The women snickered and began opening coolers and baskets, setting the food and drinks on the picnic table.

Jack joined Chance at the edge of the lake. "Chance, were Mollie and Anna just putting you on, or is there some truth there?"

"Truth? Not by a long shot. Well, maybe a little." Chance grinned. "But I was no ladies man. I've always been a bit on the shy side, and I still am." Chance watched at a black swan that was swimming nearby, looking the men over. The swan paddled past them and rounded the point. "Fact is, Jack, I knew the girls had taken the rocks, but I didn't let on to your granddad. He was a tough customer. He didn't care for nonsense. My dad was the foreman of the crew who built the stable. I was just a helper. Five dollars a day was a lot back then, and I was glad to get it."

Jack nodded and Chance continued. "Your granddad had us move the rocks up to that terrace Ruiz was building."

"Do you remember where the rocks were sitting before you moved them?"

Chance looked at the swan again and turned to Jack. "I might. The smaller ones didn't weigh much, maybe ten to twenty-five pounds. Those two that looked like women; we called them the sisters, were close to fifty pounds. I know where they were. I carried them up myself in a wheelbarrow. The big rock with all the scribbles sat on the edge of a ledge. It must of weighed nearly two hundred pounds. It took two of us to move it. Anymore and we would have got in each other's way. Your granddad hitched a skid to the bumper of that old Packard of his, and drug it to the house."

"I've seen the skid marks. I wondered who made them." Jack fished an old silver coin out of his pocket and handed it to Chance. "It's a Spanish real. My granddad kept three of them in a box on the mantle. I remember him saying that your dad found one and that one of the workman found the two others."

"Spanish silver? Yes, I know about those pieces. Your granddad paid them ten dollars a piece for the coins. That was a lot. We spent a lot of our noontimes looking for those things. At least, I did, but I never found one."

"Where did they find these?"

"At the foot of Lone Butte. Just above that wash. There was a little cave there. Your granddad had it filled in with rocks. He was afraid someone would crawl in and get bit by a snake or get trapped if there was a rock slide."

"Did anyone look in the cave?"

"I did," Chance said, "but there was nothing inside as far as I could tell. We all speculated that there were more coins, but we didn't have time to look around much. Too much work to do and summer was coming. It was already hot before we finished the stable. I was always going to come back and look around that cave someday, but I never got around to it. The Depression hit, so I went to California looking for work, and then the war came.

Anyway, I thought that those bank robbers might have stashed their loot in one of those caves."

Chance looked at Jack's surprised expression and squinted his eyes. "You're thinking that the loot was hidden under an ironwood tree, I bet." He paused. "That's what Mollie and her bunch thinks, but that ain't what happened. My Uncle Bob, Bob Goldsberry, led the sheriff's posse. They caught that bunch and there was a shoot out. The posse killed all three bandits. One of the men asked my uncle to bury him under that ironwood tree where he was laid up. He just whispered. Someone overheard him, but didn't get it right and spread the word that the gold was buried under an ironwood tree. Now, it wasn't so. The man told my uncle that the loot was hidden in a mineshaft near a cave that the Yaquis had been working. For some time after that, my Uncle Bob would ride out and look for that mineshaft, but he never did find it. As for Mollie and everyone else who want to spend their time digging up ironwood trees, well, let them look!" Chance winked at Jack. "I'm not going to stop them."

"Come and get it!" Mollie called.

Chance punched Jack on the arm and said, "Let's join the fun."

Mollie brought Jack a plate of barbecue beef, beans, potato salad, and tumbler of iced tea from a cooler. Jack ate slowly and listened to the women as they gossiped about the "good old days". She nudged Jack, "One of these days, you're going to have to carve out a benchmark of your own. Maybe not on a rock, but in your heart."

Jack nodded. "Or maybe rub out a few marks, Mollie."

The women began clearing the picnic table when everyone finished. Chance set up a chessboard. "Care for a game, Jack?"

"Sure. Why not?"

Chance hid a black and a white piece behind his back and then offered his closed fists. Jack won the white piece and made his opening move. After a few initial moves, Chance forced Jack into an even exchange. He traded a queen for a queen. Chance followed this up by forcing Jack to trade his horses and then his bishops.

"We're down to the end game, Jack," Chance said with a grin. "It's pawns and castles and position." Chance winked at Mollie who was watching over Jack's shoulder.

"Better watch yourself, Jack. Chance is a sly one," she warned.

"I think I'm in serious trouble, Mollie." Jack laughed, studied the board carefully and cautiously moved a pawn forward.

"Here we go, Mollie," Chance said and grinned even more broadly. In the next few minutes, Chance moved his pawns forward relentlessly and protected them brilliantly with his castles until he pushed a pawn into the back row. Jack had no choice but to capture the piece with a castle. Chance took the castle with his own and when Jack retaliated, Chance captured Jack's remaining castle.

"You've run out of castles, Jack. I still have mine." Chance winked again at Mollie.

"I think I'll concede. Congratulations. You play a wicked game, Chance."

"I told you about him, Jack. He is an wicked man," Mollie said.

Chance laughed and leaned back on the bench. He drew a packet of papers and tobacco out of his shirt pocket. "Still make my own smokes," he said. Jack watched as he folded the paper, filled it with tobacco, deftly rolled it up, licked the edges, and then twisted the ends. He struck a kitchen match on the bench, lit his cigarette, and tossed the match into the BBQ grill. He inhaled deeply and exhaled, a puff of smoke spiraled skyward.

"You're no Marlboro Man, Chance Clark," Mollie said.

"Can't say that I am, Mollie, but hell he's dead ain't he? The chemicals in those tailor-made cigarettes probably killed him. My tobacco doesn't have all that crap," he said and coughed. "Jack, Mollie has been telling me about her problems with the cattle and the pressure from that Carver fellow. She tells me you're having your share of problems, too."

Chance and Mollie listened as Jack told them about Carver's visit, his offer and his threats as well as the sniper and the damage to his well house. Chance sat forward.

"Well, Jack. Let me tell you something. If Carver wants yours and Mollie's land, then you'd best be together on this. You're into something like a chess game. Chess is a game of space, of time, and of force. When I was young, my father taught me that I could see the world through a chessboard. It opened up my mind quite a bit. As I see it, you can force Carver to trade pieces, but if he takes a piece, you have to be sure you trade even. You can trade queens if you have to. But if not, the queens can take care of themselves. They always do. You get me?" Jack nodded.

"But you've got to play for the end game. You and Mollie have got to stick together. You're the castles. If you cooperate, in the long run, you control the space. Carver can't win. Even if there's a stalemate, Carver loses. Time's running against him, not you two."

"Time isn't exactly on my side," Jack said. "There're some debts and taxes. I can borrow some money from my sister, but there are limits. What I really need is water."

"Water? There's plenty of water under your land. Enough for the house and the citrus grove anyway," Chance offered.

"What I need is an aquifer, enough water to sub-divide Mollie's land and mine."

"What you want is a 'dowser', a man who knows how to use a willow or a witch-hazel wand."

"I don't think I would bet the farm on a witching wand."

"It's not the wand, Jack. It's the man. The wand is just part of the dowser's bag of tricks. Your real dowsers study the land. They know where the water is or where it's likely to be. The magic is getting some farmer to put up the cash for the drillers! It's all smoke and mirrors. Ruiz is a dowser. He picked the sites for at least two of the wells on your property."

Jack laughed. "Ruiz is still mad that the drillers put in the well south of the house. They had to go 600 feet down. He says there's water beyond the orchard and that's there water down by the arroyo."

"I'd trust him, Jack. He's Yaqui. His people have always lived in hard country. They know how to find water. Yaqui town was built around their wells. In those days, you had to truck in water by wagon from the Salt River."

Mollie touched Jack's arm and said, "Chance's right, Jack."

"I know he is, Mollie. I'll think about it. Thanks for the advice, Chance, and the chess lesson."

"Take care, Jack. Don't let those cookie cutters get you down."

"A storm's brewing," Mollie said. "We'd best get going, girls."

Jack jotted down their names and addresses on an envelope and stuck it into his shirt pocket. "Thanks for everything. I'll let you know what's happening. Anna, thanks for lending me the diary. I'll get it back to you as soon as I'm finished." He said good-bye to everyone and got into his truck.

He headed down old highway 60, crossed the Mill Avenue Bridge and parked in an empty lot behind the Hayden Flour Mill building at the foot of "A" Butte. He climbed to the top and sat on a flat rock overlooking Sun Devil Stadium. From this height, he could see the cities of Scottsdale, Mesa, Phoenix, and Tempe straddling both sides of the dry Salt River bed. Beyond the I-10 freeway to the southwest, he spotted Lone Butte towering above the Ocotillo Ranch.

He started reading and taking notes from Virginia Evan's diary. When he finished the sun was dropping behind the Estrellas far to the west, nearly obscured by storm clouds. He could smell the rain in the air as he picked his way down the slope. He got into his truck and took the side streets through the ASU campus to the Hayden Library.

"What are we looking for this time, partner?" Patrick Garret said as he eyeballed Jack's straw Stetson.

Jack grinned and removed the hat. "Gold. Lost or stolen treasures."

"Like the Lost Dutchman?"

"That would be a start, but perhaps anything connected to missing Spanish gold, looted churches, payroll robberies, that sort of thing. Something your namesake would be interested in."

"You mean like Billy the Kid?" Garrett thumped his sheriff badge nametag. "I'd say about 1530 to the 1850s then." He sat down at the computer keyboard. "I'll see what I can find."

"Can you add Mormons to the search?"

"No problem. This should prove interesting," Patrick spoke to the computer. "Twenty-three items, more than I thought." He hit a key and the printer began clicking out a file sheet.

Jack scanned the list. He checked off five references and handed them to Patrick.

"Easy. These are all indexed in the Arizona Room. You're in luck." Patrick went into the stacks and returned in less than five minutes with a thick tome, *Lost Treasures of the Old Southwest*, and four thin worn tracts. "I'm afraid you can't check these out, but you can use the copier if you need to."

"Thanks. Do you have anything on bank or stage coach or mine robberies, Mormon or Christian missionaries, also the Mormon Battalion in Central Arizona, say from 1844 to 1925?"

"Whew! It'll take some time. Why don't you use one of the cubicles?" He led Jack to a row of small rooms and opened a locked door. "It's usually reserved for visiting professors. But no one will mind." Jack sat down at the desk and reviewed his notes from Virginia's diary:

> *Virginia married John Evans, a recent graduate from the Christian Training School on Indian School Road in Phoenix in 1899. He served as a minister on the St. John's Reservation. On the way back from a trip to Tempe*

to have wheat ground into flour at Hayden Mills, her driver, Tyrone, took a shortcut through Doc Chandler's land and stopped to toss a rag-doll onto the knob with the cairns and glyphs.

She noted that a large panel on the side of a boulder had a spiral and a set of eyes and an arrow slanting upward. Tyrone said that it meant "look this way". He told her that this was HA-AK's place. It was where she got pregnant from the kickball a suitor had thrown at her. She hid it under her skirt and told him to go away. Anna told Tyrone not to mention any of this to her husband.

In 1906 the Pimas left the reservation to attend a celebration in Sacaton at what the Pimas called HA-AK laying. John got upset because the tribe got drunk on nawait. There was a lot of dancing and vomiting. The women made straw effigies of HA-AK and tossed them into a fire and sang songs to, according to her husband John, propitiate the pagan deity. Following that, the clans walked and rode miles to the cairns on Chandler's land. They met some Pimas from the Salt River Reservation and held another celebration. A few went to a canyon in the South Mountains, past Hieroglyph Hill and set offerings in a cave.

At the next Sunday meeting, John harangued the backsliders and blasphemers. Virginia later questioned Tyrone. He denied that they were worshipping HA-AK; they were just asking for good luck and protection for their children. John tried to stop these celebrations, but they continued on both sides of the Salt River and at St. John's at irregular intervals. Virginia's diary corroborates with Susan's brief description of the HA-AK legend. Virginia was an eyewitness to the burning of straw effigies. Yes, there is a blue owl, Virginia. And she will go on living forever in Papago and Pima hearts no matter what disbelievers may say.

About an hour later, Patrick knocked at the door. "I've found some interesting materials." He laid several references on the desk. "If you come up with some characters or descriptors, I can narrow the search."

"I'm not exactly sure what I'm looking for. I'll let you know." When he was finished, Jack carried the materials back to the desk. "I've tabbed these reprints. I'd like to have them copied."

Garrett gave them to a clerk, "Please copy these for me, Anne. I'd be interested in what you develop from the materials, Jack. There was more activity here in Arizona than I'd imagined. Unusual requests make my job more interesting. The other day, a man was searching for references on the construction and maintenance of tunnels from old forts as a means of escape or to locate water when under siege from 1600 to 1940."

"Did you find anything?"

"Well, actually I did," Patrick beamed. "The Army engineers constructed quite a few forts in Arizona. That was long before 1940 of course. Good hunting," he handed Jack the copies and winked conspiratorially.

CHAPTER 9

A convoy of three jeeps, a camouflaged International Scout, an ancient Suburban in gray primer, and a camper, came to a halt on the track behind the well house. Paco raced out of the orchard and barked wildly as drivers and passengers disembarked warily. "Circle the wagons," shouted a large beetle-browed man wearing a red-checkered shirt. Jack called Paco back and went to meet the group of visitors.
Susan stepped out of the Suburban.

"Hello," she shouted. "I've brought the Rat Pack. This is Wes Gardner." Jack shook hands and tried to keep track of their names as Susan reeled them off: Lee Begay, Kris and Star Pappas, Rex Miller, Bill Carlin, and Dr. Felix Hartman. Jack quickly lost track.

"We came to see the glyphs. We're all rock nuts, but everyone is an expert on something," Wes said.

"True, absolutely true," Kris said. "What we don't know, we make up. I hope the glyphs are close by, I sure don't want to walk in this heat." Kris wiped his neck and forehead with a bandana.

"Just follow the path," Jack stepped back and let Susan lead the others single file up to the terrace. The party fanned out and began examining the glyphs.

"Kris is leader of the pack," Wes explained to Jack. He nodded at Kris who was aiming a video camcorder at the petroglyphs. "He's a lawyer and an author. He has contributed a number of articles to the *Desert Trails Magazine* and has published a couple of texts on Native American myths and legends. His bite can be worse than his bark. That's his wife Star." Wes singled out a comely woman in a bright yellow sunsuit with orange flowers and wispy straw hat. "She's his navigator, copy editor, secretary and PR lady. She keeps him on a track somewhere between writing and goofing off with us pack rats."

"Doc Hartman, the man over there," Wes said and pointed at an elegant, silvered-hair man near Susan, "is the director of the Pacific Rim Institute in Los Angeles. It houses the largest collection of primitive artifacts in the country. Doc cut his teeth on the early HoHoKam and Anasazi cultures. Fakes and frauds are his specialty."

"Lee's part Yavapai-Apache. He was born on the reservation near Camp Verde. He learned cryptology in the Navy and now works for NASA; he encrypts and deciphers codes -- that sort of thing. He's created a method of comparing petroglyph symbols with Indian sign language," Wes explained. "He's made quite a science out of it. Puts it all on his computer at NASA, on his own time, of course," Wes laughed.

"Rex's editor of the *Desert Trails Magazine*. He just did a piece on petroglyph sites in Central Arizona. Over there, that fellow with the black beard is 'Curly Bill'. He's an astronomer from Colorado. He found a space ship pecked on a rock slab in New Mexico and some marks that trace the elliptical orbits of the moon, Venus, and several comets. You could call them amateurs, but the academics of a dozen universities can't match this bunch's combined knowledge of pre- and post-Colombian cultures."

"I'm impressed," Jack and Wes joined the group on the terrace.

"High art," Doc Hartman said. "I've seen nothing like it anywhere." Lee nodded and began pointing out some details on the rocks.

"There's no doubt about it. These glyphs are telling the Legend of HA-AK, the Blue Owl. This glyph is the woman-who-makes-sleeping mats. Here is the kick-ball player coming towards her. The kick-ball was made of stone. When runners traveled from one village to another, they used a kickball to break the monotony, kicking it along, half-slipping it under their toes and giving it a forward fling. The leaning arrow means to strike or hit," Lee said, pointing at the ball symbol. "You can see that the ball has swirls, indicating motion. On this panel, she is rejecting a suitor: her thumbs are turned down. And here, she is hiding the ball under her skirt. In the legend, she tells the kicker that she hasn't seen it. It's sort of a creation story."

Lee continued, "The hump on the side of the rock indicates that she's become pregnant. Over her head is the sign for hidden. That convex rock with a set of circles indicates that her stomach's growing larger and larger. Look at the sign between her legs – fire," Lee said, putting his hand on the rock. "And look at her belly; the child inside her stomach is wearing braids, its hands are claws. Her mouth is a slash mark; that's the sign for horror or alarm. And on that slab over there, HA-AK is gathering children and putting them in a basket."

"God," Kris spoke. "It's like a Peanuts cartoon. One panel follows another. You make it sound easy, Lee."

"Well, it helps if you already know the legend," Lee replied. "There are more symbols on the back of the rocks. Some I recognize and some I've never seen before, but they are crude compared to the front panels. It'll take some work to figure these out. The pictographs in front… clear as spring water, if you know the story. And thanks to Frank Russell, we do."

" Who was Russell?" Jack asked.

"Russell was on the faculty at Harvard and he pioneered cultural anthropology. He developed tuberculosis and was given a leave to do field work on the Gila River Reservation in the 1890s. He was still young, 35, when he died, but he had completed the standard reference work on the Gila River Pimas."

"It was published by the Bureau of American Ethnology in 1904," Felix said.

"Thanks, Doc," Lee said. "Russell got the HA-AK story from the last living shaman. It's the same story I get from the Pimas and Papagos every time I go to a Pow Wow. Last year on the St. Johns Reservation, I talked with an old man who must be at least 90 years old. He mentioned the large boulder by your front gate. Somewhere around 1910 on his way back from the Hayden Flour Mill, he left a rag-doll on the ridge"

"I found the same story in a diary written by Virginia Evans. She mentions a young man, a wagon driver named Tyrone," Jack said.

"Tyrone Three Persons!" Lee exclaimed. "It must be him. I'd like to see that diary."

"It's up at the house. I'd really like to meet Tyrone if he's the same man."

"It can't be a coincidence," Rex said. "I think I smell a story for the magazine."

"And, I'd like to write it," Kris offered. "I can't pass up a myth like this, uncovering the Legend of the Blue Owl."

"You got it!" Rex agreed. "We have a legend, the HA-AK intaglio, and obviously, something like the Rosetta Stone to tie it all together, with Lee's help of course. And I think I've got something else. We featured Ted De Grazia, the artist, in one of our issues. He's a friend of the Papagos and I remember a series of painting interpreting the HA-AK legend. Glorious, phosphorescent colors showing her gathering up the children in a basket and another of HA-AK burning."

"A rare find. It's going to be a great story... Sorry, go on, Lee," Kris said.

"Well, this glyph, look at the double lines; that's clearly a cave. That's a ceremonial fire at the bottom. They are burning HA-AK. Look closer," Lee said and everyone leaned forward. "Little drops of water are pecked between her legs. She's urinating to put out the fire. Just like the legend says. This panel slowed me up a bit." He pointed to a frog and a butterfly that were scratched deeply into the patina. "Any ideas?"

Lee waited. No one said anything. ""My guess is that the storyteller is showing us that HA-AK transformed herself into an owl. There are some jade sticks that look like that at the Northern Arizona Museum. Things that change fascinated the Old People.

Everyone used frogs and butterflies as symbols of transformation," Lee said. "You find them from the Grand Canyon to Mexico to the Rio Grande to California."

"Lee, how do you know this is a blue owl and not a red owl or brown owl?" Kris asked.

"Well, the rock is triangular in shape. There is a triangle surrounding the owl, and there's another triangle over the owl's head," Lee answered.

"What's a triangle mean, Lee?" Wes asked.

"Blue! Or turquoise," Kris sputtered.

"You got it, Kris. We've found this symbol on blankets, rocks and in Indian sign language. We've got ourselves a bona fide blue owl."

Lee squatted in front of the petroglyphs. "I wish I knew where they were originally located. It would help in the interpretation. There are some missing panels. At least four belong in the middle, if the storyteller kept to the legend. And I think one would tell us what happened here, or maybe why they left." He drew some more circles and lines in his notebook. "They could look like this...." He handed the pad to Susan.

"Why would they look like this, Lee?" Susan asked.

"If I find a sign a hundred times, and it always points to the same thing, then I know it's a recognized symbol. Sometimes you only find a sign once in a lifetime, like the solar panels Bill found in Colorado. We also found some in New Mexico and down in Old Mexico that record a nova, same sort of stuff that Bill found. In some cases, the symbols inscribed on the backs of glyphs or on nearby rocks are as important as what is found on the front."

"So, the frequency of signs is important?" Jack asked.

"Not only that. When I visit a reservation, I talk with the old people and sometimes they tell me something useful. Even though I'm half Yapavai-Apache, I have to visit with them for years before anyone tells me anything. Since the days of the Spaniards, Native Americans have learned not to trust the white man with their thoughts or religious practices." Lee walked over to a bench on the side of the terrace and sat down. He took a drink of water from his canteen. "Talking makes me thirsty," he said with a smile.

"Don't stop now," Doc said. "This is fascinating stuff."

"Well," Lee continued, "you know that big boulder by the front gate? It has several direction signs. One of them says 'Go this way.' Actually, it means 'look this way'; the sign for eyes is "look!" This rock with the circles," Lee pointed to a square block beside his foot, "it works like a gun sight – 'look this way'. But which way was it pointed? It could have pointed to the San Tans, or South Mountain, or Lone Butte. If we knew where to look, maybe we'd find the set of circles hidden behind a boulder, or on a canyon wall. You locate that spot and you might find a sign pointing somewhere else. But you need a starting point. In this instance, we're starting with a known legend. Some of the symbols on the backsides indicate they ran out of water, or they were going to look for water. Maybe the signs say they have too much water, a flood or drought. I can't tell which. For sure there was a cave. Something of value was hidden in it, but I don't know what. Maybe they're talking about the cave where you found the icons, Jack."

Lee pointed and said, "That big slab over there says that HA-AK hid all the game in a cave. Maybe that's what they're talking about. Anyway, whoever inscribed the rocks was a damn clever man. He chose the rocks carefully so they helped tell the story."

"It is called *incorporation*," Felix offered. "It's when holes, striations, color streaks, and shapes are deliberately incorporated into the petroglyph picture."

"Thanks Doc," Lee said and continued. "He's also left a warning. He's telling us you can't blame or sacrifice someone every time life turns sour. The moral is plain: scapegoating doesn't work. HA-AK turned into a blue owl and came back to trouble the people."

"In other words," Kris said, "they kept having problems. Same as us."

Susan spread some aerial photos on a table. "Gather 'round folks. Tom needs confirmation that this is another HA-AK intaglio. We need to do some surface work gang. I brought some pennies." Susan opened her handbag and put several rolls of pennies on the table. "Help yourselves."

Wes and Rex grabbed a roll of pennies. Star grabbed two rolls and handed one to Kris. "No pennies for me. I'm going sit here and study these glyphs some more," he said. "At least, they are in the shade."

"Come on, Kris," Star said. "Move your carcass. We're going out on the ridge with the others." Kris groaned and followed her.

"What are the pennies for?" Jack asked.

"We're going to do some surface archeology. If we see something, we might pick it up, look it over, and put it back where we found it. We put a penny on the spot to indicate that someone has found an object. Then, depending on what's there, we might make a note of it," Wes said. "If we are out on forest or BLM land, we inform the district office about a find and it's location so they can mark a site on their maps. That way they know there's something there if they are planning a timber sale or bulldozing a fire road. Those maps are for their department only, not for the public."

"Why not?" Jack asked.

"If the site is in a remote area, they are afraid that curiosity seekers, pot hunters, or vandals will destroy it. They can't protect the sites and enforce the artifact protection laws even in the national and state parks," Wes answered. "In spite of stiff penalties and fines, cactus pirates still steal saguaros from the Saguaro National Park. The big ones weigh two tons, and they still take them right under the park service's nose. The tourists have been robbing the Petrified National Forest since the 1940s."

"But that doesn't have anything to do with what you are doing today here."

"The reason we are using pennies here, Jack, is because your site is on private land. Under the Indian Artifacts

Preservation Act of 1906 and 1975, private land is specifically excluded, only Indian and public lands are protected. No one can enter you property and even examine artifacts without your permission. You can destroy, sell, or give away the artifacts if you choose. It's your property. The only exception is if any Native Americans are buried on the property, a tribe can claim cultural affinity and they have to right remove the remains and inter them elsewhere, provided that they do so in a reasonable amount of time and restore the land to its former state."

"What if they found remains underneath my home or an outbuilding?"

"That's another story, Jack, and the subject of many lawsuits. Anyway, we are just going to mark and map your site. We won't disturb anything. No digging. I promise."

"I can promise you that I won't be doing any digging out here," Kris said.

"Let's go moving," Susan said. "Hit the trail."

"Susan," Jack said, "Mollie Gentry has some petroglyphs that her grandfather may have taken from the ridge back in the 1930s. Her dairy farm is only a couple of miles down the back road."

"Why don't you take Lee there?" Susan suggested. "I'll keep an eye on the others."

"I'll go along with Jack and Lee," Wes said.

They drove down the long, dusty lane. The cows, fresh from the milking stations, were patiently waiting as Dave and his brother Pete broke up bales of hay and forked them onto the conveyor belt that dropped them into the feedlot.

"Mom's out back," Dave shouted. Jack drove past some rusting, dilapidated farm machinery whose days were long past.

"Farmers never seem to throw anything away," Wes said. A chicken flapped off an old baling machine, and half-flew and half-scrambled into a grove of citrus trees behind an old stone farmhouse.

"Over here," Mollie shouted as she made her way through the waist-high grass and thick weeds behind the barn. She turned over an old rusted 5-gallon can. "I'm going to have the boys clean this up one of these days. Too busy most of the time to bother." Some chickens flew out of the grass. "No wonder I'm short of eggs. These hens are nesting back here." Mollie pointed to a clutch of eggs. "The rocks are back here somewhere." The men joined Mollie and began kicking through the weeds.

"Here's one," Mollie shouted triumphantly, as if she had discovered a cache of robber gold. "I knew it was here someplace."

Lee stood in front of the glyph. It was a large, almost round rock with petroglyph symbols. "A helping hand," Lee said. "There's the hand print, and that long mark means 'to carry or to help carry'. And there's a horse, and that's wild game trapped in a cave. See how that circle encloses it. And those are arrows. And there's Elder Brother opening the entrance to the cave. It's all part of the legend, Wes. The blue owl trapped the game and Elder Brother turned it loose."

"You're right. It's pretty obvious, if you know the legend. Otherwise, the helping hand and the arrows are clear, but it could lead to conflicting interpretations," Wes said. They examined the other petroglyph rock. "It has six different sides. There's a pair of eyes."

"Follow the trail," Lee pointed to a second panel. "That's a cave or a box canyon, I'm not sure which, and there's something there ... could be water or something else."

"There's a reverse cross over here," Wes said.

"I'm not sure what that means," Lee said. "Never saw a symbol like that before."

"Can you figure it out?" Wes asked.

"Maybe, in the context of the other figures and the other marks. If we could just get them on the site."

"I've seen that glyph somewhere before, Lee. I have some old photographs," Jack hesitated, "of my mother standing in front of the hill. I'd forgotten until I saw the glyph."

"I have some photographs to show you, too." Mollie said, "Let's go up to the house."

They sat around a worn picnic table under a majestic queen palm tree where Mollie thoughtfully provided iced tea and lined up the photographs on the table.

"There, look. Just like you described them, Lee. How did you know?" Wes said.

"The man who made these glyphs had a distinct style and a story to tell. I just filled in the blanks." Lee pointed to the photograph of a stick figure on a rock sloped like a deer's hoof. "That's Elder Brother drawn on the side of the cleft and Younger Brother on the other." Lee said, pointing at the figure. "There's an arrow penetrating his anus and coming out his mouth." Lee turned to Mollie. "The legend says that Elder Brother told Younger Brother to shoot him with that arrow and to walk away and come back four days later. There's Younger Brother walking away." He pointed to a photograph. "In other words, he sacrificed himself to help the people. These figures are part of the Origin of the Horse Myth," Lee finished.

"Well, they don't look like that to me," Mollie said. "That one looks like a lizard. And the other looks more like a mule than a horse. Anna Evans has the horse rock. It figures, she loves to raise horses."

"Lee, how are these petroglyphs connected to the HA-AK legend?" Jack asked.

"Often one legend leads into another. In this case, after HA-AK turned into a blue owl, she captured the game and the tribe's most valuable possessions and hid them in a cave. As is often the case, other magical tribal heroes come to the rescue. Elder Brother found the cave, released the animals, and killed so much game that he needed help to carry it back to the tribe. And as the story goes, a new story emerges. He sacrificed himself and transformed into a horse. When the tribes first saw horses, they considered them mystical and magical beings. And they believed that the spirit of Elder Brother is in them."

Lee pointed at the rock. "The glyph that has a faint outline of a lizard on it is part of the legend. The tribe found turquoise in a place where there was a lizard that looked like the ground. How do you show a lizard that looks like the ground? Well, you incise a definite triangle on the backside of the rock and then you peck a faint outline of a lizard on the top. Lizard that blends with the rock. Underneath turquoise. Add a pair of eyes."

"Look here," Wes said. "That's right! Morning Blue had a turquoise monopoly. All these glyphs belong together," Wes said. "They should be restored to the site."

"I've talked to the girls," Mollie said. "They would be happy to return the stones."

"How did they come by them?" Lee asked.

"You tell him, Jack," Mollie said with a wink.

"Mollie and her friends took the glyphs one night to get even with Chance Clark because he didn't show up to take one of them to a prom dance. He was working at the Ocotillo Ranch."

"We knew that he was sleeping in the construction shack," Mollie interrupted. "He was supposed to keep an eye on the property and tools overnight when the workmen were gone. We thought we would drive around, honk the horn, and roust him a bit, just to shake him up. But we lost our nerve, and couldn't think of what to do. One of the girls, I don't remember who, said let's take the rocks. We didn't know what else to do. In a way, it kind of worked. Chance had to move the rest of the rocks up to house. So, in a way, we got even. Chance knew we did it, but he never let on because if anyone asked us, we'd tell about him."

"So, they drove up in a pickup truck, hauled them off and divided them up. Fifty years later, they still have them," Jack finished.

"That's a miracle in itself," Wes said. "Kris and Rex will want to hear about this for their article."

"We need to move these rocks back to the site. If we can put them where they belong, we may find more clues," Lee said.

"We can wrap the rocks with burlap bags and put them all in the bucket of the backhoe. It wouldn't take much time to move them," Mollie said.

'Thanks, Mollie, I'll let you know when I'm ready," Jack said.

"We better get back," Lee said.

Jack drove down the road. "She's a good woman," Wes said.

"She's a tough savvy lady," Jack said. "She has managed the farm and raised those boys all by herself since her husband died."

"She sure does keep them in line. You can tell they respect her. Not many families like that today," Lee said.

Jack turned onto the main road, drove a few yards, and crossed a narrow bridge over the feeder canal and followed the service road until he found an obsolete rutted track that led to the ranch.

"Pull up, Jack," Lee said. Jack stopped the truck. "Tom's right. They used the shape of the ridge and made it part of the intaglio. It looks like HA-AK lying on her side with her knees drawn up. It's similar to the Sacaton intaglio."

"Then the cave where they burned HA-AK has to be over there in the South Mountains," Wes said pointing toward the blinking lights atop the TV towers.

"That's rough country. It will take some doing to find," Jack said.

"I need time to check out the panels. Someone needs to take some photos to Tom," Lee said.

"I'll do it," Wes said. "He wants our confirmation to go with the videotape they took the other day."

The group sat around the fire ring on the upper terrace staring at the glowing embers. The steak, beans, and tamales were finished. Someone sighed happily. Kris pulled out his flask and swallowed deeply.

"It's HA-AK's intaglio. There can be no doubt," Lee said. "The early Papagos probably really burned a woman in the cave. They felt she was the cause of all their problems. The truth was, they were exposed to the Spaniards' diseases: glory, gold, God, and small pox."

"Don't forget measles, tuberculosis, and venereal diseases. Their immune systems never developed to handle them. One epidemic followed another. The common cold and the flu could have set them up for pneumonia, whooping cough and diphtheria. They never knew what hit them," Doc Hartman finished and stared into the fire.

"The shaman who inscribed the rocks had part of the solution. He told the people to leave this place and scatter to the four winds. The Hopis have a similar legend. They scattered after they came up from the Fourth World. The shaman truly believed they had done the wrong thing when they burned the woman."

"How do you know that, Lee?" Doc asked.

"It's on the rocks. They burned a woman in a cave. When their troubles continued, someone decided that the Blue Owl transformed out of smoke and came back to trouble them. They had hoped to trap her spirit in the mountain when the tribe sealed her in the cave. Anyway, that's the Papago version," Lee said.

"A fascinating story, Lee, but who would believe it?" Wes asked.

"It's on the rocks. It's a recorded document of an oral tradition. These are truly Rosette Stones, like you said, Wes. There's no guesswork -- it's a fact."

"Are you going to include the HA-AK story when you give your preliminary report to the ARAS conference, Susan?" Kris asked.

"I might."

"I wouldn't miss that meeting for anything in the world. Buck Weaver and his gang will go crazy," Wes said.

"It would take a major research effort to unravel everything we have found here. We'll never know everything. But there's something magical about this place," Doc Hartman said, looking around the cactus garden. An owl cried like a telegraph key in the distance.

"A tecolate… an elf owl," Wes said. "You don't hear or see them very often. They're on the endangered species list."

"You mean like the spotted owl?" Jack asked.

"Yep. You can't log or mine or do anything that interferes with their habitat," Wes replied. Jack stood up and tossed another log onto the fire, sending the sparks flying. They all felt rather than heard the wings of an owl as it brushed by their heads and passed over the fire.

"What was that?" Star cried.

"HA-AK is calling you," Kris teased.

"We're all endangered species, if HA-AK's around," Star replied.

"Who do you think sent the owl?" Kris asked and everyone laughed.

CHAPTER 10

Jack, Tom, and Wes, sat together in the section of the auditorium reserved for the American Artifact Association members. "The Amerindian Rock Art Society rents this space every year for its annual conference. There are plenty of cheap hotels and restaurants in the area. We're not talking wealth here, but we are talking fanatics," Wes informed Jack. "The ARAS and old school archeologists believe that petroglyphs are nothing more than art forms, primarily just prehistoric doodles and graffiti. How they come up with their ideas is beyond me," Wes said. "Unfortunately, morticians and cemeteries are responsible for most major paradigm shifts in the scientific world."

"What does your group believe about petroglyphs?" Jack asked.

"We differ in that we believe that glyphs are symbols with ascribed meanings, often containing spiritual significance. Some could be classified as hieroglyphs, meant to be understood, not just enjoyed. The fact that today we appreciate them as primitive art forms is incidental to the historical truths they reveal. We support lobbying and education to preserve that past."

Wes pointed across the room and continued, "That's Buck Weaver, the founder and president. 'Buck Wheat' is a one-man show. He's managed to convince several influential people to save the 'rock art' sites. Our group, the AAA, is with him on that. Politically, Weaver has more clout than we do. He gets the grants. We think he's in bed with a congressman from his district..." Jack looked at Wes. "I should say congresswoman, but it's hard to tell. That's her over there!"

Buck Weaver introduced Susan and informed the audience that her presentation would be based on preliminary information she had assembled on petroglyphs located on the Ocotillo Ranch.

Jack spotted a dowdy-looking woman wearing a dark blue trim hat and dark blue suit. Large purplish veins etched her face.

"She looks like HA-AK," Tom laughed. Jack elbowed him as Susan began her presentation.

Using transparencies and graphs, she marked off the lines of cairns she had mapped on the ridge. The crowd was silent when she followed with close-up slides of the animal fetishes, but "ooh'd and aah'd" when she showed several views of the petroglyphs. The audience applauded. Susan sipped a glass of water and stood behind the podium. Weaver raised his hand, cutting off the applause.

"She stayed right on course. She didn't make any reference to the intaglios. Very professional," Tom said.

"Questions? One at a time, please," Weaver said.

A gaunt, bespectacled, owl-faced man rose. "Fakes," he shouted at the podium and turned to the audience. "Those fetishes are not HoHoKam and the glyphs are not Pima. They are all fakes."

"Who the hell's that?" Wes asked.

"That's Tom Owens. He's Draper's assistant, a graduate student at ASU," Jack said.

"Well, he doesn't know his glyphs." Wes stood up. "Fake what, sir? They sure as hell are authentic as far as I'm concerned, and as far as a lot of the people I know are concerned." He glared at Buck Weaver as the audience began tittering.

"We all know Mr. Gardner's position very well. He speaks glyphically," Buck Weaver smiled behind his fist as a short ripple of laughter ensued.

"The glyphs are real, Buck, and so are the animal fetishes. Several experts have visited the site and they concur," Wes insisted.

"But a real what?" asked Buck Weaver. "They could be a real anything, but they are apparently rock art."

"Yes, they are rock art, extraordinary examples of rock art," Wes agreed. "But they clearly contain a message from the past, beautifully inscribed using Indian sign language." Wes sat down.

"They are fakes!" Owens shouted. "They were made by a dealer on Indian School Road who peddled them to tourists in the '50s."

Wes stood up. "Mr. Owens, if they were made in the 1950s, could you please explain the fact that in the 1920s, these fakes you refer to were moved to the ranch house by several people, that photographs was taken of them in the 1930s and that they are mentioned in an1890s diary? There are other eyewitness accounts, one by a Pima Indian who visited the site in 1908. At that time, Mr. Owens, the population of Tempe numbered no more than 500 people and the site was twelve miles away. Why would someone ride out, carve the fetishes, and encipher the glyphs? So we could have a debate here tonight? Dr. Reed," he gestured towards Jack, "has talked to the dealer you are referring to. The dealer admits that he has copied petroglyphic images on sandstone for the tourist trade. But he denies having any knowledge of these artifacts and has stated categorically that he is incapable of doing this type of work."

Wes waited until the buzzing quieted in the audience. "Are you an authority on rock writing, Mr. Owens? No? Then, who is your informant? I think you should cite your authority or withdraw your statement." Owens turned red and sat down abruptly.

"Good job," Tom said to Wes.

"Dr. Reed, if I may ask, what is your interest in the matter?" Buck Weaver asked.

Jack stood up. "I own the Ocotillo Ranch. I can assure you that the petroglyph rocks and the animal fetishes have been on the property since 1903. Recently these objects have been examined and authenticated by Ms. Schaffer, Dr. Chernov, Dr. Tracy and a few others."

"Well, then you obviously have a vested interest. In any case," Weaver said with a flourish, "the animal fetishes are not within our society's provenance, although the petroglyphs are. Perhaps you would allow me and other interested members to visit your site."

"I'd be delighted. You are all welcome," Jack said addressing the audience. Several people cheered and clapped. Wes tugged at his sleeve and Jack added, "As well as the members of the American Artifact Association." A few loud boos and hisses followed the invitation.

Weaver rapped his gavel. "Our time is short. There are several position papers to be heard. We'll take a ten minute recess and then resume the proceedings." He stalked off the stage, leaving a slightly perplexed Susan alone on the dais.

"Well, Jack, you certainly know how to orchestrate a cattle call," Tom said.

After the meeting, the Pima Room was filled to capacity. The overflow spilled out onto an open veranda that overlooked the stockyards. Beyond the city lights, lightning flashed around the TV towers atop South Mountain. The ARAS had reserved the banquet room. The Stockman's Club served as a watering hole for socially and financially prominent Phoenicians. The cookie cutters and wheeler-dealers bent elbows with legislators, university presidents, and heart surgeons.

Jack was standing at the bar with Tom and Wes. He eyed Susan on the far side of the room, who apparently was having a serious discussion with Chernov and Buck Weaver.

"Why do you call yourselves the Rat Pack?" Jack asked, directing his question to nobody in particular.

"It stands for Recycled Action Time," Kris said with a grin. He swallowed his drink, slammed it onto the bar, and called for a refill. "We're all former actors, lawyers, teachers, professors, car dealers, rock hounds, nature lovers, and ecologists. You name it. The only thing we have in common is a passion for preserving the past and in the long run saving the future. Idiosyncratic amateurs, you might say. We have different ideas about rocks that talk. 'Buck Wheat's' bunch believes all rock writings are merely art forms."

He waved his glass to Buck Weaver and Susan. "Curly Bill over there thinks visitors from outer space left messages for us. The truth of it all is probably somewhere in between. Anyway, we all meet once a year to sound out our discoveries and ideas. It gets pretty hairy sometimes," Kris and Wes laughed. "Except for a few scholars like Felix and Tom here, we don't hold much for the establishment archeologists and anthropologists."

"Why not?" Jack asked.

"Scholars need to publish to keep their jobs and to get promoted," Wes said, "and to do that, they need foundation grants which means, too often, they have to sell their souls to private interests."

"Many archeologists are confused by their education. If a new idea isn't in a textbook, or if the scientific leadership has made an excathedria pronouncement against it, then it's professionally unwise to embrace the idea. To get any grift, some of them have to drift," Kris said.

"In what way?" Jack asked.

"Well," Wes said, "here's a case in point. The separate digs done in Ciudad de las Ornos, about two miles from my house. Excavations took place only because the constructions were on public land. First they put in a canal. Second, the electric company put in an utility substation. Third, the Highway Department built a ramp for the Superstition Freeway. When the mall was built across the street, did they do a dig? Nope! Why not? Because it was a private development on private land. It was fenced off and the backhoes sent the pot shards flying."

"You're standing on another good example. This restaurant was built on a HoHoKam site." Kris added, "A significant number of sites have been destroyed and that needs to end. There's been a lot of building on sites that should have been studied more thoroughly. While excavating to lay a foundation for this building, the contractors found pottery shards, jewelry fragments, remnants of homes, and burial remains"

"Why wasn't the development stopped?" Jack asked.

"Well, it depends on who runs the archeological investigation. Sometimes, they refer it to the State Archeological Department and recommend that a site by preserved and sometimes they don't. In most cases, they aren't going to call a tribal leader and admit that something may be in the ground to set off a bunch of cultural affinity lawsuits, claims, and counterclaims. In this case, it was Draper or 'Doctor Dastard'," Kris motioned to a corner table where Draper was sitting with three other men.

"That's Charlie Carver with Draper," Jack said.

"You know Carver?" Kris asked.

"He wants to buy the Ocotillo Ranch."

"Well, if he does, you'd better put your cajones in a safety box," Kris said gruffly.

"Who are the other two guys?" Jack asked Kris.

"The heavyset fellow to Carver's left is Dominic Colucci. He runs the sports arena; it's also built on a burial ground thanks to Draper."

"You can't put the blame for everything on Draper," Tom snapped.

"Can't I?" Kris asked. "Why is he selected for these committees?"

"The Salt River sites are in his geographic zone," Tom replied.

"Come on, Tom, the natives didn't have political boundaries like we do. The Pima are The River People, settling along the Salt and the Gila Rivers, same as the Maricopas who came later. The Apaches, the Mountain People. The Yumans, well, they came after the Old People. If those jokers have their way, we'll never get it straightened out," Kris finished his drink and ordered another round.

"You don't get any plums, Tom, not even in Tucson, thanks to Marshall. He's the fat one," Kris said to Jack. "He owns a couple of ranches south of Tucson that run to Nogales. Marshall has seen to that since Tom advocated saving the Santa Cruz River Ruins outside of Tumacacari. Luis Obregon and him are as thick as thieves. That's the little guy, " Kris said to Jack. "He owns a chain of Trading Posts. He's a Spanish Jew, came here after World War II. He persuaded the ASU alums to build a field house and golf course on top of a HoHoKam site."

Mike Chernov joined the group. "Kris is partially correct, Jack."

"You aren't bad mouthing one of your bosses, are you Mike?" Kris jeered loudly.

"Obregon and the others are on my Board, as you well know, Kris," Mike said calmly. "But I have the final say on exhibits, and I sit on the state Archeological Review Board. One voice, one vote is all, Kris."

"Of course," Kris said, "One voice and one vote. Did you vote for the HoHoKam? Who votes for the Papagos? And the Pimas?"

The men stepped aside to allow Susan to join their circle. "Weaver said that he would like to go with us tomorrow when we go looking for HA-AK's cave," Susan said.

"Oh, really," Wes spoke first. "I invited Dr. Carros from New Mexico State to join us."

"Two's enough from the other side," Susan sniffed and dabbed her nose with a tissue.

"I'd like to join you, if that's all right, and if I don't have a conflict," Mike said. "The museum has an interest in Jack's glyphs. I'm hoping we can fit them into the entryway in the new addition."

"Better off left where they are," Kris snipped.

"They'll be safe in the museum, Kris," Chernov said.

"Yes, and from developers," Wes said.

"But these particular developers could possibly be persuaded to purchase the rocks from Jack and donate them to the museum," Mike defended.

"They aren't for sale," Jack said. "If and when I sell the ranch, I'll decide where to place them. Right now, it's too soon to say." The group grew quiet.

"Is next Sunday okay with everyone?" Susan said, breaking the silence.

"No problem. We can stop at Jack's place on our way to San Xavier," Wes said.

"See you all then," Susan replied, crossed the room and began an animated discussion with Tom Owens and Trisha Simpson.

"Who is that guy and why did he get so hot under the collar about the glyphs?" Kris asked.

"Tom also makes replicas; he needs the income. Maybe he's afraid he's got some competition," Chernov said. "Tom was a graduate student, but he somehow managed to put a foot in his mouth and was dropped from the program. However, Draper still employs him from time to time on restoration projects and we find work for him at the museum. He has some abilities."

"How about the slim blonde next him?" Kris asked.

"Trisha is a first rate ceramist with a deep concern for preserving antiquities," Chernov said. "She restores pots for the museum and for the universities. You can't tell her work from the real thing. She uses original materials. She could mend that broken pot of yours, Jack, for a sizable fee. Probably cost you more to mend it though than to buy a replacement."

"That's an interesting idea. I'll have to think about it," Jack said.

"Tomorrow will be a long day. I'm off to find a bed," Wes interrupted. "Do you and Star need a ride, Kris?"

"No thanks, Wes. We're staying at the Western across the street," Kris answered.

"Anyone else need a ride?" Wes asked.

"I don't think so. I have other plans," Tom said, glancing at Jack.

"I'm out of here. The storm is moving closer," Jack said. "Don't want to run into a gully washer. See you next week." Jack passed through the main bar and made his way to the men's restroom.

Carver entered a few moments later. He joined Jack at the basin, washed his hands, dried them slowly and caught Jack's eye as he combed his hair. "Only ten more shopping days 'til Christmas, Jack," Carver said and headed toward the door.

"It might take you longer than you think," Jack said to Carver's retreating back.

"Not the way I count, Jack." Carver stopped, his hands on the door and his smile turning into a sneer. "There's no way I can afford to let you keep Lone Butte or twenty acres for an arboretum, or whatever you call it. And I don't need a bunch of drunken Indians running around screaming, 'sacred land, sacred land' and bullshit like that to hold me up. A squaw lawyer put my ass in a bind over in Orange County, and it cost me a half million to get clear. Don't want to do that again. I've been there, done that, got the tee shirt and the tattoo. Your cactus huggers and Indian lovers don't have any clout, Jack. Tonight you established that those artifacts on your property, and any found on mine, were there before the 1906 Antiquities Act. Your granddad bought the land in 1903; your land is 'grandfathered'. Thanks for the help, Jack."

Jack smiled. "Are tecolates covered?"

"What the hell are tecolates?" Carver snapped.

"Elf owls. They're an endangered species. They make burrows and nests in the saguaros from the freeway to South Mountain Park. They are protected under the Endangered Species Act. I'm sure the environmental protection people will want to conduct a survey before any construction is allowed. Shouldn't take long. No more than three or four years, I would guess. Even a preliminary survey could run your costs up $200,000 overnight. Then there's the Conepatus leuconotus, the Colinus virginainus ridgewayi, the Heloderma suspectum, and the Testudinata Mexicalous. Ah, I'm not sure about that last one, but I think it's correct."

"What the hell are those?" Carver asked.

"That's the Mexican spotted skunk, the bobwhite, the gila monster, and the Mexican tortoise." Jack smiled and pushed past Carver. He turned as he opened the restroom door. "And then of course, there's a whole list of endangered butterflies and beetles that breed in the area."

Carver balled up the paper towel he was holding and threw it into the sink.

The valet, a blond, blue-eyed, lanky young man with an infectious grin, parked Jack's battered '36 pick-up truck under the canopy-covered entry. The door creaked loudly as he stepped out. "Your car, sir," he said stifling a grin. He looked surprised when Jack gave him $5 tip. "Thanks a lot, sir," he said as Jack climbed into the cab.

"What's you name, son?"

"Ahron," he said and pulled an umbrella out from under the valet stand.

"You must be expecting rain Ahron."

"You bet."

"Bigger tips?"

"You bet!" Ahron smiled.

"See that caddy limo over there? I'll drop by tomorrow or the next day. If you should remember who drives it out of here, what the passengers look like, well, it's worth a ten spot to me."

Ahron grinned. "That's Charlie Carver's limo. He doesn't tip. Always stiffs you. I'll be here. What's your name?"

"Jack Reed."

"I'll remember."

Susan walked down the steps and approached Jack's truck. "Taxi?"

A few scattered raindrops splashed on Jack's dusty windshield.

"Sure thing. Get in." Ahron held an umbrella over her head and opened the door for Susan. "Where to?"

"Right across the street. I'm staying at the Sands Motel."

"That's a long two blocks on a windy, wet night."

"You're right. I was going to walk before I saw you and that lightning."

Jack drove slowly down the boulevard, the branches of the sour orange trees whipped in the wind. An occasional lightning bolt forked across the black sky causing the wet pavement to blink pink and orange. Jack paused at the intersection. There was no traffic, so he made a left turn and then a quick turn and parked near the entrance of the Sands Motel.

"I'm going to have a cup of coffee, decaf before I turn in. Join me?" Susan asked.

"Sure. Love to." Jack reached out of his open window, found the outside door handle and opened the door. It seemed to creak even louder than usual. He got out, went around the truck and opened Susan's door.

Susan jumped out, and they sprinted through the light rain to the lobby door. Jack followed her into the nearly deserted coffee shop. Susan slid into a corner booth that had windows facing outward. Jack sit cater-cornered from Susan. A waiter approached and laid menus in front of them. A short swarthy-skinned waiter asked, "Something to drink?"

"Coffee, decaf and some sweetener."

"I'll have some coffee, too."

Susan flipped through the menu. "I think I'll pass. I'm not hungry. Are you?"

Jack laid the menus on the edge of the table. "Not really."

The waiter brought the coffee and asked, "Would you like to order anything else?"

"No thanks. Just coffee." The waiter smiled, picked up the menus, and returned to the counter.

"Are the ARAS meetings always so contentious?" Jack asked.

"Always. Tonight was mild compared to some I've been to."

"You did a nice job."

"Thank you. It was nice of you to ask Buck and the others to visit your place. It could be fun. Buck's all nonsense but in a way the ARAS are sincere."

"Speaking of clashes. I had a run-in with Carver… in the restroom."

"What about?"

"He started pressing me to sell the ranch. I told him about the elf owl and a few other endangered critters the EPA might be interested in."

"What could the EPA do?"

"If they conduct an environmental impact study, it could throw a wrench in Carver's plans. Slow him down a little, anyway."

"He's well connected, Jack. I'd be careful. Think things through before you do anything rash." A bolt of lightning forked and struck the ground near the stockyards. Seconds later, an ear-splitting crash rattled the windows. Susan slid close to Jack. "I'm scared of lightning. I'm just a baby. When I was a kid, I used to hide from thunderstorms in the bedroom."

"Not a bad idea."

"Does lightning bother you?"

"Sometimes, but not much. I'm not afraid, but I'm not going to stand on a golf course and wave a club in the air."

"Why not? Some idiots do."

"Well, I'm not a golfer for one."

"What do you do, Jack?"

"Well, I used to be an oceanologist. Right now, I'm thinking about making some career changes."

"Will you go back to a university?"

"I doubt it. My academic days are over for now. I want to settle the ranch business and then I'll decide what's next."

"I never asked, but are you married?"

"I was, but it didn't work out. It takes some time, but most of the scars have healed. You?"

She hesitated. "A long time ago. We were just kids. We both went straight from a ticky tacky middle class barrio to a ticky tacky university. We graduated, got married, and moved on to gin and tonics and icy stares. He walked out one day. Me – I went on to graduate school and eventually landed a job with the state."

"Mike Chernov?"

"We were close, real close for two years. Then he had that damn accident," Susan sipped her coffee. "Well, I still care for him, a lot, but it got complicated, too complicated. I'd rather not talk about Mike."

"And what about Tom?"

"We had something going for awhile, but now, we're just friends. Tom loves the bachelor lifestyle. He's having too much fun to even think of making a commitment. None of the men in my life want to make a commitment"

"How about you? Did you want a commitment?"

"No, not really, not anymore. Actually, I'm pretty selfish. I prefer being alone, most of the time. I have my work and the Rat Pack. I love the desert and the mountains. They're less complicated."

Susan glanced at her watch. "We better call it a night. I have a tough day tomorrow."

Jack stood up and she slid out of the booth. She touched his arm. "Finish your coffee. I'll see you next week. Thanks for coming."

"Take care, Susan." Jack watched as Susan crossed into the foyer and disappeared down a hallway. He finished his coffee, laid a couple of dollars on the table and left.

Lightning flashed and a dustdevil whooshed across the parking lot, scattering paper and bits of debris into the air. A light rain began falling. Jack checked the lights, turned on the wipers, tried to wind up the window, and cursed as the handle came off in his hand. He drove slowly out of the parking lot and headed for Baseline Road, avoiding the freeway but not the rain.

CHAPTER 11

The front gate was swinging back and forth in the wind. Jack put the truck into first gear and drove slowly up the ridge. A yellow blur crossed the track in front. Jack stopped the truck at the ramada, stuck his head out the window and called the dog. Paco, belly slunk down close to the ground, circled the truck.

The mercury vapor lamp casts an eerie light onto the gravel yard in front of the darkened house. Jack turned off the headlights and switched off the engine that died with a convulsive clatter. He listened to the silence that flowed back and felt the heat from the engine. The door creaked loudly as he swung it open. His feet crunched the desert gravel as he walked toward the house.

An owl hooted off in the distance. Paco yipped, slunk past Jack and crossed into the yard. Jack followed slowly. Paco stopped beside Ruiz, who was lying face down in the yard, one hand clutching his shotgun. "Ruiz!" Jack yelled and knelt beside him.

Ruiz raised his head and shoulders and then sagged back onto the gravel. A trickle of blood was oozing out of a tangled mass of hair onto his cheek and neck. Jack checked Ruiz's carotid pulse: it was slow but strong. "Hold on Ruiz. I'll get help," he said softly.

Jack stepped inside the stable door and switched on a light. He picked up the phone and dialed 911. He quickly described Ruiz's condition to the operator and waited until he was sure the dispatcher had verified the location.

"No worries. There's an ERV at Williams Field Road and the I-10, less than five minutes away. It's on the way there now."

"I'll check on him, and leave the phone open," Jack said and let the phone dangle by its cord. He pulled a rough Navajo saddle blanket off a shelf and took it outside to cover Ruiz. Jack knelt and checked to see if Ruiz was breathing normally. "It won't be long. Help's on the way." He held the blanket over Ruiz's head, sheltering the old man's face from the dust and wind that was beginning to blow. "Who did this to you? What made you come up here tonight?"

An emergency vehicle turned onto Ocotillo Road; the blue-white lights lit the road and disappeared beneath the ridge. The siren echoed from behind the hill, and its lights reflected off the cloud cover. "Here comes the cavalry, Ruiz."

The ambulance plowed up the ridge and stopped in front of the yard entrance. Two men leaped out of the vehicle, one carrying a respirator. "What happened?" he asked.

"Someone hit him with that, I think," Jack said, pointing to a two-by-four. "He has a head injury. He's been bleeding. His pulse is slow, but his breathing is normal. I don't know how long he's been here."

The medic checked Ruiz over and signaled to the driver to bring a stretcher. One medic gently raised Ruiz's head as the other two rolled him onto the stretcher. Without wasting a motion, they lifted the stretcher and loaded Ruiz onto a rack in the rear of the vehicle. The medics strapped the stretcher in place, flipped open an oxygen mask and slid it over Ruiz's mouth and nostrils.

"Where are you taking him?"

"To Desert Sam."

"I'll follow you." Jack slammed the rear door shut as the driver got behind the wheel. Jack started his truck as the ERV moved cautiously down the twisted trail. He closed the gap as the driver slowed to negotiate the turn through the front gate and carefully crossed the widely spread rails of the cattle guard.

The driver turned on the siren, and Jack stayed a respectful distance behind. The emergency crew was already wheeling Ruiz through the automatic doors when Jack pulled into the hospital's parking lot.

Jack gave the admissions clerk Ruiz's vital statistics as well as he could recall them, laid a credit card on her clipboard and signed papers taking responsibility for all medical charges. He made his way to a row of telephones inside the hospital waiting room and fumbled through a phone book. Skimming through at least forty Vargases listed in the East Valley, he spotted a Raoul, Ruiz's son, and dialed the number. Raoul picked up on the first ring. He recognized Jack's voice.

"My mother just called. She's worried about Ruiz. She said he saw a car headed out the ranch road from Ocotillo Road. He went to look, but hasn't come home."

"I'm with him, Raoul. We're at Desert Samaritan. Somebody hit your father in the head. I'm calling you because I thought you would want to tell your mother. I think he's going to be okay, but you better bring her over."

In less than an hour, the Vargas clan filled the waiting room questioning Jack and the hospital staff. Ruiz's daughter sat hugging her mother. The granddaughters and nieces clutched each other's hands, and from time to time, glanced nervously down the hall. The sons, grandsons, nephews, and cousins stood in tight groups outside the emergency room doors.

Everybody wanted to know who struck Ruiz. "Who would do such a thing?" they asked each other. "Gringos? Thieves? Dopers?" Everyone had a different opinion.

Jack listened as a sheriff deputy questioned Maria. According to her, Ruiz had been outside the house, tying down things in the orchard before the storm came. A van with its lights off had driven slowly past the house and turned up the road to the ranch. When the van did not return, Ruiz picked up his shotgun and started down the footpath to the ranch house.

"I told him he should call the sheriff. But he wouldn't listen to me. Then I waited and when I saw the flashing lights, I called Raoul. But who would do such a thing?" Maria began to cry and wring her hands. Raoul put his arm around his mother.

A young doctor approached them and spoke to Maria: "Your husband has a mild concussion, but, fortunately, he has not lost much blood. He's out of danger, but he should stay here overnight for observation. You can stay with him, if you want to."

"I want to see my husband." The doctor took Maria's arm and led her down the hall.

"You better head back to your place," the deputy said to Jack. "There are some deputies there. It looks like there's been a break-in,"

"Tell them I'm on my way." Jack shook Raoul's hand. "Your father will be taken care of. I'll be back as soon as I'm finished."

"There is no need, Jefe. I will call you if anything changes here. You better go back to the ranch and take care of things there."

The headlamps of the sheriff's Bronco lit up the sides of the whitewashed adobe walls and the front of the ranch house. The blue-white flasher bracketed the palm trees in the driveway, casting erratic dancing shadows on the side of the stable. Jack parked the pickup on the left side of the sheriff's vehicle. Deputy Smith was behind the wheel, one foot on the ground, one hand clutching a radiophone. He said something, turned down the squelch box and waited. A distorted voice squawked back.

Cierra was kneeling in front of a petroglyph rock that was blocking the path leading to the terrace. She beamed a flashlight in Jack's face, droplets of rain filtered through the beam.

"Sorry," she said and lowered her flashlight.

"I followed the ambulance to the hospital. Ruiz has a mild concussion. The emergency room doctor said he'll be okay. They're keeping him overnight for observation."

"He's a tough old bird," Cierra replied. "He'll be all right."

Jack shrugged his shoulders. "I hope so. I wasn't so sure when I first found him."

"Any ideas about what happened here?"

"They must have been after the glyphs because this one belongs up on the terrace. Whoever moved it had to be pretty strong. In the rain and in the dark, it would have been awkward to handle. So I'm guessing there must have been at least two people here."

An owl flew between the house and a palo verde tree. Its wings fluttered softly as it almost brushed Jack's Stetson. "A tecolate, a blue owl," Cierra said, "they're bad luck." The owl circled the terrace and swept off toward Lone Butte.

Jack borrowed her flashlight and checked the petroglyph rocks on the terrace, HA-AK's mother's frown glistened in the light. "As far as I can tell, that's the only one that's been moved." The sunroom door swung in the wind. "Someone's been inside."

They entered the glassed-in sunroom and Jack snapped on a light. The display shelves were empty. "The icons, baskets, and animal fetishes are missing." Jack walked into the living room. "They took the Navajo rugs, too," he said as he glanced around the room. "They knew what they were after, but it wouldn't have taken long. That heavy rock must have slowed them down. If Ruiz hadn't shown up, they would have taken the petroglyphs, too."

"Yes, and if you had been here alone, you would be the one lying out there, and no one would have known," Cierra said. They joined Deputy Smith who was examining the tire tracks.

"They came after the Indian artifacts. They didn't take anything else." Smith nodded. "Have you got anything?" Cierra asked.

"Not really. The rear treads are wider than the front set, like an off-road vehicle. No chance of getting a plaster casting in this weather. There's nothing unusual about the treads."

"My radio's on the blink. Can I use your phone to call in?"

"In the stable. There's no line to the house." Cierra adjusted her yellow slicker as the wind increased and the rain fell harder. Jack and Cierra moved under the ramada.

"Why don't you have a phone in the house?" she asked.

"My mother thought ringing phones were a nuisance. She came here for peace and quiet. But Ned wanted a phone. So, they compromised and put a line in the stable for emergencies and for Ruiz."

"Wasn't it a nuisance to walk to the stables at night or during bad weather?"

"Not for her; she never answered the phone. One of those endearing family traits, I suppose. I don't want to bothered either."

"We're out of here," Smith said. "There's nothing more we can do here. You do the report, and I'll drive," Deputy Smith said to Cierra and walked to the Bronco.

Cierra turned to Jack, "You sure you want to stay alone here tonight?"

"Would you be willing to keep me company?"

"Not likely, but I'll drop by tomorrow. If you find anything else that's missing, I'll add it to my report."

"I'll make an inventory tonight. I probably won't be able to sleep anyway."

Deputy Smith turned the Bronco around and headed towards the front gate. The headlight beams bounced off solid gray clouds that dipped down, almost touching the top of the ridge.

Jack closed the bottom of the dutch door, leaving the top open so he could hear the rain. The stable seemed to be sinking under the weight of the churning clouds. He sat down at the desk in the alcove, opened a notepad and began making a list of the missing items. When he was finished, he started a new sheet and listed the recent visitors to the ranch: Susan Schaffer, Tom Tracy, the helicopter pilot, and the heavy equipment driver, Mike Chernov, the Mallorys, Rudy Lazar and Charlie Carver. Reluctantly he also included the names of the Rat Pack.

He drew a circle around Lazar's name. "I'd bet money on him," Jack said to Orange Cat who was lying across his foot. The kitten stood up, stretched, yawned, and then strolled toward the kitchen. "I suppose you'd like some milk?" Jack said and followed Orange Cat into the kitchen. He snapped on the light, opened the door to the refrigerator, and pulled out a carton of milk. He started to open a cupboard door when something moved on top of the refrigerator. The waxed carton flew out of his hands, spattering milk on the cupboard and ceiling.

"Keerist," Jack shouted and nearly stepped on Orange Cat as they both scrambled out of the kitchen. He edged cautiously back to the doorway and watched as the skunk eyed him warily and began lapping up the spilt milk. Jack scooped up the kitten. "O.C., it's the porch for us again tonight. Momma skunk owns the kitchen after midnight. Better hope she leaves us some milk," Jack said to the protesting kitten.

CHAPTER 12

Jack just finished his morning coffee when an older model Toyota Land Cruiser pulled into the yard. Cierra waved to Jack. "I stopped by Ruiz's. He's home. Other than complaining of a bad headache, he's fine. Can you use some company?"

"Sure, I can always use company," Jack said. Cierra stepped out of the Toyota. She was wearing Levis, a red shirt and moccasins that rose to her knees. A pearl-handled pistol rested in a brightly beaded holster on her hip. A matching beaded headband kept the shock of thick black hair off her forehead. A well-worn buckskin vest completed her outfit.

"You look like an Apache brave," Jack commented. Cierra removed her sunglasses and adjusted her headband.

"I told you that I'm half Yaqui. Sometimes I dress like a Hollywood Indian to impress the Sheriff," she laughed. "My Toyota has been Hollywooded, too." A bar of K.C. lights adorned the top, four lights pointed forward and two pointed to the rear. A powerful spotlight was attached to a roof support on the driver's side. "I can light up the desert with these." Cierra smiled. The dash was covered with vivid red velour and the seats were upholstered in bright red-black-and-white squares. An interior roll bar was padded with black leather.

Jack opened the hood; a Chevy 327, headers, and a heavy-duty truck radiator were underneath. Cierra pointed out the four pairs of gas shock absorbers, mounted two to a wheel. "It's a bit rough on the freeway, but off road, it handles like a Cadillac." Jack closed and locked the hood.

"It's my day off. I thought I'd do some target shooting and check the trail up to the Proving Grounds. I've been thinking that whoever took the objects last night might have gone out that way."

"There's no back way out of there, Cierra," Jack said. "Unless you've got a rig like yours. The hills alongside the highway slope twenty degrees or more. My stepfather was going to blast a road in from the south side, but he never got around to it. All the trails loop through the flats and end up back here. The Pimas from St. John's used the old trail that runs in front of the ridge where you turn into the ranch. No one's used that trail in years, but I think the thief or thieves left that way. They didn't go back by Ocotillo Road, or if they did, Maria didn't see them. And she was watching for Ruiz. If they hit the road to the south, they would have been back on the freeway in minutes."

"Did you make an inventory of your missing property?"

Jack opened his shirt pocket and took out his notes. "I made a list of recent visitors, too."

Cierra scanned the list of names. "I'll run a check on them tomorrow."

"Start with Lazar. He's Carver's driver. I think he's bad news."

"Why do you say that?"

"I found some of his snubbed cigar butts in the trash can. Ruiz put them there after he and Carver left that day." Jack handed her a plastic bag.

"You're learning." Cierra tucked the bag into the Toyota glove compartment. "I'd like to see the petroglyphs," Cierra said. "I didn't get a good look at them last night." Jack led her to the upper terrace and watched as she squatted on her heels and studied the patterns of the rocks.

"Apparently they tell the story of the legend of HA-AK. She was sort of witch figure to the Pimas and Papagos."

"Really?" Cierra stood up. "I first heard that legend when I was a girl. My grandmother took me over to the St. John's reservation. I remember a lot of people dancing around a big bonfire. My grandmother told me that they were burning a witch. She said it was like our Cinco de Mayo and Fourth of July. I cried when they threw the beautiful rag-dolls into the bonfire. If these rocks tell that story, it would certainly make them valuable to a collector."

"Maybe that why, the thieves tried to take at least one of them. I'll make sure they're all here, just in case I missed one last night."

"Okay. I better get going and get in some practice time. I have to re-qualify next month. I'll check with you my way out. See you later."

"Hasta luego. All the trails loop back to the flats." Jack watched the cloud of dust streaming behind the Toyota as it disappeared over the ridge.

Jack went into the stable, picked up telephone, and dialed the Vargas number. Ruiz answered the phone, "Bueno, Ruiz. How are you feeling?"

"I'm fine, Jefe. I was coming to see what those coyotes took…"

"Not today, Ruiz. They took nothing important. You scared them off."

"Well, I was coming up to the house. I wanted to see for myself, but Maria says I shouldn't."

"You stay put, Ruiz. Maria's right. It's too late. I'll come by this afternoon, and we'll talk then."

"All right, Jefe. Is Cierra with you? She came by this morning and said she was going to practice with her pistol in the canyon."

"She's been here and left already."

"Tell her Maria wants to see her. Adios, Jefe."

"I will. Adios, Ruiz."

Jack returned to the adobe and went into the den, the coolest room in the house, and turned on the electric window air conditioner that his mother installed. This was the only concession she had ever made to the summer desert heat. The thick adobe walls normally kept the inside temperatures within tolerable limits due to the cooler desert nights, even in the summer.

"Sunny days and starry nights," Jack said to Orange Cat who crawled up onto the ottoman, licked his paws, groomed himself a little and settled down for a siesta. Jack opened one of the *Treasure of the Southwest* volumes. He read for awhile and began taking notes. He looked through some of the monographs and articles that Pat Garrett had given him. He made additional notations, leaned back in his chair and stared at the imposing tapestry that covered one wall of the den.

A series of figures depicting early Spanish missions had been woven into the wool. The buildings were gray with contrasting black bells, black somber crosses, and black doors and windows. The accent was set against the dark red background. Jack identified the missions by their distinct shapes and locations: "Guaymas, Nogales, Tubac, San Xavier, Tucson, Casa Grande, and that last one I don't recognize. What do you think, O.C.?" The kitten looked at Jack, made a half-hearted attempt to rise, but gave up and closed his eyes.

Off in the distance, muffled rapid pistol shots echoed in the canyon. "Must be Cierra," he thought as he yawned and sank deeper into the comfortable chair.

The beeping of a horn brought Jack to his feet, startling Orange Cat. He crossed the room quickly and went outside.

"Wake you up? You look like you've taking a siesta. Both of you," she shouted from the Toyota. Orange Cat allowed himself the luxury of a lengthy stretch.

"Could be. I must have dozed off. The last thing I remember I was making some notes." He glanced at his watch. "It's almost six. I was going to see Ruiz. I called him and told him I would drop by this afternoon. He said Maria wanted to see you. I think she's worried that you might shoot yourself in the foot."

"Maria is always worried. Hop in. We can both go. I'll bring you back before dark." Cierra laughed.

"Give me a minute. I'll feed the cat and grab my Sunday hat." Jack started for the door, and then turned around. "Cierra could you drive me to the airport after we see Ruiz? I don't want to leave my truck there, and I don't want to ask Ruiz."

"Be glad to."

"I'll hurry."

"I'll feed O.C. Take your time."

Jack went inside to his bedroom. He stripped off his clothes, tossed them onto a chair, and went into the bathroom. He turned on the shower and managed a shave while the cool water rinsed his body. He stepped outside the shower and half-toweled his body dry and let the dry desert air finish the job while he brushed his teeth and combed his hair. Jack slapped on some aftershave, stepped into the walk-in closet and pulled a down duffel bag with a shoulder harness from the overhead shelf. He opened it and set it on a stand. He grabbed three of everything: socks, shorts, tee shirts, and shirts. "One for me and two for you." He stuffed the bag full and jammed a prepared toilet kit into a side pocket. He put a shirt, Levis, and a belt. As he put them on in order he muttered, "I should have been a fireman." He looked over his dress shirts and chose a light cotton one and slipped it on. He snapped the pearl clasp buttons together on his way to the kitchen.

Cierra was pouring milk in a saucer for the kitten, and Jack forked some tuna onto a plate. "You're on your own, son," he said to Orange Cat. "You better eat it before Mrs. Hindsquirt shows up and tries to run you off. Don't let her bluff you. You can live and let live."

"And who is Mrs. Hindsquirt?" Cierra asked.

"Mama skunk," Jack said and pointed at the stove. "There was a weird sort of guy at St. Charles, the boarding school I attended in Ohio. He was the editor of the school paper, the yearbook, and the president of the Skunks, a literary club. He was a real hind squirt, always making a fuss or stink over something that no one cared about. A real nitpicker."

"What happened to him?"

"I have no idea. That was years ago. We didn't stay in touch." Jack chuckled. "He probably ended up in New York City with all the wanna-be editors. Who knows? Who cares?"

Jack went to the den and opened a door on the side of the bookcase. He quickly spun the dial on a small safe. The door clicked. He opened it and removed some cash. "I'll need checks, too, so I'll take these along." He pulled out a plastic bag that contained three Spanish silver reals and tucked it into his shirt pocket. He closed the safe, twisted the dial, and shut the panel door. "That's it!"

"Do you always talk to yourself?" Cierra asked, surprising him.

Jack colored slightly. "Not always, but since I've been home, I've been doing it a lot lately. I started talking to O.C., and then Mrs. Hindsquirt and then the turtle. I'll probably get it on with the coyotes next."

"Don't start howling, or I'll really get worried," Cierra said and picked up the book that was lying on the ottoman and scanned the cover. She looked at the notes on the chair. "Are you planning a treasure hunt?"

"Maybe. Something like that."

"Tell me about it."

Jack opened the book and showed Cierra the pages that referred to Fray Marcos de Niza, Coronado, and Father Kino. "They all came up the Gila River at one time or another. Marcos de Niza came through here. He made it to the South Mountains, to Hieroglyph Hill. He wrote his name and put a cross on a big boulder there: Marcos de Niza, 1539."

"Right. I've seen it many times. We used to 'park' nearby on Saturday nights," Cierra grinned. "Lots of us. It was a kind of a party place. It's off limits now. There's a chain-linked fence around it now."

"That's it. The Spaniards spent several months there while they waited for word from Estaban. They sunk a few shafts or forced the Indians to dig them. They did find some gold, but not much."

"How do you know?"

"It says so right here," Jack said, "that de Niza and Coronado set out from Mexico City together. They were searching for the Seven Cities of Cibola. They had a falling out in Sonora, so de Niza went ahead, taking Estaban. He was the black slave who was shipwrecked off the Florida coast and made a trip through hell to get back to Mexico City. Along the way the Indians told him about seven cities with streets paved with gold somewhere in the southwest. When he got back, the conquistadors bought the idea and the Marcos de Niza expedition was organized. Estaban was made a captain and a guide."

Jack flipped a few pages and continued, "When they got to Arizona, they split up and Estaban went north to Santa Fe. By now he was stuck on himself and real pushy with the Indians and his soldiers. Someone got fed up with him and killed him. The deal between de Niza and Estaban was that if one of them found gold, he would send the other a gold cross. A large cross meant a lot of gold; a little one only some gold. When de Niza got the word that Estaban had been killed, he panicked. He decided to head back to Sonora and to travel light. All non-essentials, including the gold they had mined, were hidden in a cave or a mine shaft, and they split for home."

"Was there a lot of gold?"

"I doubt it. De Niza had someone cast a small gold cross to send to Estaban, so he didn't find much."

"How do you know?"

"It's in the book. Two hundred years later Father Kino came this way looking for traces of de Niza, but he only got as far as Sacaton. He built those missions – the ones on the tapestry. I've seen most of them, but I've never seen the bottom one before."

"Oh, I know this one. It's San Xavier," Cierra said, pointing at the mission. "And that's Tubac and that's the mission in Guaymas."

"That's right."

"I've been to all of them. It's the Yaqui Trail. Father Kino followed the trail or the rivers up to Sacaton."

"Probably both."

"The one at the bottom looks like the mission on the St. John's Reservation. I was out there last month. It's a ruin now. It hasn't been used in fifty years or more. So, you think there's a treasure buried there or somewhere in South Mountain Park?"

"It could be somewhere between the park and Sacaton where they built a stockade or even somewhere near the mission. They didn't take the gold with them or Father Kino wouldn't have been looking for it up here."

"Are you seriously looking for gold?"

"Not seriously, but I am curious. By the way, I discovered that one of the glyphs is missing after all -- the odd one with three circles on it. It was smaller and different from the others. Add it to list, will you? Should we go?" Jack said.

"Who's taking care of O.C.?"

"I'll ask Ruiz to keep an eye on him."

Cierra carried Orange Cat out to the porch and said, "Take care little one."

"Buckle up," Cierra said. Jack strapped the double harness across his shoulders and chest and snapped the buckle into place. "All set."

Cierra drove slowly out of the yard and shifted gears and put the Toyota onto the sandy track on the south of the ridge. She expertly drove the track, fast but not recklessly. Jack relaxed. She stopped at the gate and let Jack pull the gate open with the rope pulley. The gate shut slowly behind them as Cierra crossed the wash. She drove down Ocotillo Road until she hit the paved road that lead to Ruiz's house.

"I like your new Sunday hat. You look good in it. It suits you."

"You know what they say about Sunday hats? Buy it on Saturday, wear it to a dance..."

"Wear it to church on Sunday. And swat steers and your gal on the behind on Monday," Cierra finished.

"I wouldn't think of swatting a steer on the behind."

"Better not try swatting any gals either. Nowadays, they swat back."

"What about a gentle pat?"

"Not even."

CHAPTER 13

Ruiz and Maria were sitting in some lawn chairs in the garden when Cierra and Jack drove in.

"Don't get up Ruiz," Jack said, but Ruiz stood anyway. "How are you, Maria?"

Maria spoke softly. "I'm fine. I feel much better now that I know that Ruiz is all right. He is better, but not as good as he thinks." Maria hugged Cierra.

"I am much better. Maria makes too much of this thing."

"You must be thirsty, Jack. I will bring some iced tea. Would you like some more, Ruiz?"

"Yes, Maria, I would." Maria took his glass. "Come with me Cierra. You can help."

"Your beans and corn look good, Ruiz."

"Yes, they are doing good, Jefe. So are the melons but the jalipenos and tomatoes aren't doing as well. The air is too dry. We need more rain."

"You did a good job restoring these chairs, Ruiz."

"There was not much to do. They are good chairs. They were your grandfather's. Captain Ned didn't like them. He wanted something new. He always wanted something new."

"You didn't care much for him, did you?"

"Verdad. It is true. He was not like your father or you, Jefe. But your mother liked him. She took good care of him before he died."

"And you and Maria took good care of my mother. I will always remember that, Ruiz."

"De nada, Jefe. It was our pleasure. Your mother made Maria very happy. She was a grand lady."

"Thank you, Ruiz."

"You must have something to eat. I have already prepared some tortillas, quesadillas, and beans," Maria said, bringing the tea.

" We'll get something later, Tia Maria."

"You should eat something first."

"If they must go, they must go," Ruiz said.

"I need to change my clothes. May I borrow something from Desiree?"

"Since when do you ask if you can borrow clothes from each other? Of course, she won't mind. I'll help you." The two women slipped into the house.

"Will you be able to keep the ranch, Jefe?"

"Maybe, Ruiz, I'm not sure. Anyway, I have a plan. I'll need help though. We need water. Do you still have your willow wand?"

"I still have it, Jefe. It knows where the water is hidden. Shall we start tomorrow?"

"Not tomorrow. I'm flying to Santa Barbara tonight. Some business, but I'll be back in two or three days. Can you keep an eye on the house?"

"Yes, Jefe, but if you are gone, Raoul should sleep there in case those thieves came back. He can stay on the cot in the stable."

"He can use the house and ask him to feed O.C.. There's food in the refrigerator."

"It's better that he sleeps near the telephone. I'll give him my shotgun," Ruiz said.

Ruiz and Jack watched as a spectacular sunset transformed the sky. A band of clouds turned orange and blood red underneath a soft golden sky, the edges shining like polished bronze. Beneath that was another band of blood red clouds. The Estrella Mountains thrust their deep purpled pinnacles into the lowest band of wine-colored clouds. The gold band shifted swiftly to blood red. The edges of the clouds burned as if they were on fire. The blood-red sky turned almost instantly wine red, then to royal purple.

"There is no sky in the world like this, Jefe. It is magic, no?"

"It is that, Ruiz."

Cierra walked into the garden. The purple light cast a pastel aura around her head, shoulders, and bare arms. She was wearing a simple white cotton knee-length Mexican dress, gathered at the waist with a pink sash. Delicate pastel-colored flowers were embroidered across the neckline, which she wore off her shoulders.

"Magnifico. You are more beautiful than the sunset," Ruiz said.

"Gracias, Tio Ruiz," Cierra replied. "Buenos noches, Tia Maria."

"Buenos noches, Cierra."

"Let's go, Jack," Cierra said and he followed her to the Toyota. Cierra buckled on her shoulder harness.

"Where are we going?" Jack asked.

"Victor's."

"Where's that?"

"In Yaqui town." Cierra crossed over the freeway and turned left at the first intersection. She picked up speed. Field workers loading melons into trucks were on both sides of the road. A huge yellow moon was rising over the San Tan Mountains. By its light, Jack could see more people working deeper in the fields. Women and children were moving towards the trucks. Young boys were carrying a melon in each of their arms.

"Campesinos," Cierra said. "It's hard work. I toted melons when I was a girl. All my sisters and brothers did. For us, it was money for school clothes and books. For them, it's survival. Melons aren't so bad. Pulling onions is worse. You do it all day when the sun is hot. Melons, you do after dark. When there's a moon, you can see, but if there isn't, they turn the truck headlights on the field."

Inside the Guadalupe city limits, framed houses lined both sides of the street. Chain-linked fences separated yards. Music blared from car speakers parked in front the fences. Smoke drifted skyward from charcoal braziers where families were gathered for the evening meal. Neighbors chattered over fence tops. The aroma of spices and roasting meat filled the air.

Men were sitting on porches drinking beer from cans. Some wore white tank tops; many were shirtless. A firecracker popped loudly in one yard as they passed. A group of children, clapping their hands, surrounded a little girl holding a green sparkler. An enormous orange piñata swung from a tree branch while someone played a guitar.

"It's a birthday party. The girls get sparklers and the boys fireworks. Sometimes boys get both. Boys are always the lucky ones. I never got firecrackers."

"So, that why you spent your day off target practicing."

"Maybe. Never thought of that." She laughed. Cierra slowed the Toyota as they passed Our Lady of Guadalupe Church. Its whitewashed walls gleamed in the moonlight. People were sitting or walking around the plaza. Young men were perched on the fenders and bumpers of their vehicles parked along the edges of the plaza. A brass band was standing with their backs to the fountain facing the crowd. They had just finished a song, and the people were clapping.

Cierra turned right at the intersection and drove into the parking lot of Victor's Drive-in Restaurant. The parking stalls were filled. Waitresses with heavily loaded trays scurried back and forth between the cars and the kitchen. A short line of people waited beside a take-out window.

"We're going to a drive-in?"

Cierra laughed. "No, we're going inside." She parked beside a long blue stuccoed building that housed the kitchen. Immediately two young boys with dirty rags appeared.

One began wiping the headlamps. "I'll clean your windshield for a quarter," the boy said and pulled a spray bottle from his jeans, stepped on the edge of the front axles and began spraying.

"I'll watch you car, Mister, for a quarter," the other boy said.

Jack fished a dollar out of his pocket. "If you're here when we get back and the Toyota is in one piece, you'll get another dollar, okay?"

"Okay! Nobody touches this car. If they do, I'll call a cop," the taller boy said.

"I am a cop," Cierra said, opened her purse, took out her wallet and showed her badge.

"You're a sheriff! Please don't arrest me."

"Yes, Pedro. I am a sheriff. Now get out of my way. I'm going in to see your father and eat dinner. You can sit in the seats, but don't mess with anything. You either, Antonio."

"Yes, Cierra," the boys chorused.

"I mean it."

"We won't touch anything."

"You better not or I will arrest you." She led Jack through the back door of the kitchen. "Victor is my cousin and those are his boys. We always play this game. I have to show my badge every time they see me."

"You have a lot of cousins."

"We're a big family. If we ever all got together, we'd fill the church plaza."

"Oh, I thought that was your family."

"Knock it off, Cowboy," she said and playfully pinched his arm, "or I'll arrest you."

"For what?'

"For talking back to a police officer." Cierra led Jack through a short hallway into a tiny dimly lit room. A catering cart partially blocked an aisle that led to four dining tables spaced a comfortable distance from one another in a semi-circle. Two circular booths upholstered in deep rich-looking red leather, one at each end of the room, completed the seating. The floor was covered with Spanish tiles. The sidewall was decorated with a red, white, and green Mexican flag and a pair of Mexican sombreros, the type worn by Mariachi players. On the side nearest the kitchen, a short bar took up most of the space. Two high-backed leather stools stood in front of the bar.

Jack followed Cierra over to the bar. Cierra stepped on the bar railing and raised herself onto the barstool. Jack slid effortlessly onto the seat. "This place is great!"

"So is the food," Cierra said. "You'll see."

"Where is everybody?"

"I don't know. It's usually full. This place is a well-guarded secret. Mostly only friends of Victor's come here. It's not an 'in' place."

One of the swinging doors that led to the kitchen area opened. A tall, large-framed and big-boned man with dark almond eyes came through. His long, luminous hair was tied back with a red ribbon. He set a tray on the table and smiled.

"Cierra!" his rich baritone echoed off the ceiling. He walked around the bar and embraced her. "We have missed you. And this is Jack?"

"Yes. This is Jack Reed. Jack, this is my cousin, Victor." Victor extended his hand and clasped Jack's arm with his free hand.

Victor pumped Jack's hand vigorously while he kept talking. "Maria, has told me about you. She tells me you saved Ruiz's life the other night."

"I didn't do much; I just called 911. They did the rest. I just waited for them to show up."

"Well, no matter. If Maria thinks you saved Ruiz's life, then it's true. Verdad? Now Cierra, what will you have this evening? Do you want a margarita?" Victor asked and moved behind the bar.

"No, thanks. Just some Cuervaca with ice and lemon."

"And you Jack?"

"I'll have the same."

Victor filled two round glasses with ice cubes, poured the tequila over the top, and set the drinks on a tray, and carried them over to the booth. Cierra and Jack followed. He placed a saltcellar in front of them and a shallow bowl of curled lemon slices. "And dinner?"

"Your specialty, Victor. The works."

"Of course. The whole enchilada," Victor turned and went back to the kitchen.

"The whole enchilada?" Jack questioned.

"No, we're not having enchiladas. Actually it's a kind of marinated flank steak."

"Flank steak?"

"Shh," Cierra whispered as Victor approached them. He sat a Mexican plate in front of each of them. He piled a generous mound of guacamole on the plate. Next, he ladled a thick green sauce over the guacamole. He inserted huge fried corn chips into each mound. "It's a family recipe," he said. "Since the days in the mountains above Sonora. Try it. It's not hot. Well, it is hot, but in a mild way."

Victor brought his cart back to the table. Strips of romaine lettuce filled a wooden bowl. "A Victor's salad," he said as he opened a bottle of Worcestershire sauce and dribbled some around the edge of the bowl. Next, he dotted Tabasco sauce around the sides of the bowl. Then he ladled olive oil and garlic dressing over the lettuce. "Ah," he sniffed. "The oil is perfect. I aged it myself. A little cumin, some cilantro, and elephant garlic from Mexico." Victor tossed the salad lightly with two wooden forks. He cracked an egg on the side of the bowl, separated the yoke from the white, dropped the yolk into the salad and gave it another toss. He sprinkled the salad with fresh grated Parmesan cheese and set it on the table. He pulled two large Mexican bowls from the ice tray and wiped them with a flourish.

"A Victor's salad. Add anchovies and it's a Caesar, but a little bit better maybe. Enjoy! I'll be back."

"Incredible," Jack said as he finished the salad. "I'm ready to lick the plate. I'm ravenous."

"You're supposed to be. My brother Angel actually licked his plate clean one night. I wanted to, but I didn't have the nerve."

"Go ahead. I'll turn my head."

"Stop saying things like that. You make me want to do it."

"Okay then. I'll watch as you lick the plate," Jack teased.

"Just watch Victor; he's an artist." Victor was slicing a thick rib-eye filet into horizontal strips and spreading them onto the charcoal grill. The flames shot upward. In a minute, he turned the meat and braised the raw sides. He layered the meat with a mushroom sauce. "The mushrooms have been marinating in Tequila and flour sauce with some brandy," Cierra said.

Victor stacked layers of mushrooms and meat onto serving platters and carried them to the table. "The specialty of the house, flank steak marinated in beer," Victor said and laughed.

"It's a joke, Jack," Cierra whispered. Victor went back to the bar, lowered the bar lights and turned on a stereo player. "If he plays *"Blue Spanish Eyes"* I'll kill him," Cierra said.

Englebert Humperdink's mellow baritone voice flowed softly from the speakers, hung in the corners of the bar: *"Blue Spanish eyes, prettiest eyes in all of Mexico."*

"I don't need this."

"No worries. I have to catch a plane, remember?"

Cierra kicked him in the shins under the table. "Eat your steak."

"Okay, I will." Jack finished before Cierra. "Delicious. That's the best steak I've ever had."

"Be sure you tell Victor. He'll be pleased." Cierra sipped her drink.
"Ruiz and Maria talk a lot about your mother, but not much about you. The last thing I knew was that you went into the Marines after college."

"I spent three years in the Marines. Then I went to graduate school to study oceanography. I was offered a research fellowship at Scripps and later a teaching position in Santa Barbara. In the meantime, I got married and divorced and quit my job at UCSB. The whole bit. I sort of drifted for a while, then when my mother died, I had to come back and sell the ranch or find the cash to hold on to it." Jack avoided Cierra's eyes and stared at his drink.

"If you sold the ranch, where would you go?"

"Probably to the South Pacific, maybe to the Tonga Islands. The government there wants me to do some work. The coral reefs are disintegrating and the Japanese are over-fishing the region. If I go, I'll drop off at the Galapagos and check out El Nino. Climate dynamics, air-sea interaction, ocean circulation, marine biophysical chemistry are my areas of specialization. I study the whole catastrophe. It's my job; I'm an oceanologist. The ocean is my beat," Jack teased. "Sorry. I'm not sure where I'm going. When I first got back, I was sure I wanted to be anywhere but here. But now I'm not so sure." Jack looked directly into Cierra's eyes.

Cierra dropped her eyes and then looked up to meet his. "Is the ocean a source of power for you?"

"I'm not sure I feel power anywhere, Cierra, but I love the empty spaces."

"My uncle leads men on vision quests. They fast and visit the sweat lodge to purify. They beat drums and dance to ground themselves. Then they offer prayers. It's not a place they are searching for, but the sacred source of power and energy."

"Do they find it?"

"If they look within themselves, they do. It's not easy; it's not for everyone."

"Okay, now it's your turn. I'm curious why did you decide to become a sheriff."

"I was majoring in art with an emphasis on Native American studies. I had to earn my keep, so I thought about opening a roadside shop in Yaqui Town. Then I decided I didn't want to eat dust waiting for tourists to stop. Too hot. Besides, there's too much competition. Obregon has twenty shops in Arizona. He buys from the Zunis and the Navajos, and imports cheap imitations from Taiwan and the Pacific Islands. Unless you have a lot of capital, you can't compete. My uncle with the FBI turned me on to criminal justice. I'm also studying the Yaqui way with him," Cierra said softly.

"Someday, I'll become a deer-dancer and pass down our traditions to the children. Most young Yaquis today no longer believe we are really 'Indians.' My own father knows little about the Yaqui ways. Both my parents are teachers," Cierra said proudly. "Before I met my uncle, I knew very little about the Yaquis, or our language, or our history. The Sheriff assigned me to this end of the county. I'm supposed to be useful if there is a scrape on one of the reservations or over in Yaqui Town. But that's a joke. The Mexicans in Guadalupe don't like Yaquis. During the Revolution, Yaquis fought on both sides and some fled here afterwards. A few, like my grandfather, married Mexican women."

"A beautiful combination, especially in your case. You've explained everything except the blue eyes," Jack said.

"That's not so easy. Some Yaquis believe we are descendants of the Wanderers, a nomadic group who crossed the Atlantic and intermingled with the Mayans. It's legend; no proof except that some Yaquis had blue eyes before the Spanish came to Mexico."

Victor approached the table, carrying desert, a small cake covered with rum sauce and a sparkler blazing in the center. Bright green sparks cascaded over his linen napkin and fell to the floor. He sat the cake on the table and said, "Happy Birthday, Cierra."

"It's wonderful, Victor. Thank you."

Victor carefully removed the sparklers stub when it played out and extinguished it in a container of water. "I wish you many years of joy and prosperity, Cierra. I'll bring your King Alphonso." He headed for the bar.

"Today is your birthday?" Jack asked.

"Yes, July 19."

"I don't believe this, Cierra. It's my birthday too, add a few years, of course."

"You're kidding. July 19th is your birthday!"

"As far back as I can remember I thought of myself as a crab."

"You mean hard on the outside and soft inside," Cierra touched Jack's arm.

"Yeah, crabby was what I had in mind. I tend to move sideways. You know back and forth."

"You were going to be alone on your birthday?"

"Well, I think O.C. and Mrs. Hindsquirt were going to organize something, but that's about it. What about you?"

"I had plans, but I changed them. Well, I put them off. My brother is having a party for me at his house."

"You'll be late for your own birthday party."

"It won't even start until ten or eleven. I'll stay until midnight and then go home and get some sleep.
I have the morning shift this week, from six a.m. 'til two p.m. I'll be okay. You get used to changing shifts."

"I hate to say this Cierra, but I need to get going or I'll miss my connection from LAX to Santa Barbara. It's the last one until tomorrow morning. Thanks for bringing me here. I've enjoyed the food and your company. Really."

Jack walked over to the bar. Victor waved him off saying, "There's no charge; it's my gift to Cierra…and to you."

"Muchas gracias, Victor," Jack said.

"De nada."

Cierra came over and gave Victor a hug. "Muchas gracias. You're wonderful to have remembered!"

"De Nada, Cierra Rose."

Outside the boys were waiting by the curb. They approached Jack with their hands outstretched. "One dollar," Pedro said.

"Ah, get out of here," Cierra scolded. "Jack's my friend."

"Okay, Cierra. Free parking for you."

A 1950 Mercury, its frame a scant four inches from the ground, eased its way into the parking lot. The driver edged it cautiously into an empty space. Its deep blue lacquer paint glistened under the blue neon lights.

"A low rider," Antonio yelled, and they raced towards the car. The driver, a dark Mexican youth, tried frantically to wave the boys off. Cierra and Jack laughed.

"Now, those boys know what they are doing. A business that you get paid for offering to do a service that no one wants you to do," Jack said.

"I suppose I could arrest them for extortion or bribery or being public nuisances or for having fun. The boys will be okay. Their father has a restaurant, but most of the children in Yaqui town aren't as lucky. They learn very early how to survive."

Neither spoke as Cierra took a side road out of Yaqui town, turned the Toyota onto 40th street and then into the back entrance to the Phoenix airport. The east-west runway lights flashed by as Cierra turned into a s-shaped curved ramp and followed it to the terminal. Jack unhooked his safety belt and got out of the car. He picked up his bag, looped his arm through the strap, and slung it over his shoulder.

"Thank you for the ride, Cierra, and for Victors. It was…it was fun. It was the best birthday I've even had."

"I'm glad. I had fun, too. When will you be back?"

"I booked a 3 p.m. return flight on Thursday. I'll call Ruiz."

"If he can't make it, I'll pick you up. Buenos noches, Jack."

"Buenos noches, Cierra." Jack watched as she checked the traffic over her shoulder, found a break, and eased into the through traffic lane. He watched the red Land Cruiser until it disappeared on the down ramp that led to the tunnel back to 40th street. "Adios, Cierra Rose."

CHAPTER 14

"Good afternoon folks. This is your co-pilot Dave Warner. Our estimated time of arrival in Phoenix is 2:43 p.m., Mountain Standard Time. We'll be starting our descent in a few minutes. The Salton Sea is coming up ahead on the starboard side," he announced over the intercom. "It's the largest lake in the U.S. It hasn't always been there. It was created by accident when a levee on the Colorado broke back in the early 1990s. You could say it was manmade." Beneath the aircraft and to his right, Jack could see the wind-driven salt froth coating that lines the flat sandy beaches.

The co-pilot continued, "Due to the high salt content and no natural outlet, one day it'll become another American dead sea. That brown ribbon of water just ahead is the Colorado River. That's Lake Martinez to the south. At the far end of the lake, you can see the top of the Imperial Dam. The Colorado provides electricity and irrigation water for five states. The crops are sold all over the world. You are looking at the American Nile, folks. A miracle in the desert."

The overweight passenger on Jack's left put down his newspaper and edged over to peer out the window. "Would you like to switch seats?" Jack asked.

"No thanks. I'm a commuter. I've seen the miracle of the desert before," he sighed. "It's polluted and it's over-salinated. By the time it reaches Mexico, its nothing but wastewater. The Mexicans can't use it. They quit using DDT twenty years ago, but salt and pesticides are still leaching off the croplands, killing the bird and sea life. The whole food chain is screwed up. The fish aren't fit for human consumption, and the larger birds are developing eggshells so thin that chicks can't survive. Dead Sea, huh? If we keep on polluting, it's going to be a dead planet. Too many people are migrating to the Southwest. The desert can't support croplands and all of these people. Even if we quit growing things out here, they will drink the river dry. San Diego, Orange County, and LA want the water. Las Vegas, Phoenix and Tucson need the water to expand. Everybody wants water. There's not enough to go around. You follow me?"

"I follow you," Jack said. "But some smart people are trying to solve those problems."

"Yeah, like who?"

"The ecologists, the government, and other land and water resource people. Legislators."

"Politicians don't listen to those people, sonny. They don't care about tomorrow. Just so they get elected today," the man said. "The only they know how to do is to say yes to everybody. We need people who can say when enough is enough. But politicians can't say no and get re-elected."

"Maybe public education is part of the answer."

"The public? What's that? The public doesn't give a damn. Oh sure, lots of people care – the Greenpeace Movement and the Nature Conservancy people and a few eco-terrorists are out there demonstrating and stirring things up. But it's an old story – too little, too late." The man continued, "That's Blythe. See those figures just south of town?" Jack nodded his head. "Stick figures. Can you make out one that looks like a bird? There! It's almost on the edge of the river."

"I see it."

"They say there's hundreds of them. They say they're strung all the way along the Colorado from Lake Havasu to Yuma. Some flyer spotted them back in the twenties. Nobody knows who made them or when exactly. I read about them in *National Geographic*. They were here before Columbus. Coronado spotted them when he was looking for the Seven Cities of Gold. You ever hear about that? One of his men found the Grand Canyon, but they never did find any gold. You hear about that?"

"Yes, I've read a little about Coronado," Jack answered and studied the figures below him.

"Makes you wonder whatever happened to them. It wasn't DDT that got them," the man said, "must have been something else."

"I'm sure it was." Jack leaned back in his seat and closed his eyes. He touched the packet of Spanish reals in his shirt pocket. What had dealer in the plaza next to the mission called them? *Cobbs*. His reals were hand struck in the 1530s. The Fray Marcos de Niza party must have left them behind. Coronado came a year later, traveling a different route. They could have been stolen or traded. Kino came up the Gila two hundred years later. The dealer said something about Kino's men would have carried stamped coins because they started minting those in 1720s.

He opened his eyes and sat up when the landing gear popped open. The plane was descending from the east, following the Salt River. The Tempe Buttes and the Sun Devil stadium were underneath the port wing tip. Off in the distance, Lone Butte Mountain rose up above the Salt River.

"Welcome to Phoenix," the stewardess announced. "Please remain in your seats until we have landed."

Ruiz was waiting for Jack in front of the terminal entrance, his '52 Chevy truck parked in a 5-minute loading zone. An airport cop was edging toward them holding a ticket pad in one hand and a pen in the other. He stopped to check a car, and kept a wary eye on Ruiz's truck.

Jack threw his duffle bag in the back of the truck, opened the door, and slide across the hot vinyl seat. "Whoa! That's hot. How long have you've been parked here, Ruiz?"

"Five minutes, maybe a little more."

"Let's go," Jack said. Ruiz switched on the starter and ground the engine. When it kicked over, he pulled away from the curb just as the airport cop put a whistle to his lips and blew it shrilly. "He wants you to pull over, Ruiz."

"Who wants me to pull over?" Ruiz grinned. "I didn't see nobody." He tapped his ear, "I didn't hear a whistle." Ruiz took the 40th Street cut-off and followed the surface streets to Baseline Road. "Less traffic this way. It's not so noisy either."

"How can you tell the way this Chevy rattles?'

"The truck rattles a lot, but I like the sound. It's like having your wife snoring beside you. You get used to it, and if it stops, you miss it and wake up."

"You'll never fall asleep in this truck, Ruiz. Not while it's moving!"

"Cierra offered to pick you up," Ruiz said, his eyes twinkling under his raised eyebrows. The corners of his mouth twisted into a smile. "Are you disappointed, Jefe, that I came for you instead of Cierra?"

"Me? Disappointed? I wouldn't want to miss a chance to ride with an old goat like you."

"That's what I thought; so I came for you." Ruiz turned south on 56th Street. "What about the ranch, Jefe? Did you find someone to help you?"

"Yes, Ruiz, I did. One of my old friends specializes in land investments. I can get a short-term loan on the property with or without water. He might find an investor to back me if I come up with a reasonably priced water source. There are a lot of variables, Ruiz. I'll need an environmental impact study done. If they find a sensitive archeological area or an endangered species, it could add $100,000 to a million overnight for my development costs. A sewage system poses a bigger problem, but… Well, that's something I'm going have to think about."

Ruiz pulled into the yard. "He also gave the name of a hydrologist, Paul Manring, in Carefree. I called him from Santa Barbara. He says the fault lines and the down slope from the South Mountains indicate we have a good chance to find a source of water here."

"I could have told him that."

"Then you can be my hydrologist!"

"What's a hydrologist?"

"A man who knows how to find water."

"Then I am a hydrologist."

"That you are, Ruiz. That you are," Jack said as he climbed out of the truck and picked up his bag.

"When do we start, Jefe?"

"In a couple of days. I'll let you know. Adios, Ruiz."

"Adios, Jefe," Ruiz said, and he wheeled out of the yard.

Jack went into the stable, found the Gentry's phone number on the clipboard, and called Mollie. After five or six rings, she answered.

"Hello, Mollie. It's Jack. I'm fine. Yes, I've been away. I went to Santa Barbara. Uh huh...Uh huh. I went to see a friend, Ray Stanford, who's an investment broker. I asked a few questions and Ray gave me a few things to think about. Do you know about the Arizona Underground Water Act? You do? Your land falls under the grandfather clause, so does mine. But Mollie, Carver's property isn't grand- fathered."

He paused to let Mollie consider the information. "That's right. He needs our wells, period. Ray made a few calls and checked out Carver's development company in Orange County. Carver tied up a lot of land. Then built a model tract development on borrowed money. He lost money; actually he lost more than he should have because he got into a controversy over Indian burial grounds. They took him to the cleaners. Yes, yes, Mollie."

"Well, he sold the rest of his holdings to a venture capital company. Yes, that's right Mollie. Now, according to Ray's sources, Phoenix has turned Carver down cold. They won't set up a water or sewage treatment plant unless Carver proves that a large population can be maintained in this area without drawing on Phoenix's resources."

"That's right, Mollie. As it is now, they would have to bring water all the way around the South Mountains. Phoenix might be interested if they could annex our area. But we all have a voice in the annexation process – that means you, me, the Warners, the Evans, and Shorty. We are propinquant."

"Never mind, Mollie. Let me finish. The city of Chandler has annexed ten miles of land, all the way to the freeway. The city fathers are way ahead of Tempe. Tempe is cut off from expanding southward. A couple of years ago, Tempe tried to annex Guadalupe and Yaqui Town, but got snubbed. The Yaquis and the Mexican-Americans want to stay just the way they are; they want no part of Tempe. So Carver is caught in the middle. Tempe won't provide water and sewers. Chandler is still too far away, and they would have to annex us. Yes, that's right Mollie. And Phoenix would still have to cross part of Yaqui Town to reach us. You and I, Mollie, we're the corks in Carver's bottle."

"Yes, Mollie, Phoenix might annex this area in time, but Carver doesn't have enough time. He needs our water now! He needs just enough to prove the feasibility of one tract development. You've got it. Mollie, talk it over with your boys. I'll drive down later, and we talk some more. I've got a few things to do first. Chance Clark was right, Mollie. You and I are the castles in this game, and we need to pull together. Thanks. I won't sell unless your do; you've got a deal. See you soon. Bye," he said and hung up the phone.

Jack crossed the front porch and picked up the orange kitten that had began rubbing against his legs while he was using the phone. He began to stroke him behind the ears and the kitten began to purr. "I'm home, O.C. It's good to see you."

The door of the modest older territorial-style adobe opened about six inches. A tall almond-eyed woman stared coolly at Jack. "Yes?"

"Mike Chernov gave me your name. He told me that you're a first-rate ceramist. That you can make a broken pot look like new."

"Mike would say something like that," Trisha Simpson said. "I've seen you someplace before."

"I was at the ARAS meeting the other night."

"You own the ranch where the petroglyphs came from."

"You mean the 'fake' petroglyphs. Your friend Mr. Owens seemed concerned that the petroglyphs aren't authentic. You appeared to agree with him. May I ask you why?"

The door opened wider. "They're too well done."

"The design?"

"No, the incisions... the inscriptions were done with such care, almost with devotion. Whoever did them was part artist and part sculptor. I couldn't detect any mistakes, so I don't believe someone with a stone tool could have done it. To be certain, I'd have to see the glyphs up close."

"That's it?"

"No, there's more, but I haven't thought it through."

"Do you mean how or why?"

"Both."

"What about my broken pot?" Jack smiled.

"Bring it around back to the workshop. I'll meet you there." Trisha closed the front door. Jack picked up the box and followed the flagstone path to the rear of the house. The faces of the stones were incised with figures copied from petroglyphs: Kokopelli, the humpbacked flute player, a menacing mountain lion and a standing bear. A basalt slab with dark patina was covered with stick figures, a stenciled hand, and a reverse cross. Trisha came out to the workshop a few minutes later and unlocked the door.

Jack sat the box on an old wooden bench just inside the workshop door. Trisha snapped on a powerful overhead halogen lamp. "Did you do the designs in the yard?"

"Yes. I do some things, mostly tables and plaques. Sometimes I do work for landscapers." Trisha opened the box and quickly laid out the larger pieces, studied them for a moment and deftly began to piece them together. "This pot is water damaged. A lot of the material has deteriorated."

"It's been hanging on the front porch at the ranch house for forty years. Sometimes the monsoon rains get blown in there."

"Well, I can fix it, but you can buy one in better shape for less money."

"What's it worth?"

"Undamaged? One hundred to $150. After I repair it, maybe $50. Unless it has sentimental value, I'd chuck it. It's a Navajo horse canteen. It has character...." Trisha's voice trailed off.

"Let's do it," Jack said. Trisha smiled and began to gently place some of the smaller pieces on a tray. "Tough job, these tiny pieces. Some of these are damaged beyond repair, but I can replicate them. You won't be able to tell the difference. I repair a lot of broken pots for museums. I authenticate them down to the last detail. Same clay. Same oxides. Same sand, even." She began to fit some pieces together.

Jack noticed a wide assortment of animal fetishes lining the shelves behind the workbench. "Are those replicas?" he asked.

"Some are, some aren't. Can you tell the difference?"

Jack pulled a large bear and a frog off the shelf and inspected them closely. "Not really."

"I mark mine." Jack turned the two pieces over. The bear had a small + on the base; the frog had no marking. "The frog is HoHoKam. I make copies of early pots and mark them the same way."

"I had some pieces like this, but they were recently stolen."

"Really?" Trisha arched her eyebrows. "What did they look like?"

"Well, there was a pair of human icons carved from matates. Two bear fetishes. Some birds, an owl, a dove, maybe two doves because one looked more like a chicken. A mouse with an open mouth. I called it the mouse that roared," Jack said and Trisha smiled. "There was a beaver with a tail, a cat-like figure that could have been a mountain lion. One that looked like a porcupine. A mountain goat. And a skunk."

"What material were they made from?"

"A reddish pumice. The kind you find up around the San Francisco Peaks, outside of Flagstaff."

"When were they taken?"

"Last week. They also took some Navajo blankets and Papago baskets."

"I might know where your fetishes are."

"You're kidding. Where?"

"In the basement of the anthropology department at ASU. I saw Tom Owens cataloguing a donation which included pieces like those. At least some of them match your description."

"I'd like to see them."

"The archives are open to the public, but only a few people ever go down there. After the stuff is boxed up, it's usually never seen again. I go there from time to time to study the period pieces. Adds to my authenticity." Trisha laughed.

"Would you go with me?"

"Sure."

"When?"

"How about now. I need to pick up some supplies at the art shop. I'll meet you in front of the anthropology building in, say, an hour."

"I think I should call the sheriff's office. I know a deputy sheriff there. She filed the robbery report and has the inventory of the stolen items."

"Good idea." Trisha grinned mischievously and handed Jack the telephone.

Jack took out Cierra's card and dialed the number. Trisha sat on a storage shelf and waited until Jack completed the call. "Cierra will meet us in the basement of Old Main. She knows her way around campus."

"You go ahead, I'll close up and meet you there. I hope they're your objects. I could be wrong."

"I hope your right. See you in a bit. Thanks Trisha."

"Don't thank me yet."

CHAPTER 15

Jack, Trisha, and Cierra, in her sheriff's uniform, stood in front of a table in the semi-darkened basement storage room. Trisha sat on a carton on the table, stepped back, and waited quietly beside a tall shelf. A worried- looking Dr. Draper opened the carton, unwrapped several objects, and laid them on the table.

Cierra opened Jack's packet of photos. "Well, let's see if we have a match."

"Six of them are obvious matches, but four aren't," Draper sighed.

"Those four aren't mine. I've never seen them before," Jack said.

"Where did you get these?" Cierra asked Dr. Draper.

"A donation." He handed an invoice to Cierra. Jack and Trisha looked over her shoulder to read the document:

> *Donation. Value: $100,000.*
> *Dr. Carl Baxter. Scottsdale, Arizona.*
> *Appraised by Manouch Azad*
> *Antiquities Appraisers Association*

"One hundred thousand? For these fetishes?" Cierra exclaimed. "That doesn't sound right." Cierra looked at Jack and then at Trisha for confirmation and turned back to Draper.

"That's Azad's appraisal, not mine. I just accept the donations 'as is' from the private donors. It's for the students, you see. It's the only way we can get material like this. We can't take it from the digs ourselves, can we? And now, because of the cultural affinity issues, our access to objects is severely limited.

The museums won't let us touch their collections. No other way to study the real thing. No one really cares but us," he explained.

"One hundred thousand dollars and stored in a basement." Jack handed a bird fetish to Trisha. "Is it authentic?"

"It's the real thing," Trisha said, "but you can buy one for less than a hundred dollars, or I could make you one just like it for fifty."

Cierra took the fetish and placed it in a carton. "Thanks for your cooperation, Doctor. I'm taking these items into custody until we can verify Dr. Reed's ownership. Until then, it would be best to keep this matter confidential, Dr. Draper."

"I suppose. I suppose. I hope there won't be any problems about this."

"You're in the clear, Doctor, and so is the university. It's a good thing you record these transactions."

Jack, Cierra, and Trisha stood in the Old Main parking lot. "Something's fishy here. I don't get it. You obtain a $100,000 appraisal and then donate the material to the anthropology department? Why not to a museum?" Cierra asked.

"Maybe no museum wanted them," Trisha suggested. "Maybe they were afraid of the cultural affinity implications like Draper said."

"Or maybe the donor didn't want them publicly displayed," Jack suggested.

"I think you and I should go see Dr. Baxter. He may still have your animal fetishes and maybe the rest of your things," Cierra said.

Jack hugged Trisha. "Thanks so much for your help. I'm really grateful."

"I hope I didn't compromise myself with Draper. He gives me work from time to time. I wish Tom Owens had been there. He's so damn smug. He takes himself too seriously. I'd like to have seen his face when he discovers the fetishes were stolen. I'll call you when the olla is ready. Take care."

"Thank you, Trisha. You've been a big help," Cierra said. Trisha hurried towards her car.

"Jack, you're part of an official investigation now. I may need you to identify material evidence. You can ride shotgun. We'll take the scenic route." Cierra exited the parking lot and turned west on Mill Avenue. Driving through the Old Town Tempe shopping district, they passed the Old Shoe Mill on the corner Fourth Street and Mill Avenue. "They have the best inventory in Arizona. They carry Birkenstocks, Doc Martins, and Mephistos."

"How do you know that?"

"I worked there part-time when I attended ASU. My cousin Jake owns the store. I could get you a discount on some desert boots, to go with your hat."

"How many cousins, aunts, and uncles do you have Cierra?"

"Too many to count."

They crossed the Salt River on the Mill Avenue Bridge and turned right onto the Galvin Parkway at the first intersection. The Parkway led to a massive wind-sculptured sandstone hill with a gaping hole in the center. "Hole in the Rock," Cierra said. "I love coming up here in the evening when there's a full moon. When the angle's right, the moon fills the entire circle," she sighed. "We do too many mountain rescues here. Kids, tourists, and people who should know better can't resist the temptation to climb to the top and cross over the arch. It should be declared a public nuisance. The sandstone grit is treacherous. Sometimes they slip and fall partway down the mountain. Some don't survive the fall. If hikers stay at the lower levels, they're okay. Some people just can't stay within their limits."

"Maybe they don't know what their limits are."

"Speaking of limits, I'm going to do some 'knock and talk' work today. If anything comes up, do what I tell you, okay?"

"Sure. What do you mean by 'knock and talk'?"

"If you're doing an investigation and don't have a warrant, but you have a strong suspicion, you knock on doors and ask questions. If I suspect that say someone's running a 'crack house' or is maybe a small-time trafficker, I knock, and if someone answers, say it's the dealer or his girlfriend, I introduce myself and ask if I can come in. They usually let you inside. Then I say something like, 'We've been getting complaints from the neighbors. They tell us there's a lot of people coming and going here at odd hours. Your neighbors think you're dealing drugs.' Before they can deny it, I say 'Do you know that sales of illegal is a serious offense? That you could spend a lot of time in prison?' Before they can answer I ask 'Do you mind if I look around?' Half of the time, they just take me to the junk. Wherever it's hidden. Now, if they say 'You can't come in,' I leave the premises. If they don't want me to look around, I have to go."

"That's it?" Jack asked. "Even if you know there are drugs or contraband in the house?"

"Yes, that's it. Unless I get a warrant that states specifically what I'm searching for. If they do ask me to leave, I drop the hint that I'm going to get warrant. Then I radio in a request for someone to get me a warrant from the D.A.'s office. Sometimes I just call in and tell the duty officer what's coming down. If the guy inside is a dealer, he's in a bind. If he owns the drugs, he may flush them down the toilet. I don't get an arrest, but at least some drugs are off the street. If the guy doesn't 'own' the drugs – if he 'owes' a dealer, he might make a run for it. As soon as he hits the street, then I can stop and do a search."

"That's devious."

"The bad guys are more devious, Jack. They can do almost anything. Actually the laws work in their favor. What I do is legal if I stay within the guidelines. That's it." Cierra drove through Old Town Scottsdale and parked in front of a long, low adobe territorial building on the south side of Indian Bend Wash.

"Look at this place. It's built like a fortress. Wrought iron grills and shuttered street-side windows," Cierra said.

Jack opened a heavy wooden gate. As they walked across a flagstone patio, Cierra pointed out a surveillance camera. Another camera covered the entryway. A yellow Land Rover eased out of the driveway and turned down a side street. The passenger, a large man, peered over his shoulder and then turned away abruptly.

"The Mallorys!" Jack exclaimed. "What are they doing here?"

"Who are the Mallorys?"

"They own the Indian Traders Den. They came to the ranch house to appraise my artifacts. They're on my visitors list."

"Did they give you an appraisal for the animal fetishes?"

"Yes, but it was nickels and dimes compared to Baxters."

"Hmmm. This gets curiouser and curiouser."

The speaker box came on: "Yes? Can I help you?" a woman's voice asked querulously.

"Sheriff's Department, Ma'am. Deputy Cierra Alcaraz. I'd like to speak with Dr. Baxter."

"He's not here; he's at his office."

"May I come in and use your phone. I'd like to speak with him."

"May I ask what this is about?"

"Ma'am, I need to ask Dr. Baxter about a donation he made to Arizona State University. May I use your phone, please?"

A buzzer sounded and the door opened, automatically admitting them into a small foyer. An elderly, neatly dressed woman met them.

"Please wait here while I call Dr. Baxter," she said and pointed to an ornate wrought iron bench that faced a Mexican-tiled fountain. She was back in less than five minutes.

"Dr. Baxter is busy with his patients. He wants to know if this can keep until Saturday? He says that you absolutely are not to enter the premises," she said firmly.

"Tell Dr. Baxter that won't do," Cierra said. "Tell him I will get a search warrant if necessary."

The woman reappeared moments later. "Dr. Baxter says do as you wish, but please leave."

They walked back to the sheriff's car. Cierra was furious.

"I should have brought a warrant." She picked up the radiophone. "Sally, I need a warrant. Ten minutes ago for twenty

HoHoKam fetishes. Yes, HoHoKam, not Ho-Ho-Ho. I'm here at the Baxter address. Dr. C. Baxter. Yes. You have it. This is hot."

Two hours later an exultant Deputy Alcaraz walked out of the adobe fortress. "Two more, the doves," she said triumphantly. "I wish I had a broader warrant because that guy's place is loaded with stuff. I'll bet it's all stolen. The dragon lady nearly had a fit. I think she's scared to death of Baxter."

"Are you going to arrest him?"

"No, I can't. The dragon lady showed me a bill of sale. Baxter paid cash and traded some Indian baskets for the fetishes. He got them at the Anasazi Galleria in Old Town. I need to check this out."

Cierra drove across the canal into Old Town Scottsdale and wove her way down the tourist-packed avenues and boulevards. She parked in a green loading zone in front of the Anasazi Galleria.

"This is one impressive place," Cierra said as they walked through the high ceiling turquoise-tiled show room. A row of animal fetishes lined a back-lighted showcase in the center of the room. Two miniature bears were highlighted by an overhead track light. A card indicated their retail value: the smaller black bear was marked at $1,500 while the larger reddish bear was being offered for sale at $1,000.

"Those are mine. They were the best specimens."

"Look at the price tag, Jack. If all your pieces averaged say $1,000 that only adds up to $12-15,000. Yet the appraisal is for $100,000 for just six pieces, and they aren't as nice as these. Something is wrong here. Look around Jack. See if you spot anything else that's yours."

Jack walked around the showroom. A few high quality Navajo blankets were dropped over fake pueblo ladders. Some Papago baskets were piled casually near a window. He examined jewelry cases filled with expensive turquoise and coral inlaid silver bracelets and delicate silver and turquoise squash blossom necklaces. "No dice, Cierra. Nice things, but they're not my mother's."

"There's an office in the back. I want to talk to Arnold."

Peter Brandt, a well-groomed, young man or no more than twenty-five to twenty-eight years old, wearing a paisley tie and an off-white linen suit seemed disconcerted at having a uniformed sheriff in his office.

"I'm Deputy Alcaraz. I'm investigating a theft. Those fetishes in your front showcase belong to Dr. Reed. We just collected some fetishes from Dr. Baxter's home. According to a bill of sale, he paid $5,000 cash and traded several Indian baskets to your gallery in exchange for the fetishes. Perhaps you could explain how you happened to have them here."

Brandt looked stupefied. Then blurted, "I'm afraid I can't. I've never seen them, and I don't even know Dr. Baxter...."

"This is a bill of sale from your business, stating the conditions of the trade." Brandt looked it over critically.

"Yes, it is, I'm afraid. That's Mr. Arnold's signature. He might have traded the items to Dr. Baxter. Mr. Arnold does the buying, and the private trading and selling; I handle direct sales for the gallery."

"Where is he?"

"In Washington D.C. He won't be back for several days. He's having some things appraised."

"By Manouch Azad, I believe."

"Well, er..., uh..., yes. As a matter of fact he is. That's why he went to Washington."

"Those bear fetishes in your front case...."

"Yes?"

"I'm taking them into custody. They match the description Dr. Reed provided the sheriffs department. He has identified them as being his personal property. Would you please put them in a box for me?"

"I can't do that."

"If you don't, I'll call in a robbery detail from Scottsdale and have them do it for you."

"That won't be necessary. I'll take care of it," Brandt reluctantly agreed. "What's this all about?"

"Theft. I told you that when we came into your office."

"We haven't stolen anything."

"Possibly. Probably not. But you are dealing with stolen items."

The young man paled and walked hurriedly to the front of the gallery. He returned in a few minutes and handed a carton to Cierra. She scribbled out a property tag receipt and handed it to Brandt. "Please have Mr. Arnold call me at this number when he returns."

"I'm certain you'll be getting a call."

"What's next?" Jack asked as he stowed the carton on the rear seat of the Bronco.

"I don't know. I need to talk to Arnold."

"And the Mallorys?"

"No probable cause to search their place. No link."

"They were at Baxter's."

"So what? That doesn't prove anything."

"Look! Brooks Brothers is off and running." Jack pointed at the alleyway behind the gallery. A bright red Mercedes roadster peeled out of the alley. Brandt was behind the wheel. He crossed the canal and turned south.

"This should be easy," Cierra said, "all south roads lead to the river. Get in." Cierra started the vehicle and followed Brandt.

"Now what?"

"I'll hang back and keep him in sight."

"There he is," Jack said. The Mercedes went through an open chain link gate and disappeared around the corner of a blue-painted steel building. Cierra parked the Bronco behind a block fence under the shade of a sour-orange tree.

Cierra called the dispatcher. "This is Maricopa 19. My location is 225 South River Road. I have a suspect under surveillance. This is four-four."

"All right Maricopa 19. Your location is noted. Do you need assistance?"

"Not at this time. If anything develops, I'll let you know. 10-4." Cierra got out and peered over the top of the block fence just as the Mercedes pulled out of the driveway. She ran back to the Bronco. "Did he spot us?"

"I don't think so. He's in a rush. Are we going to follow him?"

"No, there's a van coming out." Cierra climbed into the Bronco and started the engine.

A white van pulled out of the driveway and turned west, the opposite direction Mercedes had taken. Cierra followed the van, closed to within a few yards, and then hit the siren. The driver jerked the van to the side of the road, slid across the gravel yard, and skidded to a stop in a vacant lot. The driver stepped out, pulled his Stetson down over his forehead, and walked slowly towards the Bronco.

"That's Rudy Lazar. Carver's driver."

"Stay put." Cierra slid out the door as Lazar approached.

"Do we have a problem, ma'am?" Lazar drawled.

"May I see your driver's license?"

"Yes, ma'am." Lazar pulled his wallet from his hip pocket and shoved it towards her.

"Not your wallet, sir. Just your driver's license, please." Cierra took the license, looked it over and handed it back. "Well, Mr. Lazar, I'm investigating a theft. Would you mind if I looked inside your van?"

"I would unless you have a warrant."

"Excuse me, Mr. Lazar. Please wait here." Cierra walked to the front the van and spoke to the passenger. A tall, big boned, Hispanic man with a black mustache and high cheekbones stepped out and walked slowly to the front of the van. Cierra spoke to him in Spanish. The man turned around and put his hands behind his back. Cierra quickly cuffed him and returned to where Lazar was standing.

"Well, Mr. Lazar, it seems that your employee is an illegal; he doesn't have a green card."

"He's not my employee. I don't have any employees, ma'am," Lazar said, pulling off his blue-mirrored sunglasses.

"Who does he work for then?"

"I dis-remember."

Cierra called her dispatcher. "I need a Border Patrol or a Customs, if there's a unit in the area." Cierra waited beside the Bronco.

"It's your lucky day, Alcaraz," the dispatcher said. "There's two border patrol units in your area. They just closed a warehouse at 333 River. They are one block from your location and on the way."

In less than five minutes a green US Border Patrol van pulled alongside the curb. "Shit!" Lazar said.

Cierra uncuffed the suspect and led him to the van. The Border Patrol officer opened the side door and the man slid onto the seat, eyes downcast. The officer and Cierra approached Lazar.

"Mr. Lazar, Mr. Rodriguez tells us that there are several more illegal workers in your yard," the Border Patrol officer stated.

"It's not my yard," Lazar said sharply.

"But it is your van?" Cierra asked.

"It's mine."

"I'll ask you one more time, Mr. Lazar. Would you care to open your van, or shall we all wait here until I get a warrant?" Cierra continued and Lazar shrugged his shoulders and swaggered over to the van and opened the door.

"Help yourself." Lazar stepped aside and jammed his hands in his pockets. There was a carton just inside the door. Cierra opened the lid and peered inside. She picked up a flat bird-like figure and another figure shaped like a cat and brought them over for Jack to see.

"Two more, I believe, Dr. Reed."

"They aren't mine."

"Are you sure?"

"I've never seen them before."

"Great!" Cierra carried them back to van and put them in the box.

"Is anything wrong deputy?"

"Are these fetishes your property?"

"Aren't you supposed to read me my rights?"

"Only if I intend to arrest you. I'm asking you again, are these fetishes yours?"

"No. I was returning them to the Anasazi Galleria."

"To Mr. Arnold?"

"Yes."

"And did Peter Brandt tell you that they were stolen?"

"No. He only told me that a deputy was looking for some fetishes. Are these the ones you're looking for?"

"Mr. Lazar, you're free to go."

"You're not going to arrest me?"

"Not if your story holds up, I don't see any problem. Do you?"

"No, ma'am."

Lazar climbed into his van, looked around carefully, executed a U-turn and headed down River Road as several more Border Patrol vehicles pulled into the wrecking yard.

"This isn't over yet?" Jack asked.

"Not by a long shot. There's a lot of wheeling and dealing going on here. If those aren't your fetishes, they might have been stolen from someone else. Why else would Brandt come here? I don't get it," Cierra said. "Why would a reputable art dealer use a wrecking yard that employs illegals to store artifacts?"

"Well, for sure no one would come looking for them here," Jack said. "Maybe Brandt wasn't as scared as we thought; maybe we should have followed him instead."

"You're saying that Brandt led us on a wild goose chase?"

"Sort of looks that way, doesn't it?" Jack smiled.

"That cuts it." Cierra revved up the Bronco. Jack wisely said nothing. "I'm going to check on everyone on that list of visitors you gave me. Someone on it is connected to Arnold and Baxter."

"I'd start with Lazar. And, what were the Mallorys doing at Baxter's house? The Mallorys wrote an appraisal on the fetishes before they were stolen. Carver or Lazar could have spotted them the day they came to the ranch house."

"Why would Carver want them?'

"I don't know. Maybe Rudy's short of cash and Carver has nothing to do with it. But I'd check on him anyway."

"I'll drop you off at your car, Jack. I need to go downtown. It's going to take some time to write this all up. I don't even know what we've got here, but it's going to take more than one person to check it all out. I'm going to need the Sheriff's okay on this one."

"Thanks, Cierra. I appreciate what you're doing. I'm impressed. You did a good job with that 'knock and talk' routine."

"Yep, right up until we ran into Lazar. He's been around the block." Cierra dropped Jack off at the parking in front of Old Main at ASU. "I'll call you as soon as I know something."

"Make it sooner than that," Jack said. Cierra laughed and drove off.

CHAPTER 16

Jack looked out the window of the utility room. A white late-model Lincoln town car slowly eased up to the ramada and parked. The driver set the emergency brake and stepped out. He closed his door and opened the rear door on his side of the town car. A portly woman emerged and leaned on the door. She shaded her eyes with one hand even though it was twilight, scanned the mountains to the west, then the desert in front of her. A tall angular man got out of the front passenger seat and walked around the car.

"It's pretty, but how could anyone stand to live out here alone? I'd be afraid to. Wild animals, snakes. No one to help you," she said.

"Be still, Martha," the taller man spoke sharply. "Let Arnold do the talking to this Reed fellow. Don't butt in. This isn't a social call."

"I wasn't going to say anything," Martha sputtered.

"Let's get this over with, Arnold."

"Take it easy, Wynn. Like I've been telling you, I'll take care of it. No problems, all right? Both of you stay out of the conversation. He's bound to be suspicious. Why wouldn't he be? We drive out here to make him an offer after his fetishes show up."

"That's not my fault, Arnold. You assured me that no one would ever see them in that damn basement at ASU, and you were a damn fool to display them in your gallery."

"How was I supposed to know that they were stolen? Just cool down. Look, Reed is no dummy. I can explain how they ended up with us, but he will
want to know why you want to buy them back. So, you're the Good Samaritan. Got it? I'm the straight man."

"I don't care how you do it, Arnold. Just get it done."

"All I can do is make him an offer. If he turns it down, well, that's his right."

"He'd better not. I've got too much at stake. I can't have the IRS snooping around and I certainly don't want any surveillance. Understand?" Wynn said and looked at Martha. Arnold shrugged his shoulders.

"Let's go," Baxter said and they started across the yard.

Jack walked through the kitchen and dining room and went to the gun case. He took a Remington 12-guage automatic shotgun and loaded three shells into the magazine. He set the safety, walked back to the dining area and stood by the window. Waiting until the trio had stepped onto the porch and Arnold was about to knock on the door, he pumped a shell into the breech.

"What was that?" Martha said loudly.

"Sounds like someone has a shotgun."

"Oh, God! Let's go." She grabbed her husband's arm. "He's going to kill us.

Jack set the shotgun beside the front door and flipped on the porch light.

"He's coming."

"Damn it, Martha, of course he's coming."

Jack opened the door. "Good evening, Dr. Reed. I thought I heard a shell being pumped into a shotgun," Arnold said.

"You did. We've had a few problems out here lately. Robberies, arson, vandalism. My caretaker was assaulted, so I'm not taking any chances."

"Well, we mean you no harm. I can assure you. I'm Robert Arnold," the bland pleasant-looking man in his mid-fifties offered his hand. "Thanks for seeing us. This is Mr. and Mrs. Baxter."

"Please come in. Mi casa su casa." Jack held the door open and waited as Mrs. Baxter, a heavyset woman with sagging jowls, hesitated and then, reluctantly entered the house. A tall, thin, cadaverous looking man with hollow dark circles for eye sockets nodded at Jack and followed her inside, moving like a cautious crane.

"This way." Jack led them into the semi-darkened living area. He flipped a switch and the wagon wheel chandelier started to circle slowly; its candle-like bulbs casting flickering shadows on the fireplace and ceiling.

"How quaint," Arnold said. Mrs. Baxter sat perched on the edge of the sofa as if she were ready to fly off at a moment's notice. Carl Baxter sat across from her, with his hands folded in his lap. He avoided making eye contact with Jack and fixed his eyes on the circling lamps.

"My grandfather made it. Quaint wasn't part of his vocabulary; rustic would have been his choice."

"Yes, it is quite rustic. Dr. Reed, I'll get right to the point. The Baxters are embarrassed by this whole incident. So am I. I purchased the animal fetishes in good faith from Mr. Lazar. We have done business in the past and there was never any problem. Rudy is a quite a collector. I had every reason to believe the articles were his and that the appraisal was a sound one. My manager apparently handled the officer's inquiry rather clumsily, but you can imagine his
concern. It's not everyday a police officer inquires at our gallery, especially regarding misappropriated articles."

"Stolen articles," Jack interrupted.

"Yes, in this case stolen articles. You're absolutely correct." Arnold paused and glanced at Mrs. Baxter who was twisting a ring on her finger. "It's all right, Martha. We can work something out with Dr. Reed. I'm sure he understands your concern."

He turned to Jack and said, "I've offered to return Dr. Baxter's investment fully. When Mr. Lazar is located, perhaps I'll recover my losses. In any case, I'm responsible, but that's not why we are here. Dr. Baxter is genuinely interested in obtaining the fetishes, if you would be willing to sell them for 40% of the figure given by Mr. Azad. That would be approximately their wholesale trade value." Mrs. Baxter's hand stopped fluttering. She held her breath. Jack said nothing. "Mr. Baxter is willing to go as high as

60%. And I assure you that that is a very reasonable figure, Dr. Reed." Arnold waited for Jack to respond.

"I may be able to help you move your rock art as well. The Baxters have no interest, but there are buyers in New York and Germany and even some interest in such items in Japan. It would take some time, of course. They aren't your everyday item, so to speak." Arnold sat back.

The odd trio looked at Jack expectantly. Jack studied the chandelier overhead as it made a full circle. Mrs. Baxter was startled when Captain Ned's ship's clock on the mantle began ringing eight bells. Jack waited until the reverberation ceased. "To be frank, this whole business is puzzling me. I'm just beginning to make inquires, so right now I'm not ready to sell anything, even if I could. The Sheriff's Department is holding the fetishes as evidence. They will probably prosecute Lazar if they prove he stole them."

"I can only tell you what I told the deputy, and that is that he sold them to me. I can't say that he stole him," Arnold said. "In the meantime, Jack, you could use some cash, couldn't you? The Baxters could make a substantial advance on your promise to sell them."

"Thanks just the same, but no thanks," Jack said. Mrs. Baxter sighed audibly and directed a pleading look towards Arnold. "I'll dispose of them in my own way and in my own good time."

"The antiquities market is a mine field, Dr. Reed," Arnold said. "Please don't be offended, but it's no place for amateurs. There are a lot of dishonest characters in the business. The Native American Protection Act means that any tribe may claim your property if it can prove any spiritual or cultural affiliation. Even museums have had to return items. If I were you, I'd consider selling while you can. I've made you a generous offer. You can check around, but I doubt if anyone else would take the risk. Your animal fetishes now have a tainted reputation. Most dealers will shy away. Dr. Baxter is a private collector and ultimately will see that a proper museum houses your artifacts."

"Proper? You mean proper as in the basement archives at ASU? I don't think so," Jack stood up. "Let me make it perfectly clear. I'm not interested in selling the fetishes now or at any time in the future." Mrs. Baxter clutched her bag and hurried to the door. Baxter stared hard at Jack; his dark eyes were blazing coals in their sunken sockets. He turned away abruptly and followed her outside without saying a word.

Arnold offered his hand and handed Jack a card. "If you change your mind." Jack didn't take either. Arnold shrugged his shoulders and laid the card on the table in the entryway. "Good night."

"Buenos noches." Jack waited until Arnold left the porch to bolt the door. He slipped quietly into the darkened utility room, eased open a window, and listened to the two men talking outside the town car.

"I must have those artifacts," Baxter demanded.

"Now is not a good time to discuss this," Arnold said and looked back at the house. "You heard him. The Sheriff's Department has them."

"Now's as good a time as any," Baxter raised his voice. "I don't have time. I don't need any IRS investigators on my tail."

"I doubt if there will be any problems with the IRS. But you might call your attorney. We can establish that you acted in good faith."

"I don't need my attorney. I just want those damn fetishes. This is your damn fault and Manouch's. And if the IRS or the Sheriff comes snooping around, this is just the beginning of our troubles. We won't be able to move a foot." Baxter looked at Martha and closed his mouth tightly. "I'm riding in back with her," he said to Arnold and crawled into the rear seat and slammed the door.

Arnold turned on the headlights; his hands rested on the wheel. "Yes. Yes. I think we should be on our way." Arnold turned the car in a tight circle, spun the wheels, and showered the side of the house with gravel as he pulled away from the ramada.

Jack watched the headlights bounce off the ridge and then lift skyward as Arnold missed the track, drove up a hillock, and skidded down the opposite side. "Break an axle, why don't you?" Jack said.

A clinking sound in the stove startled Jack, and he stepped away from the window. "Hello, Mrs. Hindsquirt. I think I smell something rotten here, and it's not you."

In the morning Jack called Doc Hartman at the Pacific Rim Institute. Felix listened as Jack explained the Baxters' strange offer and said, "Talk to Will Culver in Old Town. He's a straight arrow. He's into pre-Columbian materials. He sold an Aztec piece for six figures in Santa Fe. Maybe he can help you."

Jack drove all the way through Tempe on Rural Road only catching one red light. He crossed the bridge over the Salt River. It was nearly at flood stage due to the release of millions of gallons of water from the project dams, overflowing from the monsoon rains. Out of curiosity, he drove past the Indian Traders Den and noticed that its front doors were padlocked.

He crossed Scottsdale Road and left his truck on a parking island in the middle of Main Street. Tacked onto a massive indigo blue door, a modest copper plate simply stated "Will Culver." Pre-Columbian effigies posed on a bed of white sand stared morosely out of the narrow sun-tinted window. A violin in an open antique leather case lay on a shelf suspended by gold-braided cords. A hand-lettered card made an unpretentious statement: Stradivarius.

Inside the shop, a glass case held a variety of gemstones; another case was devoted to Australian black opals. The wall opposite the cases was lined with tins and bottles that appeared to have been salvaged from an apothecary's shop or an alchemist's laboratory. A doorway at the rear opened into a tiny cubicle with just enough room for a desk, filing cabinet, and a swivel chair that was occupied by a ruddy-faced fortyish man with a thick reddish mustache.

Will Culver leaned back in his chair. "Can I help you?"

"Doc Hartman suggested that I talk you. He said you might be able to find a market for these." Jack handed Will the packet of photos.

Will studied the photos and then studied Jack. "What do you want for them?"

Jack handed Culver Azad's appraisal. He read the bottom figure. "Holy Toledo! $350,000. I wouldn't pay $700 for the lot. Are you trying to con me? What the hell's Azad pulling here?"

"Felix said that you sold an Aztec piece for six figures."

"That was a magnificent piece. A full-bodied figure trimmed in jade. One of a kind. It had a legend – an Aztec noble woman put a red ball under her skirt and became pregnant."

"These glyphs have a legend, too," Jack said. "In fact, a similar one." Jack briefly summarized Lee's interpretation of the petroglyphs and their relation to the Legend of HA-AK, the Blue Owl.

"Lee's pretty sharp. He may even be right, and if he is, the glyphs could be worth that kind of money, but I wouldn't want to get involved. I'm into gemstones nowadays. The Indian market is too unstable. No museum is safe. The glory days are over. Cultural patrimony is in today, Jack. Respect, repatriation, and reburial are the watchwords. In light of that, the appraisal is a piece of crap unless you can prove your items were obtained from private property."

"The ranch has been privately owned since 1888."

"Then you are probably home free, but some tribal authority may bring a suit against you anyhow. Tell me about the ranch. The site."

Jack briefly described the ranch, the cave, and the site. Will thought this over. "I think you're telling the truth. The word is out on you. Arnold is telling everyone you sold the fetishes to Lazar for $600 and when you found out they were worth more, you called the cops and reported them as stolen."

Jack sputtered. "I didn't sell the fetishes. I called the sheriff when they were taken. Ruiz, my caretaker, had his head busted."

"Anyone see who did it?"

"No, and Lazar hasn't been seen since the Sheriff Department recovered the fetishes."

"My friend," Will said, "I'd say you're up to your ankles in crap. Only you're walking on your hands. These fetishes are worth something to someone, but damned if I can see why. Wait a minute, I think I can."

"Why?"

"It looks to me like the Baxters tried to set up a tax scam with Arnold's help. Don't quote me on that because I'll deny it. They need to get the fetishes in an unpublished location, out of the sight and mind of the IRS. But I think the IRS will contest their donation even with Azad's appraisal. The word gets around pretty fast. If I were you, I'd deposit those items in a safe place. Find an art storage vault, preferably out of state. If you understand what I'm saying." Will stood
up and shook Jack's hand. "Felix vouched for you and I think you're straight arrow. Take care of yourself, Jack."

CHAPTER 17

The lead jeep was following an old track hidden behind the last ridge of the South Mountains. "I haven't been here since I was a kid," Jack said. "My mother and her friends used to ride their horses this way. Sometimes they'd overnight behind that rock house. There's an artesian well there."

"The WPA built it back in the '30s," Rex Miller volunteered. "Back then you could drive all the way to Laveen from here. That was before they put in the Proving Grounds."

The Rat Pack parked their vehicles on a ridge that overlooked a wash. South Mountain Peak towered over the canyon. A pair of bald-headed buzzards circled a flood plain at its base.

"Look here at these," Felix said. The Rat Pack converged on several rock panels that were covered with petroglyphs.

"The locals call this place Hieroglyph Hill," Wes said. "Somewhere there's supposed to be a curse on the rocks. Marcos put it there. He thought the Indians were worshipping the rocks or the spirits inside the rocks."

"Well, they did believe there were spirits in everything. But they weren't really worshipping the rocks. They just used them to write on."

Lee looked around. "Here it is. These inscriptions were made with a metal chisel."

"It's clear as day. There's the Chi-Rho mark. Marcos cursed the rock all right and then made a bee-line for Sonora," Wes said when the others joined him. "Look here, 1539 and de Niza are chiseled deeply into the rock."

"Over here, that arrow there and these eyes mean – 'Look down this way' or 'Go down this way'. Let's see what's at the top of the ridge," Lee said. They walked down the slope and crossed to the center of a clay pan that was ringed by a low rock wall. "The WPA didn't build this wall," he said, "the clay has been crushed solid. They held their dances here."

"Or that cairn," Wes said. "It's huge." The group circled the rock pile.

"It's narrow at the top and widens at the base," Susan said excitedly. "Could it be…"

"HA-AK? Nonsense." Weaver spoke up. "Why it's just a pile of rocks. Anyone could have done it."

"Not anyone," Lee said, "certainly not the WPA. Their surveyors didn't make marks like this." Lee pointed to a glyph. "That's a sighting rock, and it points up that trail." Lee moved to the center of the dance ring, raised his arms, and began singing a song.

"What's he doing?" Weaver asked.

"He's singing to I'itoi to make us a path," Susan answered.

"Tell him to make it a wide one," Kris said, "and not too steep."

The Rat Pack looked at each other sheepishly, and one by one bowed their heads reverently. Lee finished his song and dropped his arms to his side. "Let's take a look see," he said and started up the canyon.

The Rat Pack shuffled into a single file and trailed behind him, admiring the creekside desert olive trees, the cats claw in full flower, the mesquite, and the white flowered plumage. A pair of white-tailed deer darted out of the bush and crossed a knoll racing towards the other side of the canyon. A pack of javelina exploded across the trail and crushed into a cluster of hackleberry bushes, startling a covey of quail and two Mexican jays darted skyward crying raucously.

"It's breath taking," Susan said. "Awesome."

"We are going to sneak up on I'itoi today," Kris said.

"You aren't going to sneak up on anybody, Kris. You move like a constipated elephant," Wes joked.

They came to a halt in front of a narrow ledge where the trail forked. Wes started up the trail and then hesitated. "Which one?"

Lee pointed to some zigzag white traces on a rock overhang. "I'd say this way." He looked at Rex who nodded his agreement.

"It's a long way to the top. We'd better get started," Rex said.

The group strapped on their light packs and canteens and started up the steep path. Desert spoons, cholla, barrel and prickly pear cactus barred their way. A Gila woodpecker flew over laughing. A Harris hawk soared overhead and spiraled higher up the side of the canyon.

"If I only had the wings of an eagle," Kris sang.

"Come on, Kris. Keep your eye on the trail," Wes said.

"What trail? A mountain goat wouldn't call this a trail." Perspiring heavily, Kris sat down on a rock. "If y'all don't mind, I think I'll wait for you here. I'm just a tender-foot." He took a stick and began removing a cholla cactus from his boot. "Anybody bring tweezers?" They watched as Kris knocked off several clusters of cholla. "Y'all go ahead. I'll stay here and keep an eye on the vehicles."

"Come on, Kris. You'll be all right. You're doggin' it," Star said.

"No thanks honey. I'll stay here. It's a dirty job, but someone has to do it."

"Okay. Let's get moving," Star said.

The Rat Pack climbed the trail for another thirty minutes and came to a wide spot at the base of a thousand-foot cliff. Lee called for a break. "Whew! This track is steep." Lee said. "The rocks up above are more weathered and face to the east. That's where we'll find the cave."

Jack sat apart from the others and stared out across the desert floor.

"What are you thinking?" Susan asked.

"Oh, about if a man lived here, he'd have a world of his own. I love the empty spaces, I guess. It's the only place besides the ocean where you can't see a traffic light. In fact, it once was an ocean. It spread from here to the Rockies."

"It's still the widest beach in the world," Susan said. "From up here the saguaros look like seaweed."

A dark cloud covered the sun. "We'd best move on. I'd hate to get caught up here in a rain storm," Lee said. The sky was turning darker. The sun's rays edged a cloud with a silver cusp. The Rat Pack turned their backs on the panorama and moved upward slowly. The path was so steep that everyone had to shift into a three-point crawl.

In a half-hour, they reached a series of overhanging cliffs and caves. The Rat Pack scattered out to search for I'itoi's cave.

"I never thought I'd live to see something like this," Wes said.

"This trail?" Jack asked.

"No, all these people working together and starting to agree on something for the first time. Look at them." He pointed to Weaver and Wes. The two men were studying a petroglyph figure incised into the sun-darkened desert varnish on one side of a huge boulder.

Curly Bill shouted from the top of an outcropping, "There are thousands of glyphs up here. It'll take years to photograph them all. No vandals; no one's been here. It's our glory hole."

"Your glory hole?" Weaver shouted. "It's not yours. We're on city or state land. Which is it?" he asked Jack.

"As far as I know, it's part of South Mountain Park."

"Well, the ARAS has pull with the city. We don't need your bunch mucking up this site," Weaver said and began climbing up the rock face.

"Oh, shut up Buckwheat," Curly Bill said.

"There goes your working in harmony theory, Wes," Jack said. "Maybe we should call it a day; the trail will be tricky after dark. Someone could break a leg, or worse."

"Over here. I think I've found it," Lee called. He was standing in front of a waist-high vertical slit partly concealed by a sixty-ton boulder. The entrance was only about a foot and a half wide. Lee entered feet first and disappeared inside. The Rat Pack waited expectantly until Lee stuck his head and shoulders partially from the hole.

"This is it!" Lee yelled. "It's I'itoi's cave."

"That was easy," Felix said.

"Only when you know what to look for, like Lee does. You can eliminate a lot of places not to look," Susan said.

Jack removed his pack, turned sideways and slid feet first into the cave. He snapped on his flashlight to help the others find their footing.

Its beams played along the walls of the cave. The cavern was at least twenty feet high and sixty feet deep. "Looks like someone's made a shrine here. They must have been worshipping HA-AK."

"Not really, they just wanted good luck to their children," Lee said. A stone axhead, some strings of beads, and a few hand-carved seashells were placed in tiny niches on the wall. Lee played his flashlight on a pair of small stone figurines. "Frog and turtle effigies," Lee said, "water signs. There must have been a drought." A basket with an image of a diminutive man standing at the beginning of a circular design lay on the floor. Inside the basket were some drilled shells, a pair of copper bells, and a turquoise stone pendant.

"These bells are pre-Columbian, could be from the Sacaton Period, or earlier," Susan said. The group circled the find. Curly Bill's camera flashed, temporarily blinding everyone. "Back off, Curly," Susan said and covered the objects with a sheet of plastic she pulled from her pack.

"Someone shine a light up there," Lee said. On the smoke-blackened ceiling, an arrow-like mark penetrated two circles. Jack noticed a rock with familiar markings on the floor.

"That's the same mark we saw at Lone Butte, Jack, except there are two circles on the ceiling and there are three on yours," Susan said.

"Those larger figures match the ones on your petroglyphs. The patterns are practically identical. I'm getting an eerie feeling that someone was burned alive in this cave. This cave has a musty smell. It's almost evil," Susan said and moved close to Jack. "I'm getting cold."

He wrapped his arm around her and drew her closer to him. The wind began to howl outside. A deafening boom of thunder followed by another shattered the silence in the cave. Startled by the sound, Susan moved even closer. "That was close."

Felix crawled out of the cave's entrance. A few moments later he stuck his head back inside. "It's getting as black as night out here. We're going to get a gully-washer soon. We better get going."

Jack and Susan crawled outside and waited for the others to join them on the edge of the precipice. Wind-driven slate gray clouds with dark black tops were moving rapidly through the canyon. "I'll lead," Jack shouted. "Wes, can you and Lee hang back and count heads? We don't want to leave anyone behind."

"Can do," Wes shouted back.

Jack led the way down the narrow trail. The first few drops of rain beat down the dust on the trail. The raindrops increased in tempo. Jack stopped, took off his pack, and located his nylon rain parka. He pulled it over his head and drew the drawstring tight around his chin. Flashes of lightening reflected off the terraces on the opposite side of the canyon. He waited patiently while the others put on their rain gear. "Stick close together," he shouted over the wind.

Susan grabbed the back of Jack's parka. "I'm sticking with you. Lead on McDuff." The Rat Pack followed Susan's example, forming a human chain and began slowly descending the zigzag trail.

The dark cloud overhead burst like a dam drenching the party. Seconds later a strong gust of wind nearly swept them off the edge of the cliff. A lightning bolt, hotter than the sun, seared their eyes. The concussion from the thunderclap drove them to their knees. The walls around them turned into vertical streams of water cascading to the streambed below. The party huddled under a rock overhang. Susan clung to Jack.

"A micro-burst," she shouted in his ear. A wall of water rushed down the creekbed from somewhere higher up the canyon.

"Flash flood!" Rex yelled.

"We're okay," Wes yelled over the roar. "It's beneath us." The downpour stopped as suddenly as it had begun. They watched in silence as a stream of detritus cascaded over the rocks below. "Do you hear that?" Wes asked.

"It's Kris," Lee said. "He's singing us a way down." Far below they could see the faint glow of a campfire through the gloom. The group moved slowly down the trail. An hour later they reached the stone hut. The cold, wet, scratched, and weary Rat Pack huddled at the edge of the warm fire.

"Kris says we should stay put. A chest-high wall of water came through here. It's still knee deep with nothing below but mud. The vehicles are okay; it's lucky we parked above the flood plain," Rex said. "He also saw car lights. Someone was driving around in circles out there in the flats, but the lights stopped when the cloudburst hit. Whoever it was may still be out there."

Kris tossed a log on the fire. "Lucky for us that the park service stocks this place with firewood. I don't know what kind of wood it is, but it's sure not cottonwood."

They watched silently as the fine twigs blazed first, then the pale papery bark curled and yellow bubbles of resin rose to the surface and popped, giving off a pervasive astringent lemonish turpentine aroma.

"Clears your sinuses, doesn't it?" Wes asked as he edged closer to the fire.

"They cut those logs from Elephant tree," Lee said. "The desert people made a for shampoo from the bark to kill head lice. They also made a tea from it to treat gonorrhea."

"It's sure strong smelling," Kris said.

"It only grows on the southeast slopes. This is about as far north as it gets," Lee said. "It needs the sun on winter mornings."

"So do I," Wes remarked. "I could use some morning sun right now."

The wind began to sway the palo verde trees and whistled through the saguaro needles. Jack pulled his rain parka over his head, "The temperature must have dropped thirty degrees."

Lee poked at the fire with a stick. "The elephant trees up here are connected to the HA-AK Legend," he said. "Owl Ears was a Pima shaman born in the 1830s. He was still alive in 1900s when Russell met him and recorded the Blue Owl Legend and the Blue Owl Song."

"What's the difference?" Weaver asked.

"Spoken Pima is not the same as sung Pima. It's not like English where both are the same," Lee explained. "The songs make reference to their mythology. The spoken word refers to actual events."

"Why would that make a difference?" Kris asked.

"Well, we're trying to unravel a mystery. If we follow Russell's account closely, I think that somewhere in time, the Pimas actually sacrificed a woman, burned her alive in a cave. She must have been a giantess. I'm guessing, but I think HA-AK was an acromegalic."

"An acro what?" Kris asked.

"Lee's saying that she had a defective pituitary gland," Felix said. "It's a rare disorder. Children with a growth hormone-secreting tumor grow to tremendous size. Their skulls and faces coarsen. She would have been a frightening figure; a monstrous body with a normal size head. They would have driven her out into the desert to die, or they may have burned her alive in the cave."

"Maybe they felt guilty," Lee said. "Normally human sacrifice wasn't their way. But the song tells us why they did it and why they wanted to remember. In the sung version, I'itoi lived in a cave in the South Mountains. The people asked him to help get rid of HA-AK. He told them to gather elephant wood and pile it front of his cave. Then he told them to prepare for a big dance and to mix tobacco with earth flowers to give to HA-AK. Well, according to the song, they invited HA-AK to the dance. The men took turns dancing with her and the dance lasted four days. They gave her the drugged tobacco. When HA-AK tired, they led her into the cave and told her to lie down to rest. They lit a bonfire of elephant wood hoping the aroma would dull her senses even more. You know the rest of the legend, Russell's version anyhow…"

"Go on, Lee," Susan urged.

"That blackened roof of the cave tells me that this is where they burned HA-AK. They used this wood to burn her. The entrance is I'itoi's footprint. That's what the scratches on the rocks are all about. That ground below, where we parked our cars, is where they held the dance and that cairn could be covering up HA-AK's remains. Anyway, after that I'itoi moved to a new cave. It's supposed to be the entrance to a whole labyrinth of underground chambers."

"What do you think, Buck?" Wes asked quietly.

Weaver stared at the fire for a few moments and looked around the circle before he answered. "Well, I hate to say this, but everything we've found here, in my opinion, supports Lee's notion. Eyewitness accounts, Jack's glyphs, cave drawings, and the dancing ground. It all fits." Wes and Kris hooted. Someone whistled.

Wes raised his hands in the air and shook his fingers. "Hallelujah! I've lived to see the coming of the Lord!" A loud cheer went around the fire circle.

"Mind you," Weaver said when the noise abated, "I still believe that rock art is just that – rock art. But, if this is an exception to the rule, there are bound to be others." The Rat Pack howled and clapped as Curly Bill danced a gig around the fire ring.

A hard gust of wind blew down the canyon sending the sparks flying. The drizzle increased in intensity. Susan stepped closer to Jack.

"Shoot! I'm cold. We ought to try and get out of here. I'll check the gully." Wes moved down the trail, his flashlight bobbing in the darkness. He came back in a few minutes. "As far as I can tell, we can cross. The water's down."

"Saddle up," Kris boomed. "We'll follow each other. Anyone gets stuck, we can wench each other out."

"You mean winch," Star said.

"No, I mean wench," and Kris thumped her on her bottom. "I always bring my own wench. You coming, Lee?"

"Don't think so. I'll sleep in the camper. If it's clear in the morning, I want to check that cave again."

A bullet whistled overhead. Seconds later, another round thudded into the roof of the ramada. Lee dove to the ground. Jack grabbed Susan by the arm and ran towards the stone hut. "This way," he yelled.

The Rat Pack raced for cover. Wes and Rex dove behind the stone wall. The rest quickly joined them. Wes shouted. "Keep your heads down."

Susan crawled under Jack's arm for protection. "I'm scared."

"So am I."

Curly Bill's whisper broke the eerie silence, "I'm going for my mobile phone to call a sheriff."

"Better wait for daylight," Wes yelled, but Curly Bill was up and running. They waited quietly, all eyes watching the ridge beyond Curly's Suburban. A panel light lit up the front cockpit when Curly opened the door. A metallic thud was followed by a loud crack. Curly slammed the door and ducked behind the Suburban.

Jack dodged behind some boulders and made his way to the vehicle. "Are you okay?"

"Sure, I'm okay, but there's a helluva of a hole in my door."

"Let's go back. Stay low." Curly followed Jack back to the hut. The Rat Pack was all inside, sitting on the floor, backs against the wall.

"There's some kind of a nutter out there," Wes said. "What's he trying to prove?"

"An idle prank or maybe it was an accident," Weaver ventured.

"Idle prank, my ass. Are you loco, Buck? That was no accident; he fired twice. There's a hole the size of a silver dollar in my door," Curly grunted. "I say we go out there and flush the bastard out."

"Take it easy, Curly. You know Wes is right," Kris cautioned.

Curly settled down on the floor and rested his back against the wall of the hut. "I'll wait till sun-up and then we'll see what's what. Someone's going to pay for that hole in my door."

"Whoever it is may be shooting at me. This is the second time that I've been shot at," Jack said.

"You've been shot at before?" Felix asked.

"It started before I came back. Someone shot up my well house and some of my neighbor's cows. And then someone took a shot at me."

"Do you have any idea who's doing it?" Felix asked.

"Not for sure, but I have a hunch. It may have something to do with Charlie Carver and Rudy Lazar."

"Why do you think they're mixed up in this?" Kris asked. Jack told them about his run-ins with Carver and about the theft and recovery of the missing fetishes.

"That's a whale of a tale," Wes said when Jack finished. "It sounds like the Blue Owl is stirring."

"Or I'itoi," Lee said. "It's his kind of mischief."

Everyone sat motionless and watched the fire slowly sputter out. The rain stopped as suddenly as it began and the stars began to creep out from low scudding clouds. A half-moon appeared turning the desert gray against the blackness of the South Mountains where the lights blinked red from atop the spindly radio towers.

"I'm going to get some shut eye," Wes said and leaned back against the wall.

"It's too cold to sleep," Rex said.

"Then why don't you stand guard?" Wes said.

"What if he's still out there in the morning?" Susan asked.

"No worries," Kris said. "We've got food and water. We can outlast him. If he's still there in the morning, Curly can sneak out and surround him." No one laughed.

CHAPTER 18

The first ray of sunshine broke on the horizon as the caravan pulled up at the sheriff's substation. Deputy Smith was alone on duty. He put in a call to the dispatcher's office and began taking their statements. "Is that it? Anybody have anything else to add? It's a bit wild, but I'll go take a look," he promised.

When no one answered, the deputy went outside and examined the holes inside of Curly's Suburban. He opened the door and looked inside. He stuck his hand in the front seat cushion, groped around for a moment, and then turned to Curly. He held up a slightly flattened lead bullet. "Look what we have here. It's a large caliber. It could be a .458."

"Or a 45-70," Jack added.

"It could be. Just could be. I'll send it to the lab. It's beginning to look like your shooter is back. He's a busy guy."

"The guy must be a maniac," Felix said.

"I'd be thinking about moving to town until they nail this guy. It sounds like he could be after you, Dr. Reed," Smith said. "So far he hasn't hurt anyone. But he may be trying to build up his nerve to do just that."

"Maybe or maybe he's just trying to run me out of here," Jack responded.

"Well, I'd think about leaving for awhile, if it were me. I'm going to drive out and look around, folks. He could still be out there. You are all welcome to wait here. My relief should be here in a few minutes."

"We're not going to wait around. We're out of here," Kris said. "We're headed down to San Xavier. Anybody want to ride along? Jack?"

"No thanks. I need to check the house."

"Susan?"

"I'm too tired, Kris. I'll pass on San Xavier. I'll drop Jack off and then head for Tucson."

"Take care, Jack. If I were you, I'd start carrying a piece, " Wes warned.

"Call me soon, Jack" Felix said. "We should have a talk." He crawled into Wes' jeep and waved as they drove off.

Susan drove Jack to the ranch house and parked in the yard. "I'm a mess, would you mind if I cleaned up?"

"There's a shower up in the cupola and a bathtub behind the bedroom. Take your pick."

"I'll take the bath. I need a long hot soak. My bones ache."

Jack walked into the kitchen, opened a cupboard, found some instant coffee, poured some into two mugs, added some water and set them in the microwave. "Four minutes," he hummed to himself and punched the keypad. He went into the master bedroom and pulled a terry cloth robe off a hook. He carried the robe back to the kitchen, grabbed a mug of coffee, and knocked on the bathroom door. He could hear the water running in the bathtub.

"Coffee?" he shouted.

"O God, I need coffee. Just a minute." He heard the bench slide on the floor. "Come in. I'm decent," Susan said. Jack opened the door. Susan was standing in the tub, cinching a towel around her breasts.

"Nice legs," Jack smiled.

Susan smiled back.

"You said coffee?" Jack handed her a mug. He laid the terrycloth robe on the bench. "When you're ready, there's some fry bread, honey, and powdered sugar in the kitchen. Take your time." Jack closed the door and heard her settle back into the tub. He went to the kitchen, opened the fridge, pulled out some tinned milk, and Indian fry bread. He poured a saucer of milk for Orange Cat and sat it outside on the porch.

Jack heard a loud crashing sound in the bathroom, followed by a scream and the sound of water splashing. He raced through the bedroom and pushed the bathroom door open. Susan was naked, water dripping from her curly hair. She stood motionless like a golden statue, a look of utter disbelief on her face. The floor around the tub was covered with pools of water. A mirror, an open backpack, and her undergarments were scattered around the room. She grabbed the worn transparent shower curtain, wrapped it around her body and turned around so only her buttocks were revealed. "Something shocked me," she said and began giggling.

"Are you all right?" Jack asked.

"I think so." Susan began shivering.

"Here, take this towel." Jack grabbed a towel from a wooden wall rack and draped it over Susan's shoulder. "I'll be right back. Stay away from the tub."

"Don't worry. I won't go near it."

He ran through the bedroom and closed the door. Jack rushed through the kitchen porch, grabbed a flashlight, and went out into the rear yard. He lifted the bar on the door to the crawlspace and tossed it to one side. He opened the door and turned on the flashlight. He swung the beam over to the floor area under the bathroom. He held the beam steady for a moment, reached up to the joists, tugged on a pair of wires and drew then down towards the ground. He picked up a small rock, laid it across the wires and backed out of the crawlspace.

Susan was sitting on the edge of the porch. Her long tanned legs stretched over the steps, her toes just touching the edge of the gravel. Jack went inside and picked up her backpack and laid it on the bed. The plastic bag Susan had filed with artifacts fell out along with a plastic pill case. Jack looked at the prescription instructions and put the pills back in the pack along with the artifacts. He laid Susan's mirror on the back of the tub, grabbed a towel from the rack, mopped up the floor and tossed it in a hamper. He tested the water with his hands and touched the metal faucet.

He crossed the room and went out the front door. "All set. You won't get electrocuted. You can finish your bath."

"No, thanks. I'm staying put. What was the matter?"

"Pack rats. They chewed the rubber off the wires. When they run down the wires, they make contact with the plumbing. There was a ground there, but Ruiz must have replaced the upper line with a piece of PVC. It's plastic, so there was no ground. Simple. I'll have him repair it. You're safe. You can go back in. I won't look," Jack laughed. "I should have knocked, but after the sniper last night, I thought you were in trouble."

"I was in trouble. I thought I was being electrocuted. But I don't mind. I mean, I don't mind that you didn't knock."

Jack colored slightly. "No, I didn't mind either. In fact… I'd better take a shower. I'm cruddy."

Orange Cat followed Jack across the yard and up the staircase to the cupola. Jack stooped and rubbed his head. "Did you find the milk?" The kitten purred an answer. Jack opened one of the windows. He checked the flats in front of the South Mountains. A white Bronco was parked at the edge of the flood plain. He took the binoculars off the shelf for a closer look.

A lone figure was crossing the saltpan. "Cierra," Jack said to Orange Cat. Two other sheriff vehicles were parked beside the canal. A deputy was using his radio. A second deputy was scanning the ridge with his binoculars. Jack closed the window. "More trouble," he said. He kicked on the shower, wet himself down, and then turned off the water. He lathered his face and body, and then he shaved without bothering with a mirror. He turned the shower back on and rinsed off quickly. "A Navy shower," he told Orange Cat who was eyeing him suspiciously as he dried himself with a towel.

He put on a terrycloth robe, tied the belt loosely, picked up the binoculars and stepped out on the roof deck. Cierra was back at her Bronco. A helicopter flew down the ridge and circled the flood plain. "To hell with it." Jack skipped down the steps, his robe flying. Orange Cat pawed at the robe's belt and tangled its claws. Jack freed the kitten and carried it down the stairs.

"Nice legs," Susan said.

"Hey, that's my line." Jack laughed and sat the kitten down on the porch.

Susan handed him a chunk of fry bread and a cup of coffee. "It's gooey, but it's great." Jack wolfed it down and swallowed some hot coffee.

"God, I needed that."

Susan picked up the kitten and began stroking it idly. "Why do you call him O.C.?"

"It's short for Orange Cat."

"That's no name for a kitten."

"Better than House Cat or Outside Cat," Jack said.

"You're hopeless," she said frowning. "Is that a helicopter?"

"They may be looking for our shooter. I doubt if they'll find him. He probably skipped out before it got light."

"I hope so. At least, I hope he's gone." Susan sneezed twice. She sat the kitten down on the porch and went inside the house. She came back in a moment, holding a tissue to her nose. "Allergies. I seem to be allergic to everything, including cats, men, and the desert."

"Well, I used to hate the desert. This desert anyway." Jack went into the house and came back with a photo album. "The bad old days." He handed it to Susan. She began to leaf through it slowly.

"Is that you? Is this the cave?"

"Yes, that's me, big ears and all."

"What's that in your hand?"

"It's a cross. A gold cross."

"Did you find it in the cave?"

"Yes, I did."

"You didn't tell me you found this in the cave."

"Well, you're right. I have never told anyone about it. My parents knew I found it, of course. My mother kept it for me."

"Do you still have it?"

"Yes, as a matter of fact, I do. It's in the safe." Jack went inside the house and came back in a few minutes. He handed Susan the cross.

She studied it. "It's crudely made. It's a sand casting."

"Yes, that's what I thought."

Jack showed Susan the square-cut silver reals. "Were these in the cave, too?"

"No, they were found some distance away, on the far side of the wash. There are a lot of caves at the foot of Lone Butte, but there's nothing in them except rattlers. I've looked. Everyone around here thinks the Yaquis found a cache of Spanish coins somewhere. Back in the 20s, the Tempe sheriff spent a lot of time looking for it; so did our workmen when they were building the stable. Mollie Gentry and her sons have looked, but so far no one has found anything."

"I'd say these coins were minted in the 1750s. I've seen a few before. The cross, I couldn't say," Susan ventured, "could have been made at the same time. We'd need to know when the shaman was buried in the cave. I could have the lab in LA do some carbon dating."

"Why not? I'll get everything ready next week. Someone's coming," Jack said. A sheriff's Bronco pulled into the yard. Cierra stopped her car and stared out the window. Susan hurriedly slipped into the house while Jack walked out to the vehicle.

"Am I interrupting something?" Cierra snipped.

"What? Oh, no. Susan's with one of the State Historical Departments. She's the one I told you about. She was with us yesterday at the canyon..."

"And last night?"

"Yes, we were all there when the sniper shot at us. She just wanted to clean up and have a cup of coffee."

"Well, just so she's a happy camper. Sorry, Jack. I'm out of line. We found a yellow Land Rover in the canal. It's the Mallorys. They're both dead."

"Dead? The sniper shot them?"

"No, it looks like they drowned. I won't know for sure until the coroner's finished. A wrecker is coming to pull out the Land Rover. I've got to get back."

"I'll be right there."

"Take your time," Cierra spun the wheels and tore out of the yard. Jack ducked as the gravel pelted his face and robe. Jack went to the back bedroom and hurriedly dressed. When he came out, Susan was sitting on the top step.

"They found the Mallorys in the canal. They're dead. Drowned," Jack said.

"I heard," Susan replied.

Jack scribbled a note and slipped it underneath the base of the railroad lantern that hung beside the door. "It's for Ruiz. I always let him know where I'm going. It's our post office. Listen, I'll be back soon. Stick around. O.C. could use the company. So could I. There are more albums over there."

"We'll see." Susan smiled.

Jack jumped into his truck. He waved at Susan standing in the doorway as he drove by the cactus garden and headed for the power line road.

CHAPTER 19

A tow truck drove off with a yellow Land Rover as Jack pulled alongside Cierra's Bronco. He waited until she finished taking a call.

"What happened?"

"It looks like the driver didn't see the bend in the canal. He braked," Cierra pointed out the skid marks that led over the edge of the track and down the v-shaped embankment. "The Land Rover flipped and wedged the doors against the sides of the canal. They never had a chance to get out. Even when the pressure equalized, they couldn't have opened the side doors. They must have panicked. We found the younger Mallory in the rear compartment. The power door switch was broken off. He tried to smash the rear window…"

"It must have been ugly."

"It was. I almost lost my breakfast."

"You okay?"

"I'm okay now."

"When did it happen?"

"Sometime last night. The Salt River Power crew was checking the canal banks for storm damage. We got a call about 6 a.m. this morning."

"That's about when we checked in to report on the sniper. You didn't find a .458 did you?"

"No. There were no weapons inside, but we found something else." Cierra opened the tailgate of the Bronco. A large olla surrounded by several taped packets rested on the floor. "Crack. Worth at least a million on the street."

Jack shook his head. "The Mallorys were dealing drugs?"

"Apparently, and someone else was in on it or was trying to rip them off."

"How did you know?"

"I'm guessing he was waiting for them on the side of the cut. I found the spot where the vehicle was parked. The ground was drier where it was protected from the rain. Whoever it was may have turned on their lights to signal the Mallorys..."

"Or try to blind them," Jack finished.

"You've got it!"

"Any ideas, like maybe Rudy Lazar?"

"Right again. No trace of Lazar though. He never went home. He's definitely missing."

"Or running."

"I haven't a clue, but somehow I feel he's out there somewhere. He had a chance to run, but he's waiting for something or looking for something. I'm sure of that."

"Women's intuition?"

"Not exactly. Someone walked in here from where you and the Rat Pack were ambushed."

"You followed the tracks to the canal?"

"Why would anyone shoot at us?"

"To buy time. To keep you away until he could meet the Mallorys. Something went wrong."

"Someone attacked Ruiz and stole the blankets, baskets, a glyph, and fetishes. I thought it had to be Lazar or the Mallorys, but why bother with my stuff if they were into drugs?"

"The animal fetishes are tied to this somehow, Jack. They must be worth quite a bit. Any ideas?"

"Well, they are either worth a lot or next to nothing. Manouch Azad, he's a supposedly big honcho in Washington D. C., gave me an appraisal on the glyphs based on the photos. Then rescinded it, but he stuck by his guns on the fetishes. Will Culver, a dealer in Scottsdale, thinks the appraisal is outrageous. According to him, someone's running a tax scam – buy low, get a phony appraisal, make a donation and claim a substantial write-off. Culver also told me that the word is out that I bashed Ruiz in the head, stole my own artifacts, and sold them to Lazar. Arnold brought the Baxters out to the house the other night, Cierra, and they offered to buy the fetishes back. I turned them down. I overheard Baxter tell Arnold that he had to have the fetishes back. They are obviously afraid of something."

"Maybe that's why Lazar is hanging around. It gets curiouser and curiouser," Cierra said. "I met with Arnold Saturday. He claims Lazar offered him the fetishes and some other things. Lazar told him later a 'Hollywood group' bought the rest. He says he doesn't know whom Lazar was referring to. Fat chance. I went out to Lazar's, and he wasn't there. The yardman next door said he left with two heavyset guys in a yellow Land Rover yesterday."

"The Mallorys?"

"Yep. Anyway, I drove over to their place and it's locked up tight. A sign on the door said to leave packages at the foundry next door. The owner said that Dan had told him they were going back east for a few days on a buying trip."

"Washington?"

"He didn't say."

"Arnold was in Washington! So is Azad. It doesn't make sense. The Mallorys offered me a few hundred dollars for the fetishes, and Azad appraised them for over six figures. And the Baxters offered to buy them at 60% of the appraised value."

"Beauty is in the eyes of the beholder."

"Why would Baxter donate the fetishes to ASU?"

"It sounds like Culver hit the nail on the head. It's a tax scam. Why else would he dump them in the archives? The blue-haired dragon says he left town this morning. A vacation. She doesn't know or won't say where he's gone. But one of his nurses says he has a beach house at San Carlos. She heard him tell someone he was going to check on his boat."

"You can't question him in Mexico," Jack said.

"No, I can't. But my Uncle can. The Feds have a drug crime team that cooperates with the Mexican Federal Drug

Enforcers Team. He can sniff around." Cierra grinned. "You know anyone else I should check out?"

Jack hesitated. "Well, maybe Charlie Carver?"

"The developer?"

"The same. He's trying to push me into selling the ranch. He saw the petroglyphs. He didn't seem impressed, but when I came back from Tina's, he was on the porch. He mentioned something about my interesting collection of fetishes. Either one might have gone into the sunroom; the door wasn't locked."

"That's it?"

Jack hesitated. "Well, it's not much, but Carver's on the Desert Museum Board of Directors. So was the Governor before he was elected, and they both served on the Council for the Arts."

"Looks like if you have the dollars, you can get elected to any social or power group."

"Yes. My dad used to call them 'Cookie Cutters'. He said that even the smell of dough gets them stirring. I don't like Carver, and I do know that he and Colucci have a real attitude problem with Native Americans. But there's more. Carver mentioned that he lost money in a dispute in California when a tribe claimed that a parcel he was developing was on sacred ground. When I flew over to Santa Barbara, I had a friend check Carver out. The tribe that sued him won a big settlement. When Carver pulled out of California, he had a lot of money, but not the kind of capital it takes to build a tract out here in the desert from scratch. My friend says it could be teamster money or maybe drugs..."

"Or maybe," Cierra said, "he's laundering money."

"Why don't you check with your uncle and see if Carver or Lazar have even been connected to the teamsters union and if Lazar has ever had any drug arrests."

"I've had Lazar checked out. He has no priors for drugs, but he was busted in Miami Beach."

"For what?"

"Some kind of labor union strike. I'll get more details. He was also charged, but not convicted, of labor racketeering.

However, it didn't involve the teamsters union, some other union. I'll check on it."

"Did Smith tell you about the slug he pulled out from Curly Bill's car seat?"

"He mentioned it, but there's been no time to send it to the lab."

"Cierra, if it's a 45-70, and I think it is, I think you should check out the Mallory's Trading Den."

"Why?"

"There were three 45-70s in a gun rack by the desk. I asked Dan about them when I picked up the appraisal, and he said they were already sold. If they're not there, you could check the daily sales record. It might be interesting to see who bought them."

"I'll do some checking, but I need to clear it without the Sheriff. He thinks I'm in over my head, so he's called in the CID team."

"Do you still have the list of names I gave you?"

Cierra nodded and opened the back of her notebook. "Right here."

"Let me see it."

Cierra handed it to Jack. He sat on the rear bumper and began writing while Cierra looked over his shoulder:

1. *Carver – tried his bully routine not once, but twice. He's land rich and water short.*
2. *Chernov & the Mallorys – came to the house. Mallorys gave me an appraisal for the animal fetishes.*
3. *Lazar – drove Carver to the ranch the first time I met him. Carver was driving his own car the night Ruiz was hit and the artifacts stolen. Where was Lazar?*
4. *Draper – was at Stockmens bar sitting with Carver. Some of my fetishes end up in his basement. He conducts impact studies for the State Archeological Board.*

"Has he ever done a survey for Carver?"

"Yes."

"Do you think there's connection between the two of them?"

"There could be, Cierra."

5. *Trisha – tipped me off about Draper. Trisha and Tom Owens were together at the ARAS meeting.*
6. *Draper & Owens – had seen the photographs of the petroglyphs and fetishes.*
7. *Tracy & Schaeffer – have seen photos and have been on property at least twice that I know of.*

"Wait a minute," Cierra said. "We find some fetishes in Draper's storage room, two at Baxter's house and two more at Arnold's gallery. Now why do you want me to check them?"

"Because they came with Arnold to see me and to try to buy back the fetishes which they both claim were sold to them by Lazar. When we went to the Baxters, the Mallorys were there. The Mallorys gave me the low-ball appraisal."

"Full circle, but not a full explanation. They all could be linked together by drugs? Or the fetishes? Or both?"

"If Culver is right, the Baxters and Arnold tried to pull of a tax scam and need to get off the hook. Better talk to your uncle, Cierra, and see if the IRS can check out the Baxters and get some information on Azad."

"I need to clear it with the Sheriff, but I think he'll tell me to back off and let the CID handle this."

"The more the merrier," Jack said, handing her the updated list.

"I'll do some more checking, and I think my uncle may be interested in this list and in the appraisals. 'Look for the money,' my old criminology professor used to say, 'then look for the woman'," Cierra smiled. "Keep an eye out for Lazar. He's as smart as a desert fox."

"Maybe he's dead."

Cierra pointed skyward, "Do you see any buzzards? He's alive."

"Did your old professor teach you that too?"

"No, my Yaqui Uncle." Cierra laughed.

"I'd better get back," Jack said.

"Don't want any unhappy campers, do we?" she snipped and then laughed as Jack's cheeks reddened.

Jack turned without replying. As he drove off, he glanced in the mirror and saw Cierra talking to someone in a Department of Public Service vehicle. He drove straight into the yard and parked beside the porch. A note was stuck in the railroad lantern.

"Had to run, Jack. I'm going to catch up with the Rat Pack at San Xavier. Call me soon. Thanks for the thrills and the coffee. Susan."

Jack went into the dining room, picked up the photo album, and sat down in the alcove. He picked up the book of photographs that Dr. Ryder had given him. Jack drew some sketches on his notepad. Then he studied the red, black, and gray Navajo blanket with the mission motif that hung of the wall and made another drawing on the pad. He removed the icon from the space under the window seat and laid it on the table beside the photographs. He turned the icon around and studied the backside. Satisfied, Jack stuck the closed the book, picked up the icon, and headed for the door.

Jack took the back track to Williams Field Road avoiding the cluster of police vehicles at the junction of the canal and the dirt road that led to the ranch. He drove straight to Trisha's place.

She was in the workshop. Jack surveyed the olla, "Great job."

"There's one hairline crack. I couldn't get it right," Trisha apologized.

"Looks like it belongs there to me."

Trisha smiled. "I know the difference, but no one else would."

Jack handed her the icon and took the photos out of his pocket. He picked up a felt pen and circled two symbols. "Could you copy these marks on the icon? Same style as the petroglyphs?"

"Probably."

"Could you use this to make the inscription?" Jack handed her a gold cross.

Trisha examined it closely and then grinned at Jack. "The shaman used this to tap the gold leaf into the owl's eyes on the glyphs, right?"

"Probably."

"No doubt about it. The end is furled, and he used the round edge to trace the facial features," Trisha said. "Where the hell did he get a gold cross?"

"Trade? Massacred priests? We'll never know."

"Are there any more pieces like this?"

"Not where I found this, Trisha."

"Can you use these?" Jack handed her a crude metal hammer and a chisel.

"What are these? They look handmade, hand forged metal. It has an odd feel to it," Trisha said as she lifted the pieces. "They have a good balance. Where did you find these?"

"They were in shaman's cave. I'm guessing they could have been made from a chunk of meteor. I think they're iron and nickel. Maybe the Spanish forged them, maybe the shaman did. I'm guessing the shaman used them to incise the petroglyphs."

"That explains the incisions. I knew the inscriptions were real. They have such a feel to them, but I knew whoever made the incisions used metal tools. Had to. You should get the rocks tested."

"Not enough time, Trisha. Maybe later. How long will take you to alter the icon?"

"An hour, more or less." Trisha took some tools off a rack. "If you don't mind waiting outside. Trade secrets, you know."

Jack sat on the bumper of the truck. The whir of a grinder punctuated the air and then a rapid tapping punctuated by Trisha's humming. An hour went by. The door opened and she handed Jack the icon.

"Will this do?" she asked.

Jack studied the incisions critically. "It's perfect. How do you it?"

"It looks like the real McCoy, doesn't it? The patina, the desert varnish, was easy, especially if you have the iron awl to do the carving. There was no chipping." Trisha packed the repaired olla in a box filled with Styrofoam chips. "You'd better put the olla on the seat, Jack, not in the back. It could get tossed around back there."

"What do I owe you?"

"Nothing," Trisha said. "Just fill me in when you get to the bottom of this. I'm really curious as to how this is going to turn out."

"What turns out?"

"Jack, I'm not a genius, but you're baiting a trap, at least I think you are. Those marks on the icon will fool a professional."

Jack hesitated. "Want to help bait the trap?" Trisha's almond-shaped eyes narrowed.

"Try me."

"It's not much, but it would help. Are you going to ASU today?"

"I wasn't planning to, but I could."

"I'd like you to drop in and see if Draper needs any work done. If you see Tom, mention that you altered an icon for me. I'd appreciate it. Sort of pass the word."

"Is Tom involved in this?"

"Not directly, Trisha. If he is, he doesn't know he is."

"Yeah, I'll do it. Always wanted to get a leg up on Tom."

Jack hesitated. "Oh, Trisha, there's one more thing. I saw some pots at the Mallory's. Were those yours?"

Trisha looked surprised. "Could be. I made a couple of dozen for them last year. Why?"

"The Mallorys drowned in a canal last night. Their Land Rover turned turtle."

"The Mallorys?" Trisha raised her eyebrows and paled. "I don't want to know any more, Jack. This is heavy."

"Do you still want to bait the trap?"

"Will Tom get in trouble?"

"No, I promise, and you won't either. There's no risk for either of you. You'll just be part of a pipeline. You'll be helping to put an end to this business."

"Okay, Jack, if you think so. You have a honest face." She laughed and gave Jack a hug. "Love your icons. I'll do it."

Jack drove to ASU, found a space in the parking garage, caught the elevator to the ground level, and walked quickly to the Hayden Library. Patrick Garrett was his usual affable self. "Well, Mr. Holmes. What is it this time?"

"Looking for EPA studies, engineering studies," Jack said. "Salt River, Tempe Buttes, hotel sites, City of Tempe."

"No problem. They're in the inactive file."

"You told me that you keep check out records on documents in the Arizona Room?"

"Everyone gets listed. Stolen pages, you know, can be a problem."

"Could I see the records for Section L.H. please."

"I'll bring you the list, but it could take a while."

Jack spent several hours examining the records and taking notes. Satisfied, he closed the registers and returned them to the shelves. A manila envelope was waiting for him when he returned to the Arizona Room. He glanced at the list quickly and thanked the librarian. He scrawled a quick note to thank Patrick for the list and gave it to the attendant.

"Home, James," he said as he fired up the truck. "Time's a wasting."

Jack stopped in front of the valet desk at the Stockmen's Restaurant. Ahron trotted over to the truck, his blond hair waving in the breeze. "Carver left with four people, two men and two women. I think they were both blondes. I'm not sure."

"Did you get a good look at them?"

"No, not really. I got his car and then the wind blew my umbrella away. I chased it, but they were already in the car when I got back. They took off. Carver stiffed me again."

"Was one of the men tall and lean, about 45-50?

"No way. They were younger looking, average height."

"Glasses?"

"No. I don't think so, but it was dark except for the lightning."

Jack fished a ten-dollar bill out of his pocket. He wrote down his phone number on a card and handed it to Ahron. "Call me if Carver shows up with a tall, lean, mean-looking dude, okay?"

Ahron kept the card and handed back the ten-dollar bill. "If I see him, I'll call you. It's a freebie. You're after Carver for something. I'm guessing drugs. Are you a cop?"

"Hardly." Jack laughed. "Can't say that I am, but I have a friend who is. Do you think Carver's got some interest in drug dealing?"

"Just a guess, but he's not pushing anything here. Some of the people who come here are heavy users. You can tell, but they carry their own. No one buys drugs here. This place is clean, but Carver flashes his money and plays the B.T.O. He's a flake."

"You're a good judge of character. Call me." Jack winked and drove off as Ahron tucked the card in his wallet.

Jack fixed Orange Cat some tuna. "Come and get it. Chow time." The kitten followed him into the kitchen. He went down to the stable and called Mollie. They discussed the Mallorys' suspicious accident and the possibility that Lazar was still in the area.

"I don't like the notion of someone hanging around out here. You be careful," Mollie said. "He could burn our haystack again or set your place on fire."

"Somehow, I don't think he'll try anything, Mollie, but if you see any fire or smoke, come running."

"I'm having one of the boys sleep out by the haystack, with a rifle. You better arm yourself, too."

"I'll be careful, Mollie."

Jack hung up, picked up his .243, and a light sleeping bag. He turned out the lights, eased out a side window, and climbed the steps to the cupola. He opened the door and spread the sleeping bag on the floor. From his vantage point, he could see Lone Butte, Mollie's barn and haystack and the main road to the front gate.

"A room with a view," he muttered to Orange Cat who snuggled into the sleeping bag with him. "If you hear anything O.C., call me," Jack said to the drowsy kitten. "Tomorrow we go hunting."

CHAPTER 20

Jack woke up with a start. A steady rapping of a hammer woke him. A shaft of sunlight bore into his face. A warm breeze was already promising a hot day. "Old Ruiz is pounding nails again," Jack said and moved Orange Cat off his chest and sat up.

Jack dressed quickly and made his way to the kitchen. He lit the burner under last night's coffee. While he was waiting, he poured Orange Cat a saucer of milk. The hammering began again, under the utility room this time. Jack stuck his head out the window. "Ruiz, what are you doing?"

"Nailing the holes shut, Jefe. Keep that damn skunk outside."

"Leave it, Ruiz. I don't want her trapped under the house." A long silence followed.

"Then you do it, Jefe. You wait till you see her in the yard some night. I'll leave a board here. That's the only way you get rid of a skunk."

"What about the kits?"

"You take them down to the canal in a sock," Ruiz said, "and drown them."

"I don't know about that," Jack carried two mugs of coffee outside and handed one to Ruiz.

"Muchas gracias, Jefe." They sat down together on the steps. Jack told him about the Mallorys.

When he finished, Ruiz said, "Well, Jefe, maybe we get rid of these skunks, maybe not. I don't know, but the skunks in the stove aren't as bad as those who are causing trouble out here. I think we should leave them be for now. Besides they are almost grown. The mother will take them out soon. The kits won't be back. But the mother skunk will. If not her, then another skunk will come. They always do. They always will."

"Do you mean another mother skunk?"

"Both kinds. The world is full of two-legged skunks."

"You're right." Jack laughed. "Let's go for a walk." He went to the stable, and got the metal detector and handed Ruiz the new dowsing rod. Ruiz looked it over and twisted it in his hands carefully.

"This thing is not much, Jefe. I have something better." Jack followed Ruiz to the well house. Ruiz went inside and emerged with a willow wand. "This stick can find water."

The two men walked single file across the salt flat. Jack stayed about twenty yards behind Ruiz swishing the metal detector back and forth. Ruiz held the wand, his hands crossed in front of him. They traversed the saltpan from east to west several times in the next two hours.

Jack rested and wiped the sweat off his forehead. "Anything, Ruiz?"

"Nothing, Jefe. But this is a good place. I can feel it."

Jack was standing on the edge of the circular mound where he used to sunbathe. The sun was turning the bright bits of gravel into a shimmer of sparkling colors. Jack walked up the mound, slowly swiping the detector in front of him. Suddenly, it began to hum and then it pinged as he moved forward.

"Up here, Ruiz." Jack walked to the center of the mound. The metal detector's whine increased in volume and then shrilled as he stepped into the depression in the center of the mound. Jack flipped off the switch, adjusted the knobs, and turned it back on. The detector responded with a deafening pitch.

Ruiz walked the mound slowly; the willow wand in his hands began to twitch, then abruptly the prongs twisted downward violently. Ruiz's arms were shaking. "There's water here. A lot of water," he said as the wand snapped out of his fingers. "Very close to the surface, Jefe."

"We've got more than water here, Ruiz. There's something else very close to the surface," Jack speculated.

"Gold?"

"Could be, but I doubt it. More likely, an iron deposit." Jack adjusted the metal detector. It pinged again. "It's further below the surface than I thought. Ruiz, you always knew there was water here."

"Yes, Jefe, I knew."

"How?"

"Your grandfather told me. He made a map and showed me the places to drill. The map is in the stable behind the saddle. Your grandfather was a geologist. He told me *geo* means earth."

"Why didn't you tell me?'

"You are an oceanologist, Jefe. Are you not? You should be able to find water."

Jack laughed. "Maybe salt water, Ruiz, but we need fresh water."

"It is here, Jefe. The wand also told me so. I didn't need no map, but it helped." Ruiz laughed.

It was mid-morning when they arrived back at the ranch house. Rudy Lazar was sitting on the porch with 45-70 government rifle resting against the railing. Orange Cat was toying with the laces of his boots. Lazar leaned over and roughly rubbed the kitten's head. Orange Cat seized his hand and bit hard. Lazar jerked his hand back. He stood up and aimed a kick. Orange Cat dodged the boot and scrambled off the porch. Jack started towards Lazar.

"Easy dude," Lazar said, picking up his rifle and pointing it casually at Jack's stomach. "Find what you were looking for?"

"We found water if that's what you mean," Jack said.

"Yeah, the old man's pretty good with a douser. How about the metal detector? Did you find any gold, or maybe a gold mine?" Lazar stared hard at Jack.

"You can find water with a detector if you know how to use one," Jack said, eyeing Lazar.

"Sure, sure, Dude."

"What do you want, Lazar?"

"I need to borrow your truck, amigo. If you'll just turn around." Jack turned around slowly. "Now reach in your pocket and drop the keys on the ground. Toss them behind you." Jack dropped the keys. "Now move away." Jack moved ten feet. "Far enough." Lazar stooped and picked up the keys. "You can turn around, both of you."

Lazar was standing at the entrance to the stable. "Now just stay put." He stepped inside. Jack heard him dial a number and say, "Hell, yes, I'm alive. No thanks to you, you brainless bastard. I don't want to hear what happened. It's your problem. It ain't my problem anymore. I'm out of here." There was a brief silence, Lazar went on, "You're the one who's screwed, not me." He jerked the telephone off the wall box and tossed it on the ground. "You won't be using this for awhile." he grinned.

"How did you know where the phone was, Lazar? Did you find it the other night when you slugged Ruiz?" Jack asked.

Lazar's face darkened. "You think I turned the old man into a piñata? Why would I do that?" he smirked. "I got nothing against Mexes." Lazar was edging backwards towards the truck. Something moved behind him.

"I'd watch your step, Rudy. There's a big rattler on the rock behind you," Jack warned.

"Sure, Dude." Lazar smiled and stepped backwards.

The rattler struck him in the calf. He screamed and fell backwards. The rattler struck repeatedly as Lazar tried to roll away.

Ruiz emerged from the stable with a shovel. He struck the rattler hard, severing the head from the body. Ruiz scooped up the writhing head and deftly pitched it into the cactus garden.

Jack grabbed the rifle and put it out of Lazar's reach. Lazar's face had turned a ghastly white. He tried to rise, but collapsed on his side. The severed body of the snake twisted convulsively splattering Lazar's clothes and boots. "Let's get him into the truck, Ruiz."

"Too bad he tore out the phone. You could have called 911," Ruiz said.

They carried Lazar to the truck and Ruiz ran to the stable and came back with a saddle blanket. He crawled into the bed of the pickup and covered Lazar. "We'll take him to the sub-station," Jack said.

"We better hurry. He's been hit in the neck."

Jack drove as fast as he could down the power line road, slowing only for the deeper ruts. He checked to be sure Ruiz and Lazar weren't being tossed around. Ruiz was gripping the edge of the truck bed with one hand and cradled Lazar's head with the other. Jack slid the truck to a stop in front of the sheriff's sub-station. Cierra looked out the door.

"Better call air-evac," Jack shouted. "It's Lazar. A rattler got him in the neck. It's bad."

Cierra ducked into the office. She was back in two minutes with a plastic bucket of ice and a compress. "They're air borne." Cierra crawled into the truck and applied the compress to Lazar's neck.

Lazar opened his eyes and stared blankly at Cierra. His eyes focused momentarily. "Cave... Car..." Lazar gasped and then lapsed back into unconsciousness.

"They better hurry," Ruiz said. "I don't think he has much time."

The Boeing Nortar landed in the designated area. The side door flew open and two medics ducked under the blades and raced to the truck. They immobilized Lazar on a gurney.

"Snake bit," Jack offered.

"We heard," a medic said. "Did you get a look at the snake?"

"Ruiz killed it," Jack said. "Western Diamondback. A big one."

The medics rushed the gurney back to the helicopter, flattened the carriage, and lifted Lazar inside. One man closed the panel as the other locked down the gurney. In seconds they were airborne.

"Lazar said something that sounded like 'cave'. Mean anything to you?" Cierra asked.

"Cave? He could have meant cave or cavern. Or maybe Carver. He worked for him."

Ruiz handed Cierra the 45-70. "This is his rifle. It made the holes in the well house."

"And in Curly Bill's truck," Jack said.

"What happened?" Cierra asked.

"He wanted to borrow my truck." Jack nodded at the rifle. "But he stepped on the snake."

"Old Granddad," Ruiz said. "I boarded up his hole after the rain. He couldn't get back in. He was one angry snake, I tell you."

"So that's what the hammering was about."

"I tried for the snake and the skunk, but I caught a coyote, Jefe," Ruiz smiled.

"I'd better follow up on Lazar. You'll have to file a report with Deputy Smith. If there's a connection between Lazar and Carver, the CID will want to know," Cierra frowned. "I'm off this case, Jack. In fact, I'm being transferred to the Peoria substation."

"Why? When?"

"Monday. The Sheriff gave me three days off and a pat on the head. 'Out of my league' he said. I'm not supposed to be ready for investigative work. It seems I'm too indelicate for the Scottsdale crowd."

"You got no suave? No deboner?"

"Something like that. Anyway, Deputy Smith overheard the Sheriff talking to Luis Obregon, but I'm sure that Arnold's behind it."

"In that case, do you want to go caving?" Jack asked.

"Sure," Cierra said. "When?"

"Meet me at the house in the morning around nine. Bring your gear."

"Should I bring an air tank?"

"No, just a harness."

Deputy Smith stuck his head out the trailer door. "Sheriff Cuso...line one."

"Tell him I'll be right there. Tomorrow then," she said.

"Call me when you hear about Lazar. I want to know where he is."

"For sure," Cierra waved and walked to the trailer, her pistol swinging from her side. Jack stared at her thoughtfully.

"What are you thinking, Jefe?"

Jack grinned. "About fire and ice, Ruiz."

"I would chose fire every time, Jefe. You can get burned, but life is more interesting. Women with ice in their blood don't keep you warm at night. Your grandmother had fire."

"Yep, she burned down the old ranch house."

Ruiz laughed, "That's what I mean, Jefe."

CHAPTER 21

The backpack lay open on the table. Jack checked the contents: compass; spelunker's helmet with headlamp and battery pack; safety harness; a coil of nylon rope; pitons and claw hammer; a mini maglite flashlight; chalk; a first aid kit; a can of sterno; water bottles; and a packet of beef jerky. Jack strapped on a belt and holster, checked the Colt .45, and snapped the flap shut. He stuffed the icons and the photographs into a side pocket. He scratched a note and stuck it behind the railroad lantern on the front porch.

At nine o'clock, Cierra drove her Toyota into the yard and parked alongside the stable. Jack joined her and tossed his gear onto the back jump seat.

"All set?" he asked.

"You said spelunking. Well, something like that," she opened her pack and Jack checked her gear.

"Great! You're better set up than I am." Jack went into the stables and scratched another note and placed it under a can of nails.

"What's that?"

"A note for Ruiz. I'm telling him where to look for us if we're not back by this afternoon. Just in case something comes up."

"Good idea."

Jack picked up the metal detector, walked outside and put it into the back seat of the Toyota. "What's that for? Are we going prospecting?"

"Something like that." Jack found two road flares behind the seat of his truck and shoved them into his pack. He climbed into the Toyota. "Let's go."

"Where to?"

"To the shaman's cave. Take the low road and then follow the power lines." Cierra drove around the well house and gravel mound, took the fork to the power line road and crossed over the ridge. She followed the power line road for a quarter of a mile and then turned the Toyota into the wash and drove downstream for 200 yards and pulled up in front of the slight ridge that concealed the shaman's cave.

Cierra and Jack walked over to the entrance. "Someone's been here," Jack said and pointed at the slab-like wedge-shaped rocks lying in front of the entrance. "These two rocks were on the top. I wedged them in there myself."

"Did someone go inside?"

"Let's find out." Jack moved the flagstone slab and rested it against a boulder. When he was finished, he pulled out the mini flashlight and crawled through the entrance. "Come on in."

Cierra stooped and then slid into the cave. She crouched down beside Jack, resting her knees on the cave floor. The wind shifted outside the cave and swept the slightly dank smelling air clean. "The shaman's gone," Cierra said softly, breaking the silence.

"Yes, I thought he might be."

"You thought he might be? Who would take him? Why?"

"I'm not sure who. Lazar or Carver, or maybe the Mallorys, but they must have taken him when they stole the glyphs. But which? Carver needed to get rid of the shaman's remains. He needs this land for his development schemes. He needs the water rights. Normally a developer can do almost anything he wants to with private land, including bulldozing over artifacts, intaglios, whatever. But if there are human remains, it's different. I'm sure there were remains under the cairns, but he bulldozed them off the day I got home. If he had gotten my land, he'd have done the same thing. But if an investigative process was initiated on my property before he bought it or even after, his projects would have been delayed. If it was proven to be sacred land, possibly forever. Carver couldn't wait."

"There's more to this business, isn't there?" Cierra asked.

"You're right. A lot more." Jack opened his pack and laid the icons on the dirt floor. He took out a compass and laid it on one of the sunken stones. "North by northwest." Jack moved the compass. "South by southeast. Jack reset the compass on the third in the circle. West by northwest. He laid the compass on the stone. South by southeast.

"What are you doing?" Cierra asked.

"These stones are a compass of sorts. North, east, south, west. Aligned this way, they all point to caves of some kind or another or at least to something hidden. This triangle can mean blue or turquoise and this cross is a sort of a bas-relief. The same kind of cross we found on the Marcos de Niza rock and the symbol in the corner means hidden. I whish we had the glyphs. There are two spirals on the backside. They could mean 'go up' or 'go down' and there were some arrows. Maybe, five or six, but I can't remember which way they were pointing and I can't remember if there were any other markings. So we have the four directions and up and down, but it's all just guesswork. We could end up going to four different caves and I only know where three of them could be that relate in any way to I'itoi. I checked Ryder's book and there were all kinds of arrows and spirals and trail markers, but I didn't find anything like the boxed in petroglyphs of HA-AK and I didn't see many signs for hidden.

"So, are we going up or down?"

"Let's find out. That's why we have the spelunking gear." Jack opened a can of sterno and set it in the center. He struck a match and tossed it into the open can. It sputtered and began to burn slowly as the sterno melted and spread along the matchstick.

"Now what are you doing?"

"Magic." Jack smiled. He stood the icons upright in front of the flame. "The old shaman instilled spirits in them, at least one of the them. I had Trisha make one from a photograph of the one that was taken. The secret, Cierra, is to suspend your disbelief. You have to believe what the shaman believed. That spirits of all kinds, good and malevolent, inhabit the animals, the plants, and even the rocks. They are in the air we breathe. They are everywhere."

"Yes, I believe that with all my being. The Yaqui Way also teaches that."

Jack clasped his hands together and then opened the palms upward. "I'itoi, hear me. We mean no harm. Show us the way to the sacred cave." Jack and Cierra sat silently. A zephyr of wind swirled through the cave. A black-gray lizard scampered across the ceiling and disappeared into the crevice at the rear of the cave.

"Thank you, I'itoi."

"Thank you I'itoi for what?"

"For sending us that lizard. It's part of the HA-AK legend. The lizard that looks like the ground led the Papagos to their turquoise quarry." Jack covered the can of sterno with its lid and stood up. "I'll show you. We're going this way." Jack led her deeper into the cavern. He yelped as he slipped on the floor, barking his shin.

"Are you okay?"

Jack examined his leg, "Nothing broken." He peered down the black pit that yawned before him. "Lucky I didn't step in there." Jack adjusted his pack, strapped on his spelunker's helmet, and snapped on the light.

"If Lee's theory is right, that hole is an entrance to a descending maze." Jack braced himself and pushed the rock slab open wider with his feet and stared downwards. "It's twenty feet to the bottom." Jack opened his rucksack and pulled out a wrapped nylon rope and dropped one end into the hole. "Nope, more like twenty-five feet." The light from his helmet played on the vaulted ceiling overhead. He slipped one end of the rope through a natural arch and looped the rope around his leg and shoulder. "Wait here," he said and then stepped into the hole.

"I'm not going anywhere."

"There's plenty of room. Come on down." Cierra landed beside him. "This way." Jack wedged his shoulders into a circular passage that led downward. They moved slowly crawling on their hands and knees for thirty to forty feet until there was enough room for them to crouch and then to stand, almost erect.

Jack's light glanced off a series of morphic figures lying on their sides. "The shaman must have carved them. I wish Lee were here; he could probably tell us what they mean. Maybe they are cave guardians."

"Well, if they're cave guardians, it looks like they're asleep. At least, I hope they're asleep."

"Save your batteries. I'll use my lamp," Jack said, half-crouching and half-stooping as he led the way down the tunnel. His headlamp cut a swath in the darkness in front of them. As they moved forward, the darkness closed behind them. Jack pressed his hands against the damp walls to keep his balance. Cierra hooked one hand on Jack's belt.

"This is fun. I feel like we're a choo-choo train going through a dark tunnel. Whoo! Whoo!" Her voice echoed.

"You better hope that there's a light at the end."

"There's always a light at the end of a tunnel, Jack. Whoo! Whoo!" Cierra giggled and Jack groaned.

"Twenty minutes," Jack said, glancing at his watch, "it's a long way back and it's all uphill." They were standing in a small oval chamber. A pool of water, a sump, lay at their feet. Jack searched the room and touched its smooth walls. "This could be the end of the line."

"What's this?" Cierra asked and pointed at a stick figure with an arrow entering the mouth and pointed downward from the buttocks. Peculiar pecked marks were dotted beneath the figure.

"A water symbol. It could mean 'go through here'." Jack turned off his light and squatted on the floor. There was no sound, except their breathing. "If there is a way out, Cierra, it's likely through this sump. We can turn around or I can try to push through here. With any luck, I'll probably drown. If we follow the stick figure's advice, it means this way, feet first."

"Good thinking. Maybe you don't need Lee after all." Cierra strapped a line around her waist. "I'll go first."

"No way."

"You're stronger. You can pull me out if I get stuck."
Cierra slid into the water before Jack could say no. "It's warm."
She moved her feet around slowly. "There's an opening. I can feel
it. Two tugs, pull me out. One tug, follow me through."

"Wait."

"Time to go." She took a deep breath and pushed down and
disappeared feet first into the hole.

Jack waited apprehensively and then he felt a single tug on
the rope. He lowered himself into the sump and moved his feet
around slowly until he felt the opening. "Careful, boy. No is no
time for shallow breathing." Jack took several short breaths, and
forced the air out of his lungs, then inhaled deeply, and slid down
into the sump. He shoved away from the edge with considerable
force. He could feel his legs moving through the opening, his body
and arms were clear. He doubled up his legs and stood on the
bottom and raised himself slowly.

"You can breathe now," Cierra said. "And open your eyes
if you want to."

Jack opened his eyes and mouth. The light from his lamp
danced eerily off the walls. "That's better." His voice echoed
hollowly in the chamber. Jack shook off the excess water, like a
dog. "All this gear, and I forgot to bring a towel." Their wet
clothing clung to their damp skin.

"I'm soaked," Cierra said as she squeezed her shirt dry.
"What a place to hold a wet tee-shirt contest."

"You'd win, hands down."

"You better watch your mouth, boy. I'm no honky tonk
girl," Cierra laughed.

Jack removed two packets from his pack and handed one to
Cierra. "They're thermo-wraps; no need to get hypothermia. I'll
turn my back."

"Just turn off your light," she said and Jack snapped off his
lantern, stripped to the waist, and struggled to pull the protective
covering over his head. Cierra snapped her light on. "Wow! Were
you ever a dancer at the Calvaras Club?" she teased.

"Sure! That's how I worked my way through college," Jack said. Cierra giggled.

Cierra pointed her lamp at a circle with an arrow that was aimed at a narrow tunnel in front of them. "Hey, I'm beginning to get the hang of this. Do we follow the arrow?"

"This opening is bigger."

"You don't need to shout. No one's here, but us chickens and claustrophobics."

"Who's shouting? I barely whispered." Jack stooped slightly and entered the passage. The walls were worn smooth with the passage of time and running water. The angle of descent was fairly steep so Jack had to check himself to keep from slipping. "It's all down hill from here," he said, his voice echoing down the passage.

They used the walls for support and moved rapidly. "There's some kind of shaft here," Cierra said. "It leads upward, I think."

Jack stuck his head inside. His lamp searched the surface of the shaft. Veins of white quartz crystals and iron pyrite wove their way across the shaft. He picked out traces of chisel marks on the walls. "It's a mine shaft. There's turquoise here, a lot of it. This must have been a turquoise mine. It's old. I can't tell how old. There's a fault line at this end of the valley. It crosses the ranch and ends up somewhere in the Estrellas. The Yaquis worked this canyon. They followed the fault. They were looking for veins of gold. It could be their work or maybe the Spaniards. Several shafts have been found over in South Mountain that the Spaniards dug. It should lead to the surface somewhere. It might be another way out if we need it."

Jack checked his compass. "I'm not sure where we are exactly, but I'm guessing we're well west of the wash."

They moved forward. The tunnel widened and opened into a large chamber. "There are more tunnels leading out of here," Cierra said. Eerie patterns of light and shadow danced up and down as she played her lamp around the walls of chamber.

Jack took off his pack and laid it on a ledge. "You know what? I bet we're in Se'ehe's chamber. How incredible!"

"Who's Se'ehe?"

"I'm not exactly sure. In some of the tribal legends his name is often interchanged with I'itoi's. And sometimes Se'ehe is described as having helped the Papago capture HA-AK. But in most of the legends, he's the ogre who guards the cave. He devours men and does despicable things to women who trespass here."

"Aren't you lucky it's not the other way around?"

Jack took out a notepad and made a quick sketch and some notations. He searched the ceiling with his flashlight. A spiral and an arrow pointed to a passage on his right. He sighted his compass down the two tunnels that exited each side of the chamber.

"Let's try this one first," he said and moved into the tunnel on his left. The passage divided into three branches. Jack made a chalk mark and crawled through the lowest entry. He crawled on his hands and then stepped into a wide chamber. He scanned the small room and discovered another. It led gradually upward. He pulled himself up a shaft using some hand-carved niches spaced twenty inches or so apart. The shaft opened into a larger chamber. Jack reached backward and pulled Cierra up beside him. The stench of rot and decay filled their nostrils.

Jack's headlamp lit up a ledge carved into the walls. A ring of smoke-blackened stones filled the center of the chamber.

"It looks like a kiva," Cierra said.

"I think you're right," Jack said and played his headlamp on the ceiling. "They must have entered from the top. There's traces of an opening there; it's been sealed in. There must be a ladder somewhere." The lights from their headlamps criss-crossed the room. Jack splashed through a pool of water and crossed to the other side of the chamber. He felt something soft underfoot and stepped back. He glanced downward; his headlamp revealed a human arm and then a man's face. Jack yelled and stepped backwards.

"A body!" He looked again and saw that the man's eyeballs tilted grotesquely upward. "He's dead."

Cierra splashed across the pool, her headlamp bouncing around the room. "Over here, Jack. God, there's another one. Dear God. There's more over here." He circled the fire ring and joined Cierra. "It's a girl, Jack, a little girl. She's dead. They're all dead." Cierra choked back tears. He touched her gently and she threw her arms around him. He held her tightly. "It's a whole family. They're campesinos."

"We need to get out of here," he said quietly and led Cierra gently back to the tunnel. Neither spoke as they followed the chalk marks back to the first chamber.

Cierra pulled off her helmet and sat down on it. "What happened to them, Jack?"

"This maze is a death trap, Cierra. That microburst yesterday must have flooded the tunnels. Lazar mumbled something about a cave or a cavern. He was trying to tell us. He must have hid that family here."

"If we had known, we might have saved them."

"They were already dead when he came after my truck, Cierra."

"What are we going to do, go back?"

"No, I believe the tunnel over there leads to the surface. Come on." Jack entered the opening and climbed up a series of several ladder-like steps cut into the wall. He could hear Cierra's heavy breathing closely below him. "Easy does it," he said.

The shaft opened wider and Jack crawled into a niche-like space, knocking over an olla. Several wrapped packages spilled out of its wide mouth. "It looks like more cocaine." He handed a packet to Cierra. Jack turned the pot over. "Carver," he said.

"How do you know?"

"I saw pots like these at Trisha's place. That's the mark she puts on the ones she makes for Carver." He crawled forward.

"Dead end?" Cierra asked as she crawled up beside him.

"Not quite," Jack said and pulled the pick hammer from his backpack. He clawed with the hammer and dislodged some interlaced rocks. He pushed hard against the remaining stones and the wall gave way. Jack pushed away the remaining bits of debris and crawled into the bright sunlight.

CHAPTER 22

Jack pushed through a mountain of tumbleweeds that had been swept into the arroyo by the dust storm, effectively hiding the slit-like aperture that led to the cavern.

"Oh, my God." Cierra sat down beside Jack on a split half-rotted cottonwood stump. "I thought I'd never see sunlight again."

A black-gray lizard raced across a slab of granite at their feet. "There's another lizard like the one we saw in the cave," Jack said. "They're all over this hill. Like the legend says, follow the lizard that looks like the ground, and it will lead to something of value."

"What it led to is those dead people down there," Cierra said.

"I'm sick of the legend, these damn glyphs, the coyotes and drug runners," Jack said. Cierra threw a handful of pebbles at a lizard sunning itself on a rock. It pumped itself up and down briefly and settled back down. "You missed."

"I meant to. Do you believe in God, Jack?"

Jack looked gently at Cierra. "I don't know. Right now, I'm not sure if I believe in anything or anyone."

Cierra nodded. "How could God or anyone let those people die like that? They were human beings," Cierra said. "It's not right. They came to find a better life. They came to the El Norte to find freedom, Jack, to raise a family. They were prepared to work, work hard. I know these people. They are good people." Jack put his arm around Cierra.

"I know, Cierra. I know."

Cierra slid out from under Jack's arm and stood up. "We've got to find the coyotes who did this. I need to call the sub-station and let them know what's happened here." She glanced down at her muddy shorts and tee shirt, and at her mud-covered arms and legs. "I need to clean up. There's going to be hell to pay out here."

"Let's go. You can take a shower at the ranch house. And then you can call from Ruiz's. Our phone was disconnected by Lazar yesterday." They crossed the wash and walked up the ridge towards the Toyota. "We have company." Jack stepped in front of Cierra.

"Hello, Jack," Chernov said cheerfully. "I found your note. Figured you might turn up here."

"Did you come by yourself, Mike?"

"Just me, Jack. I'm alone if that's what you mean. Were you expecting someone else?"

"Sort of, but I'm not surprised you showed up. I thought you might."

"Find anything worthwhile?" Chernov asked softly.

"Nothing but a shaman's bag full of owl feathers."

"You left your metal detector in the Toyota. Did you find the treasure?"

"Well, not exactly. It wasn't in I'itoi's cave."

"It's here then?" Chernov asked.

"I'm not sure that there is any treasure. Here or anywhere else."

"Oh, it's here, all right. You must have found something."

"Gold crosses? A breast plate worth a fortune to collectors?" Jack asked.

"Quite right! How did you figure that out?"

"The missing icon, for starters. It had a symbol for 'hidden' on the reverse side. You spotted it when you brought the Mallorys out and then you sent Lazar to steal it. You had him spread the fetishes among your dealers to cover your tracks. Then you let Trisha know where they were. You set them up, didn't you?"

"Well, something like that, Jack."

"I knew something was wrong when the icon and the glyph with a circle didn't turn up. Then, I remembered what I read in your articles on Pima legends and lost Spanish treasure. You're quite a gold bug, Mike."

"Interesting. I didn't realize that you're such a quick study. Speaking of treasure, I think we should be on our way." Chernov pulled a .25 caliber Beretta from his pocket. "Now put your pistol and holster on the ground." Jack hesitated, looked at Cierra, unclipped the holster and dropped it at his feet. "Kick it over here." Jack deliberately kicked the pistol away from Chernov. It skidded off the ledge and landed in a heap of tumbleweeds piled in the wash below.

"That really wasn't necessary, Jack. Inside, you first."

"Better do what he says," Cierra said. Jack shrugged his shoulders, turned, and crawled into the entrance.

"Now, toss out HA-AK's effigy."

"Why don't you come in and get it, Mike?"

"Don't care for snakes, Jack. Just toss it out. Don't make trouble. All I want is the treasure." Jack opened his backpack, found the icon and tossed it outside. "Thank you. Inside Deputy," Cierra crawled through the entrance. She crouched beside Jack.

"We can't let him take the drugs," Cierra gasped.

"He wants the relics, Cierra. I don't think he knows about the drugs or the family down there."

Chernov examined Jack's icon. "I'm curious, Jack. Why did you have Trisha make this?"

"Curiosity killed the cat, Mike," Jack replied.

"I've seen this symbol somewhere. Casa Grande! It's on one of Morning Blue's petroglyphs." Chernov laid the icon on the ground and pointed the head towards the cave. He opened his bag and pulled out the small glyph with the circle and the arrow. He sat the object upright, stepped back and scanned the butte.

"It works, Jack. The sight lines up perfectly with that wide opening on the side of the butte. I think the relics are hidden up there. Too bad you tried the downward spiral first. How'd you do it?"

"I just followed the arrows!"

"You learned a lot from Lee, Jack. As I said, you're a quick study. I spent years looking for Marcos de Niza's treasure and you come up with the answer in days."

"You spend too much time in the library, Mike. The message was on the rocks. You should have asked for Lee's help a long time ago. But then Lee isn't an archeologist, is he? He's just an amateur with a theory. He wasn't reliable enough for you."

"Well, I don't need Lee now, do I, Jack?"

Chernov waved his pistol. "Move back, please. I need to close the entrance, just for a while. I won't be gone long."

"Don't be stupid, Mike. You're in deep trouble and it's only going to get worse," Jack warned. "People know that we're here; I made sure of it." Mike's pistol made a quick popping sound; a bullet ricocheted off the rocks. Jack pulled Cierra away from the entrance. Chernov began piling rocks in front of the entrance. When it was sealed, they heard his footsteps crunching across the graveled shards. Jack pulled the pick from his backpack and started to dislodge the rocks. He managed to break away a pair of rocks at the top of the pile. Jack stared out the slit.

"What's he doing?" Cierra asked.

"I don't know. He's in your Toyota and he's headed this way." Jack and Cierra scrambled backwards as the front bumper of the Toyota struck the rocks. "He's pinning us in."

Mike stepped out of the Toyota. "If the treasure is there, Jack, help is only a phone call away. I'll let the Sheriff know where you two are. If it's not there, I'll come back, of course."

"Keep him talking, Cierra." Jack grabbed the flares out of his pack and crawled back to the tunnel that led to I'itoi's maze.

"You lie Chernov!" Cierra shouted. "You let those people die. You'll let us die, too."

"What people?"

"There's five dead people in here. They drowned like rats, thanks to you and Lazar."

"Did I hear you right? Were some people trapped in there? They're dead?"

"Yes. Damn you! A whole family!"

"I'm sorry, Deputy. Using illegals to bring in drugs was Lazar's and Carver's game. I had nothing to do with their dirty business."

"If you knew what they were doing and didn't say anything then you are worse than they are."

"Life is not that easy. Nothing is true; nothing is a lie anymore. It depends on the color of the glass you're looking through, Deputy."

"Why are you doing this to us?"

"No choice. Lazar will talk to save his hide. He stole the icon for me. I had him sell the other objects to confuse the issue."

"Then Jack is right. You did set them up."

"Yes, Jack, you figured it out, didn't you. And then you, Deputy, sicced the IRS on Azad's clients. They are looking for tax fraud. I didn't think things would develop so quickly. In time, my part will come out."

"Yet, you wanted to expose them."

"Very clever. She is a bright one, Jack."

"Why?"

"Why? Because they had their hooks in me, Deputy, and I got tired of playing their game. I had a chance to entangle them in their own shenanigans. It almost worked. Are you there, Jack? Jack? Nice work, Deputy. O dear, I suppose he's headed back to I'itoi's cave. That should take him awhile. I should have told him that I sealed that entrance when I was waiting for you to surface."

Chernov walked away. "He's gone," Cierra shouted. There was no answering echo. A shaft of light several feet over her head caught her attention. Cierra wedged her knees against one side of the wall, her back against the other and edged up the chimney. Cierra managed to reach the light source, push out a small rock, and then another. They rattled down the rock face.

From her vantage point, she could see Chernov working his way awkwardly up the butte. She couldn't see the entrance to the cave across the wash. The cluster of tumbleweeds blocked her viewpoint. A cloud of blue smoke swirled upward from the far side of the tumbleweeds. Cierra watched in fascination as the tumbleweeds began to burn furiously. Soon, a wall of fire scorched the base of the butte and reached skywards. She heard Jack's voice below her.

"Cierra?"

"I'm up here, in the chimney."

"What are you doing there?"

"I'm watching Chernov and your brush fire, right?"

"Where is he?"

"He's on a ledge beneath the opening."

"Has he seen the fire?"

"He has his back to it. I don't think he's noticed."

"He will. There's a lot of brush beyond the tumbleweed, and it leads to the base of the butte. It should create a lot of heat and smoke soon. The fire can't reach him, but the drifting smoke may slow him down." Jack crouched by the blocked entrance and pulled out some stones.

"I'm hoping that Mollie or her boys notice the smoke."

"Come on up. The air's better up here; so's the view."

Jack wedged himself up the shaft. They watched as Chernov turned and gauged the smoke rising up towards him. He edged himself higher up the face of the butte. He reached the ledge that was below the wide opening. He rested for a moment and then pulled himself upright in front of the opening in the rocks. He started to force himself into the opening on the face of the butte.

A huge feathered owl lunged out of the hole in the rocks. Its claws extended, it smashed into Chernov's head and shoulders. He raised an arm and tried to fend off the owl. He raised the other arm, lost his balance, clawed the air frantically, and then fell backwards. The owl swooped downwards, following the body; Chernov's arms and legs were flailing like a rag-doll. They both disappeared behind boulders. Then the owl soared upwards and circled the butte.

"Dear God," Cierra said. Neither one spoke for several minutes.

"We better get down. I'll go first," Jack said. Using his knees and back, he wedged himself back down to the cave floor. Cierra followed close behind. They heard the sound of a truck pulling alongside Cierra's Toyota.

"Who's that?" Cierra asked.

"The cavalry. I've been expecting them."

"Anybody home?" Mollie shouted.

"Nobody but us chickens and claustrophobics," Jack answered.

Cierra chuckled slightly and punched him in the arm, "That's my line."

"Whoo! Whoo!" Jack said.

"Stop it!" Cierra giggled.

"Are you two all right?" Mollie asked.

"Will be as soon as you get us out of here," Jack yelled.

"Dave, bring your truck up here." They could hear a diesel truck chugging up the slope.

"Pete, wrap a chain around the front bumper and pull the Toyota out of the way."

"Yes, Boss."

"Move that boulder, Dave."

"Yes, Boss." Dave hefted a rock and heaved it to one side. Cierra and Jack could hear the Toyota being pulled away from the cave entrance.

"Pete, come on over here and help your brother." Pete and Dave quickly cleared the blocked entrance.

"You first." Cierra scrambled past Jack and into the sunlight. Jack grabbed his pack and followed her out.

"Hallelujah brother!" Jack shouted. Dave gave Jack a hug. Jack turned and clasped Pete's hand. "Are we glad to see you."

"I'll bet," Mollie hugged Jack.

"You saw my smoke signals?" Jack asked.

"You said to keep an eye out, but I didn't think that you were going to set the wash on fire," Mollie said.

"I saw the smoke and guessed that you were in trouble," Dave said. "I took off and got Mom and Hal. Art and Pete came behind us."

"Chernov fell off the cliff over there." Jack pointed at the butte.

"We saw him fall," Mollie said. "The owl scared him. He's alive but he's shook up pretty bad. Hal's down there with him. Art went to call the Sheriff and an ambulance."

"I'm a sheriff deputy," Cierra said and she started to rise.

"Sit down, honey," Mollie said and pushed Cierra gently back onto the ground. "Just give yourself time to catch your breath."

"Some campesinos are in the cave, Mollie. They're dead."

"Dead? There are some dead people in the cave? Oh, God, what were they doing in the cave?"

"I'm not sure, Mollie, but I think Carver was running drugs through here. He was forcing illegals to carry the drugs in from Mexico."

"Is that what you were doing in the cave, looking for drugs? Who is that guy who fell off the cliff? Is he a drug runner?"

"No, Mollie. We stumbled onto the drugs and the bodies. We were looking for gold, same as you and Dave, only we had a map. I'll explain later." Jack left Cierra and Mollie and followed the wash that led to the base of the cliff. He found Art and Hal standing beside Chernov.

Chernov's leg dangled limply over a piece of jutted sandstone. His scalp was lacerated severely. There was a wide gash over his left ribcage. A deep cut ran from the corner of his right eye to his chin.

"How are you doing, Mike?"

"A bit woozy. My damn leg gave out." He glanced down, "Maybe for good this time."

A DPS helicopter landed downwind from the base of the butte, away from the drifting smoke. Deputy Smith and two paramedics jumped out. They moved quickly to where Chernov was lying on the rocks. Cierra walked towards the helicopter and met Smith halfway.

"What do you want me to do with this guy, Cierra, if he lives?"

"Book him for assault and kidnapping after they've patched him up," Cierra told Deputy Smith. "I'll be filing more charges when I get to the hospital."

"Okay, but the Sheriff isn't going to like this, Cierra," Deputy Smith said.

"He'll like it less when I file charges against some of Chernov's friends."

The paramedics carried Chernov to the helicopter and slid the stretcher inside the hatch. Chernov's maroon and cream Morgan skidded to a halt near the helicopter. Susan got out, ran over, and knelt beside Chernov. "Is he all right?" she asked the medic.

"He may have fractured his skull. His arm and leg are fractured."

"Mike fell down and broke his crown and Susan came tumbling after." Chernov forced a weak smile.

"Mike, you fool! Why didn't you wait for me?" Susan asked. She crawled in beside him and took his hand.

"Keep an eye on her, too, Smith. I'll be bringing changes against her also."

Deputy Smith grinned and crawled into the helicopter. The cloud of blue smoke around Lone Butte cleared as the helicopter lifted and headed to the east.

"Pete," Mollie ordered, "go see what's up there in that hole." They watched Pete work his way up the side of the butte. Mollie and Dave shouted advice as he attached a rope and harness to a flat overhanging rock and drew himself up to the opening above the ledge. Pete peered into the opening and took off his hat and waved.

"There's some young owls in here," he shouted.

"Be careful," Mollie yelled as Pete disappeared into the hole.

They waited and watched. Then Pete crawled out to the ledge, held up a golden breastplate and waved it in the air. "There's more stuff up here!" he shouted. "Send up a burlap bag."

CHAPTER 23

An elderly man shuffled past the hospital waiting room, almost soundlessly in his soft slippers. He paused at the drinking fountain, padded over to the magazine rack and picked up a newspaper. Jack stared at a R.C. Gorman pastel print encased in a non-glare plastic frame.

"Susan," Cierra said, "The FBI is taping Mike's statement. He is admitting falsifying data with you on archeological impact studies. It's very clear, Susan, that you helped Carver by contaminating and not reporting any evidence of existing Native American remains on Jack's and on Carver's property. Draper's signature is on the impact study, but I don't think he'll take any responsibility for the report or for any of the other false impact studies that you and Mike prepared. He'll point the spotlight on you to save his own butt. He'll testify that he relied on your statements, that he trusted you, which is probably what he did. Didn't he, Susan?"

"I'm not going to comment on that, Deputy." Susan said.

"Cierra, I'd like to buy Susan a cup of coffee. Could you spare us a few moments?" Cierra's eyes flashed at Jack and then at Susan.

"Go ahead. Take your time. Mike will be busy for awhile and then I need to wrap this up." She walked down the hall and joined Deputy Smith who was standing outside the door to Chernov's hospital room.

Susan and Jack crossed through the lobby and entered the commissary. "I'll get the coffee, Susan. Why don't you grab us a table?"

"I'll take iced tea instead. I'll be outside in the atrium."

Jack set the iced tea in front of Susan and sat down in a white polyethylene chair. A pair of sparrows was busy scrounging crumbs from a pink paper plate on the next table. One of the birds flew over and landed on the top of the empty chair next to Susan.

"Go away." Susan shooed it off. "No crumbs here." An overhead mister kicked on; a cool spray wafted over their heads, evaporating as it cooled the air. "I hate misters. They make me feel clammy."

"Would you like to go inside?"

"No, I'd rather stay out here. I hate hospitals, too." Susan sipped her tea. "Ugh!" she said and set her glass down hard, scaring the sparrows away. "Cafeteria iced tea always taste awful."

"You're upset, Susan."

"Well, wouldn't you be? What do you expect? Mike's in there and he's hurt. Heaven only knows what he's saying."

"He's hurt, Susan, but he understands what he's doing."

Susan stared at the hanging potted plants for several minutes. The automatic misters came on again. "How long have you known, Jack? When did I become a suspect?"

"Even before we met, Susan. Before I drove to Tucson, I went to the Hayden Library to get information on the petroglyphs and anything on the Ocotillo Ranch and Carver's property. Pat Garrett, you know him, found some articles and monographs; one of them described Fray Marcos de Niza's expedition. It was a collaborative effort written by you and Chernov. It contains specific references to the Marcos de Niza rock, the inscription and the curse. It's obvious that you and Mike had visited the site, yet when we stopped there on our way to I'itoi's cave, you let Lee describe the padre's adventures. Then at the dancing ground, you expressed surprise at Lee's interpretation. But the wall and dancing ground are described in your monograph. You knew all about it, yet said nothing. You and Mike were looking for the treasure."

"Mike was looking for the treasure, Jack. He was obsessed with the idea of finding it. I just did some of the research for him. I never thought he would find it. It was important to him. I just wanted to help him."

"Susan, you wrote the impact study for Carver. Mike just added a few squibbles. I read it. Both of you visited the Ocotillo Ranch several times. In fact, you had already mapped the cairns on my property and those on Carver's land before you came to see me. The day you drove up from Tucson, you pretended to be excited about the cairns. You took less than thirty minutes to chart them. No wonder, Susan, you had already been there. When I showed you and Tom the pictures of the petroglyph rocks and the mentioned the cave, you realized that if it became known that there were human remains here that would affect your impact study. Before you came out to the ranch, you met with Mike and you both agreed to fluff me off, Susan. When I asked you about human remains under the cairns, you told me the Old People never placed bodies at these sites. Well, Susan, when I was a kid, I dug up a cairn and found bones underneath. My grandfather helped me cover them back up. So I knew you were wrong or lying. The Pimas and Papagos put the cairns there and they placed the kick-balls and rag-dolls there right up until the late 1930s."

"So?" Susan asked.

"The 'so' is that you knew both tribes could forestall any development, even on private land, if they applied for permission to dig up and inter the remains. And they could possibly claim that the land the cairns are on is sacred ground. When Chernov toured the property, he scarcely glanced at the cairns. When I took him to see the glyphs on the front of the ridge, although he didn't realize it at the time, I let him lead me! He knew what was there, and he knew about the glyphs in the yard."

"Remember when I showed you the photo album and asked about Tom and Mike and commitments?"

"Yes, that was after you tried to electrocute me in the tub." Susan smiled and Jack chuckled.

"I sort of enjoyed that scene."

"I bet you did." Susan smiled again. "So did I. I like you, Jack. I like you a lot. Oh, why do things always get so damn complicated? I didn't want to do that report for Carver, and after I met you I really didn't want to do it at all."

"Why did you then, Susan?"

"It was already in the works. I'd signed off on it, so had Mike. Anyway, Carver had his hooks in Mike."

"And in you, too, Susan. You have a problem with cocaine, don't you?"

Susan opened her purse, took out a tissue and wiped her nose. Her eyes grew misty. "Who told you? Mike wouldn't have."

"Well, the sniffles for one thing. You talked of mulberry trees and allergies. The pollen season was over, but you mentioned you were going to see an allergist before you came to the ranch. When my fetishes turned up at Baxters', I knew there was a

connection. I just couldn't figure out what it was, and then after you got shocked in the tub, I cleaned up the mess in the bathroom."

"And you found my mirror with cocaine on it. That was stupid of me, wasn't it?"

"Not stupid, Susan. Cierra had just told us about the Mallorys drowning in the canal."

"I panicked and…"

"You went to Tucson the clean up your act. In fact, you called Mike and he told you to."

"How do you know that?"

"Cierra checked with the phone company. You called Mike from the stable and then you called Tom."

"You left a note for Ruiz in that railroad lantern. You said it was your post office, and you left the diary and the photograph album on the porch. You set me up, Jack and then you left that other note for Ruiz when you and Cierra went to the shaman's cave."

"I still wasn't sure, Susan."

"You weren't sure? So you let me dig myself in a little deeper."

"I thought Mike was pulling all the strings, Susan, and in a way, he was. I didn't know whether it was Mike's game or yours. There was a chance that you didn't fully realize what you were doing."

"We both knew, Jack. Mike was trying to help me get Carver off my back. Well, off both of our backs. Carver's a cretin. You don't know him, Jack"

"Susan, I didn't know about the drugs until they were found in the Mallory's Land Rover. It all began to come together, but I hadn't counted on finding the drugs in the cave or that campesino family." Susan put her head in her hands and started to cry. "Drug trafficking is serious business, Susan. If a death occurs as a result of the trafficking, anyone involved can be held responsible." Susan looked up at Jack. "Baxter has been arrested by the Federales. I shouldn't tell you this, but he's talking his head off. He doesn't want to face a death sentence in Mexico. He'd rather by extradited to the States."

"God, I'm in deep trouble, aren't I? What can I do, Jack?"

"You could help yourself a lot if you voluntarily entered a substance abuse program. And if I were you, I'd ask Cierra to let you make a statement when Mike's finished. Put the onus on Carver, turn state's evidence, well, I'm no judge, but it could be your best defense. You might get a break. The bottom line is that you're going to be arrested and charged anyway. But if you cooperate, it could help."

"It's a rotten world, Jack. Carver's a rotten bastard. So are Mike and Tom and so are you. All men are." Susan cried even harder. "I'm sorry, Jack. I didn't mean that. It's just that I'm so confused."

"I know Susan." Jack took her hand.

Cierra walked into the atrium. "Mike is finished. You can see him now, Susan." Susan wiped here eyes and stood up. "He's asked to see you, too, Jack."

"After I see Mike, Cierra, I think I like to speak with you and your uncle."

Cierra glanced at Jack and back at Susan. "I think we can manage something. Would you like to have a lawyer present?"

"That won't be necessary. I know what I'm doing. Will you stay with me?"

"Yes, Susan. I'd be glad to." Cierra touched Susan's arm and walked with her to Mike's room. Jack followed.

Cierra's Uncle, Thomas Alcaraz, dark-skinned and dark-haired, his chin and jaw freshly shaven, white shirt still morning-fresh, stood patiently beside the hospital bed. Chernov was speaking quietly into a tape-recorder.

"That about tells it all," Chernov said and clicked off the machine. Agent Alcaraz bent over and picked up the recorder.

"I'll have this typed up. I'll need your signature, Dr. Chernov. You can witness it," Cierra nodded as her uncle left the room. Chernov smiled sardonically, "My part is a bit exaggerated." Susan moved to his side and took his hand.

"You've always been a liar, Michael. You even lied to me," Susan said.

Jack cleared his throat. "Why, Mike?"

"Why did I become a Judas goat, a pilot fish? I want to tell myself that we're all thieves of time, as Franz Boas said. Adventurers, pirates, and plunderers, but that's not true." Mike looked at Susan and then back at Jack.

"I suppose I got caught in the Darwinian Shuffle," Mike said. "When I started out I was an idealist. I wanted to build a stellar museum where science, art and history blended to bring the old cultures to light and to keep ours from growing dark. I wanted people to respect the Native American culture. But all that takes time, energy, and money. I had to go begging for dollars from institutionalized intellectuals and armchair anthropologists and from board members and philanthropists who have never visited a reservation. I got tired of it, so I created the Indian Market to raise funds for the museum. I had the world begging for more turquoise, jewelry, Navajo blankets, and katchina dolls. The dealers cashed in, Jack. The prices skyrocketed for rare objects. I took a chance and swapped bones and rare objects buried in the basement for trash. Old lamps for new ones," Chernov laughed sardonically. "Then I hatched a scheme to 'blue sky' the appraisals so the buyers could cop a bigger tax write-off. It was easy. The Mallorys, Arnold, and Carver are dwarfs, Jack."

"So instead of protecting the museum, you looted it?" Cierra said.

"And polluted it, Deputy! I'm sorry to say, but at the time I enjoyed the experience. It was exciting putting on the world. I fooled everyone, dealers, experts, everyone. But, I want you all to know, that I'm sorry, truly sorry, about the family who drowned in that maze. I told myself I had nothing to do with drug-traffickers, but I did. I knew that Arnold and the Mallorys were shipping drugs in fake pots and that Susan was involved. But I couldn't do anything to stop you, Susan. You wouldn't listen to me."

"Maybe at one time I would have, but not recently. You're right," Susan said.

"I understand like no one else does, Susan. For me, it's ironic, but working at the museum was like being buried in Lazarus' cave. Now I'm headed for a real prison, but it won't change anything. It won't bring back the people who died. I hope you understand. Does that answer your question, Jack?"

"Your whole world is colored differently than mine, Mike. In my opinion, you are just as ruthless as Carver and the rest of that bunch of thieves," Jack said. "The real world is irrelevant to you. You had a responsibility, Mike. You had an opportunity to show the world the best of Native American cultures. You disregarded what was sacred to them. You could have restored their trust in us, but instead you chose to cater to anyone who was willing to buy you. You turned their cultural center into a commercial brothel. No, I don't understand you, and I don't want to." Susan laid her head on the bed and began to sob. Chernov stroked her hair, turned his face away from Jack, and stared out the window.

"I've got to get out of here. I need some fresh air." Jack walked out of the room.

Cierra followed him into the hall and touched his arm. "Thank you."

"For what?"

"I needed to hear you say that."

"You know that I wanted to sell the petroglyphs. They could have ended up in the entryway of Chernov's Folly."

"That's not what I meant. But you wouldn't have, would you?"

"Probably not, but it was a close call."

"You're a crab, Jack."

"A what?"

"A cancer. Hard on the outside and soft on the inside. And sweet, yes, sweet." Cierra smiled and took Jack's hand. "Thanks for helping with Susan. Let's go outside. We both need some fresh air."

"What's going to happen to her?"

"I don't know, Jack. If she's smart, she'll become a witness for the state while she can. If she tells what she knows about Carver's operation, it might go easier on her since this is her first offense."

"What about Carver?"

"He's next on my list. The drug control unit arrested Baxter at his San Carlos ranch. They confiscated a shipment of cocaine and arrested a couple of coyotes who had lined up another family of illegals as mules. They found maps of the route from Altar to the Ocotillo Ranch in the back of a transport van. Everyone was caught red-handed. I'm having Carver picked up and brought out to the ranch. I don't have a deposition yet from Baxter, but I know the gist of it. Carver will be at the ranch in an hour or so. Sheriff Cuso will bring him directly from the airport to the mound. I want to question him there – and I want him to see those people he let die. But before I leave, I need to talk to my Uncle and Susan after I get her deposition."

"How can I help?"

"Why don't you go to the ranch and help Dave get organized? We'll need the backhoe to expose the kiva. I'm calling in the rural metro fire department and the coroners office."

"Okay, I'll meet you there."

CHAPTER 24

Dave expertly leveled the gravel mound near the ranch house. He dropped the bucket. Its teeth bit deeply. The backhoe turned and dropped its load to one side. The bucket dropped again and again, creating a deep hole in the center of the space where the mound had been. A wide gap opened at the bottom of the pit. Dave drove the rig to one side, turned off the diesel engine and climbed off.

"I've broken through to the caves. Is the hole wide enough, Cierra?" Dave asked.

"I think so. We'll wait until rural metro gets here. They're going to take care of the bodies. If they want a bigger hole, can you do it?"

"I'm not sure, Cierra. It could cave in." They watched as a small avalanche of gravel slid down the sides of the pit and disappeared into the hole.

"We better let them check it out then. I'm afraid we ruined a part of the intaglio, Jack."

"I don't think so, Cierra. These chards are just part of the kick-ball from the legend. When you're through here, Dave can refill it," Jack said.

"I can put it back the way it was." Dave grinned.

A Maricopa County Sheriff Department vehicle pulled up on the ridge where they were standing. Sheriff Cuso got out and walked rapidly towards them.

"What the hell's going on, Cierra? This place looks like a bloody battlefield!" he shouted. "Deputy Smith said something about dead illegals and a drug bust and Spanish gold."

"That's about the size of it, Sheriff. Did you say anything to Carver on the way here?"

"Hell, no. I don't know anything. I just told him there's been an accident and that we found his driver. Rudy Lazar, that's the name you gave me."

"Lazar's dead. Snake bit."

"Snake bit?"

"Yes, Sheriff, he died yesterday. Carter and Lazar are transporting drugs and illegals, and they are responsible for the deaths of that family down there. I want to talk to Carver."

"Alone?"

"You want to make an arrest that will stick, Sheriff? If you do, you'd better let me handle this. I've got Carver by the cajones."

Cuso looked hard at Cierra, swallowed and glanced at Carver. "All right, Alcaraz, but you better be right. That joker has an army of attorneys and friends with a lot of clout."

"He'll need them." Cierra strode towards the Sheriff's car and led Carver, crisp and neat in his gleaming white shirt and narrow black tie, an epitome of flawless urbanity, across the baking gravel surface. Jack and Dave sat on the edge of the rubble that had been pushed aside from the opening to I'itoi's maze. Cierra led Carver to the opening.

"What the hell? What's going on here? Where's my operator?"

"He took a hike, Carver," Cierra said. "Said something about not wanting to work for a coyote like you."

"What the hell are you talking about?" Carver turned to Cierra. "Tell me what's going on or I'm out of here."

Cierra grabbed Carver by the elbow. "Not until I show you something." She half-led, half-drug Carver around the backhoe and stopped short of the yawning hole in the ground. Carver jerked his arm free.

"What the hell is that?"

"What does it look like? It's a hole in the ground. It leads down to a cave. Care to take a look?"

"What for?"

"I thought maybe you might want to give us a hand. There are five bodies down there. A family of illegals. They're dead, thanks to you and Lazar. You let them die down there."

"I don't know what you are talking about. I've never seen illegals out here. What's this bullshit?"

"We're talking about drug trafficking. It's your operation, Carver. Lazar hid the drugs and the illegals in the cave. The monsoon rains flooded the cave. They drowned when Lazar didn't get back in time. But you knew they were here. Lazar called your private number from Jack's stable! Remember? Ma Bell has a record of the call in case you don't remember. You're going up for second degree murder or manslaughter, at least, Carver," Cierra said. "You knew they were out here, but you didn't even try to help them. You didn't give a damn."

"I didn't have anything to do with this. If Lazar was running drugs and illegals that's his problem."

"That was his problem. He's dead," Cierra said. Carver took off his Stetson and wiped his forehead. "But he named you before he died and now you've got the problem."

"He was my driver, that's all. You have nothing."

"There're some pots down there, Carver. They're full of crack cocaine. There's a mark on the bottom. Trisha Simpson made pots for you, the Mallorys and Arnold. She numbered them so she could keep track of them. But she personalized the ones she made for you. You should have checked; they've got your initials on them."

"This is crap, Deputy. Are you trying to tell me that Arnold and the Mallorys were transporting drugs?"

"The ollas were a give away, Carver. Those were your pots we found in Mallory's Land Rover and in the cave. You had Arnold ship the cocaine in the ollas to warehouse drops in Chicago, New York, and Washington, D.C.. The FBI has already found your ollas and traces of cocaine at these drops. Arnold owns the warehouses and has Indian Art Galleries in all three cities. He had a legitimate excuse for receiving artifacts. You had Trisha treat the pots chemically with preservatives so drug-sniffing dogs wouldn't detect it. There's even a label warning the handler to call poison control if the chemicals are inhaled. You knew a shipping clerk wouldn't mess with the ollas? Arnold's shipping agents were specialists in moving and transporting artifacts. They don't use the regular shipping channels. A good plan, almost a perfect set up. Lazar dropped off the cocaine at Arnold's Scottsdale warehouse. The drugs were packed in ollas. In fact, you just flew back from Washington; you were checking on a delivery to Azad. Sheriff Cuso met your flight. Want to hear the rest of the good news, Carver?"

"I have a feeling you're going to tell me whether I want to or not."

"You're right," Cierra said. "The FBI picked up Azad as soon as they learned about the dead illegals. He's talking his head off, Carver, about you and the tax scams and how you were laundering money through your land development projects. The Federales arrested Dr. Baxter and his wife outside San Carlos. They had another shipment of crack and a carload of illegals ready to come north. They both are cooperating with Customs. They'd rather be in an U.S. prison than a Mexican one, especially since they could get the death penalty in Mexico. They're all talking, Carver, and they are putting the onus on you."

"Mike Chernov was helpful too. He kept track of your tax scams, Carver, and incidentally, helped unravel the paper trail of how you laundered the drug money into your land developments." Cierra said. "Chernov wanted out, so he set you all up. He had Lazar steal the fetishes and peddle them to Arnold and to the Baxters. When Jack took his broken olla to Trisha, she told him where some of the fetishes were. Sooner or later Chernov was going to let someone know where the stolen goods were. Jack came along at just the right time."

"You're crazy, Deputy. This is a wild story you're making up."

"When we found the fetishes in Draper's storage room, everyone hit the panic button. The Mallorys decided to make a run for it and make one last drug deal with you. When the Baxters couldn't buy back the fetishes from Jack, they went to Mexico to set up one last drug shipment. They were your connection down there, but Lazar was your link to the syndicate, wasn't he?"

"You're doing all the talking, Deputy. I'm not saying anything. Sheriff, I don't need to listen to any more of this."

"Ah, I think you should. It's interesting, Mr. Carver. Go on Deputy. I'm still listening," Cuso said.

"Well, let's see, where was I? Oh, yes, Draper. You were laundering the drug money into this tract development. You needed an impact study that would clear the way. Susan did them for you. Draper merely signed off. Why would Susan do this for you, Mr. Carver?

Carver shrugged his shoulders. "Well, why is because you paid her to do it. At first you paid her cash and later you paid her with drugs. She had a problem with cocaine; she's an addict. You used her and Mike and everyone else. Don't shake your head. Susan's signed a confession and volunteered to be a state's witness. Meanwhile back at the ranch, everyone was panicking; you needed to get the drugs, the shaman's skeleton and the illegals out of the cave. It was a busy night for you, wasn't it? You sent Lazar and the Mallorys to do the dirty work while you waited in the car by the canal. You knew Jack and the Rat Pack were going to be in South Mountain Park. You couldn't afford to have Native American corpses discovered on Jack's property or yours. So you brought in a bulldozer to scrape off the cairns and move the remains into a ditch."

"I was building a road, darling. I didn't do a damn thing like that."

`   "Give it up, Carver. The operator has already shown us where he dug a trench and filled it with the cairns and Indian remains that were on your property."

Carver again took off his Stetson and wiped his forehead. "You're sweating, Carver. Something went wrong that night. The monsoon hit. Quite a lightning show and then the flood came down the canyon. The Mallorys and Lazar were delayed. You saw the lights moving down the mountain. So you went out and did a little sniping to hold them up. You were afraid Jack would get back to the ranch before the Mallorys finished."

"I've nothing to do with any of this, Sheriff." Carver looked at Cuso. "I want out of here. Now! Or my attorney will fry your ass, Sheriff."

"Save your bluster, buster," Cierra continued. "The Mallorys sold you a 45-70. In fact, three of them, according to their records. You paid cash, but Ben marked it in his cash receipt book. It was on his desk. You know, Mr. Carver, I bet that if I check the trunk of your limo, I'd find a 45-70. Furthermore, we've got a mountain of cigar butts. You left one that day on the ridge above Jack's house when you tried to throw a scare into him. You were having a little fun. Well, Jack almost nailed you then. I wish he had and maybe we wouldn't be here now and those people wouldn't be dead. Lazar emptied an ashtray from your limo when you paid Jack a visit. Ruiz cleaned it up. You left another on the ridge when you sniped at the climbers, and a couple more where you parked by the canal. You should give up smoking, Carver. It's bad for your health," Cierra glanced at Cuso.

"You're doing fine, Deputy. Refresh our memories some more." Cuso said.

"Lazar is the one who smokes those damn things, not me."

"Lazar didn't smoke. The autopsy revealed healthy pink lungs. In fact, you have some cigars in your caddy right now. Same brand. Not unusual, but you do chew the ends a bit. We're having a lab conduct DNA testing. Your saliva has saturated the stubs. When I take you downtown someone is going to ask you to spit in a cup."

"You can go to hell, Deputy."

"One more thing, Carver. I traced your tracks from the ridge to your car. I've been wondering, were you signaling the Mallorys about the curve in the road along the canal with your headlights or were you trying to blind them?"

"I didn't signal them. There was a bolt of lightning. It…"

"Yeah, I guessed as much. You didn't do a damn thing to help them either, Carver. You just sat on your butt and when they didn't come up you thought they were all dead. The front doors of the Land Rover were pinned against the sides of the canal. The Mallorys were big men, but they couldn't escape because the back was loaded with pots and the mummy. But you didn't know then that Lazar wasn't with them. He didn't realize that the maze was filling with water and the family was trapped. By the time, Lazar realized what had happened, it was too late. He waited for you or the Mallorys to return to the cave, but you didn't. The next morning, there were too many police in the area for him to get out. Either way, the family would have drowned. And you didn't lift a hand to help. The bottom line is, Carver, the family in the pit, that little girl. They came to El Norte to get away from poverty and oppression and what they got was a coyote like you."

Carver's eyes darted furtively. A cold sweat broke out on his forehead. "I didn't…"

Cierra stepped closer to Carver, who edged back apprehensively. "Cierra! Look out!" Jack yelled as Carver grabbed a spanner wrench off the backhoe and swung it wildly.

Cierra dodged, but the wrench glanced off her shoulder, spinning her sideways. She lost her balance and slid downwards towards the open hole at the bottom of the pit. Carver slung the spanner at Sheriff Cuso. He ducked, but he was too slow. The spanner struck him on the forehead. Sheriff Cuso staggered forward, lost his balance and slid down the gravel landing alongside Cierra, who was clinging with both hands to the side of the bank. Carver looked around quickly and began running towards the ranch house.

"Come on, Dave!" Jack said and sprinted to the side of the pit. He clung to the edge and lowered his body over the side. Dave held Jack by his wrists. "Grab my legs, Cierra," Jack shouted. Cierra grasped Jack's leg with one hand and then grabbed Sheriff Cuso's shirt with the other.

"I've got him," Cierra said. "Now what?"

"Can you hang on, Jack?" Dave asked.

"I'm okay."

"I can't let go, but I'm okay for now," Cierra said.

"Hang tight," Dave said and ran to the backhoe. He began uncoupling a length of chain. Jack glanced at Dave and then back to the ranch house. Carter disappeared into the citrus grove. "He's going after my truck, Cierra."

"Don't worry about him. He won't get far. Just get me and the Sheriff out of here."

"I'm all right." The Sheriff flipped over onto his stomach and started to crawl up the slope. "I'm okay."

"Just stay put, Sheriff. You've got a nasty cut over your eye." Cuso reached up to feel the cut and slid backwards. Cierra grabbed him by his shirt collar. "Don't move."

Dave stepped over the side, one arm looped through the chain and walked himself down to Sheriff Cuso. "I've got you." Sheriff Cuso struggled to his knees. "I'll walk you up." Dave half-tugged, half-carried the Sheriff to the top and eased him over the edge. "Stay there. I'll be right back."

Dave swung back over the side, crab-walked over to Cierra and picked her up with his free arm. "Here we go, Cierra." He walked her to the top and put her down beside Cuso. Dave walked over to Jack, grabbed him by the wrists, and pulled him over the edge. Jack stood up and dusted off his hands.

"Where did the bastard go?" Cuso said, pressing a handkerchief to the cut over his right eye.

"He's going for my truck. Take care of Cuso, Dave." Jack sprinted towards the house.

Dave led the Sheriff toward his car. "I'll call for a back up. He's not armed, Cierra."

"There're guns in the house, Sheriff." Cierra took off running. "Wait up, Jack," she yelled. "Wait for me."

Jack hurdled the back fence, ran through the citrus grove and came out on the edge of the yard. He could hear the rapping of a hammer at the rear of the house. He looked around the yard, nothing was moving. Jack went to the far side of the stable and spotted his truck.

Cierra came up behind Jack. "Did you see him?"

"My truck's still here, but I didn't see him. He could be inside. He could've found my guns."

Cierra pulled her pistol from her holster. The loud hammering sounds echoed off the stable wall. "What's he doing? Carver must be outside."

"You stay here. I'll check this out."

"No way. You go around the side. I'll go through the stable."

"Okay, but be careful. He might be armed."

Jack slid through the stable door and stepped into the first stall. No one was inside. He worked his way from the dark shadows into the sunlight and then stepped cautiously into yard. The pounding stopped just as Jack stepped around the corner.

"Buenos diaz, Jefe," Ruiz said and tossed a sledgehammer to the ground.

"Ruiz, what are you doing?"

"I catch that skunk, Jefe."

Cierra came up behind Ruiz. "Did you see Carver? Did you see a man in a white shirt, Ruiz? He was running this way."

Ruiz sat down on a rock slab, took off his hat and wiped the sweat off his face. "Yes, Cierra. I catch a skunk. The one with the evil eye, Jefe. He's under the house." Ruiz grinned.

Sheriff Cuso drove his Bronco into the yard. Dave and the Sheriff jumped out. "Is Carver here? Did he get away?" the Sheriff asked.

Cierra smiled. "He didn't get away, Sheriff. My Uncle nailed him in there. He's trapped under the house. Tell him Tio Ruiz."

"I was watching from the grove. I saw the Evil-eyed One swing that wrench. You all fell into the pit, and he came running this way. I hid in the stable and waited for him. When he tried to get in the truck, I hit him with the shovel. He came at me, so I hit him again on the head. This time he fell to his knees and crawled under the house and pulled the door shut. When he began pounding on it because the skunk went off, I nailed it shut." They all moved closer to the door. A sweet, slightly sickening odor began filtering across the yard.

"Whew" Sheriff Cuso said and backed away from the door.

Carter began pounding on the door. "Let me out of here. There's a damn skunk in here. It's after me," Carter pleaded.

Sheriff Cuso walked back to his Bronco and picked up his radio. "This is Unit One. Cancel the back-up units. The situation is all clear. I repeat, all clear. I will need a fire rescue team. Secure a pry-bar and about a gallon of tomato juice. That's right; make it two gallons. Tell them it's a safety precaution. We have a skunk problem."

"Take off you hat, Sheriff. Let me have a look." Cierra checked the cut over Cuso's eye. "You're going to need a few stitches. The bleeding has slowed. Keep the pressure on until metro gets here. They can clean it up and take you to ER."

"I'll be all right, Cierra. Let's give that SOB time to think things over. An hour or so with that skunk, and maybe he'll want to talk to us. Better read him his rights."

"I wouldn't get too close, Cierra. Mrs. Hindsquirt may strike again," Jack said.

Cierra walked to the Bronco. The speaker blared from the top of the vehicle. Orange Cat dashed out from under an agave cactus. "You have the right to remain silent..."

Jack sat down on a rock slab next to Dave and Ruiz. Deputy Smith drove up and parked his vehicle behind Sheriff's Cuso's Bronco. He approached Cuso and Cierra. Smith spoke to Sheriff Cuso who listened and then ripped off his Stetson, threw it on the ground and stomped on it. Cierra covered her mouth with her hands and turned away.

"What's that all about?" Dave wondered.

Cierra walked slowly over to them. She swallowed and looked at Jack. "It's Chernov. He's dead, shot himself. Susan took his gun when they were in the helicopter. I didn't think to have her searched at the hospital when I arrested her. I forgot all about the gun. I thought he had dropped it when he fell off the ledge. I didn't go with you to the base of the cliff. I'm responsible for this. I allowed her in to see Chernov."

"God," Jack said. "Why?"

"I don't know Jack. My uncle used to say that some men are too tender to live among the wolves. I think Chernov was that kind of man. Maybe he was afraid of being in prison or trying to live with coyotes like Carver and Arnold."

CHAPTER 25

The Rat Pack stood in a circle in front of the cave watching Dave Gentry seal the entrance with mortar and rocks.

"Where does gold fit into this, Lee?" Wes asked.

"Ask Jack. He figured that out."

"The cross and the triangle symbol for turquoise or blue, and that symbol that Lee told us about, the half-circle, the Indian hand sign for 'something is hidden'. They were inscribed on the back of the glyph with three circles. The one Chernov had taken. He knew the story of the golden cross. He and Susan wrote a monograph on lost Spanish treasure. I found it in the Arizona Room when I was looking for archeological material related to the ranch. Like Kris said. The glyphs read like a Snoopy cartoon. The first one is the lizard that looks like the ground. It's described in the legend. There was a triangle on the reverse side. The triangle is the symbol for blue or turquoise. Morning Blue's people found turquoise where the lizard hole in the ground was located. His people had a turquoise monopoly. They traded turquoise from the Great Plains to Guatemala, from California to the Gulf of Mexico."

"The second glyph Lee showed us was of a kick-ball player. He was a Papago – he had a bone in his hair. He came to trade for turquoise and was a suitor, but he was rejected by Woman-who-makes-sleeping-mats, Morning Blue's daughter. She was impregnated when she put the kick-ball under her skirt," Kris said, and gave birth to HA-AK, who grew up and became the evil witch that devoured the children and they burned her alive in the cave in South Mountain. So the turquoise was real and the turquoise mine was real."

"Exactly. And Morning Blue was a real chieftain, chief of the Big House at Casa Grande. And so was Woman-who-makes-sleeping-mats who was his daughter. Then HA-AK was a real person and burned her or someone in the cave. And inscribed it on that rock. It shows a cave and a ceremonial fire under HA-AK. Then I'itoi much have existed as well," Doc Hartman said.

"Yes. In the legend he moves to a new cave. The shaman's cave on the back of the ridge," Lee said.

"And it was the entrance to I'itoi's maze, also in the legend," Felix said.

"You're right, at least, I think you are. I'itoi was the shaman we found his tools and the gold cross and owl feathers in his cave. The gold cross? How does that fit into the legend?" Wes asked.

"It doesn't fit, Wes. But remember Lee showed us there was a secondary story, not as well done on the backside of the rocks. The inverted cross, Wes said. Yes it was there. The same cross that was on the Marcos de Niza boulder. Also the symbol for hidden and a box around the sign – hidden in a cave. The Spaniards gear was hidden in a cave. I examined Ryder's book of photographs. There're all sorts of arrows, eyes, and signs showing the direction to I'itoi's cave, the turquoise mine. The photos of glyphs that Mollie's friends took back in 1930s had similar signs. Later the Papagos moved the Spanish gear and hid it in the cave with the Mormon gold." Felix said.

"Yes. And Chernov and Susan were looking for the Spanish treasure and the Mormon gold," Wes said.

"Chernov had the icon and the petroglyph that Lazar stole, but he couldn't interpret the symbols. That's why Susan brought Lee to see the petroglyphs in the first place. Both of them were trying to fit the pieces together, but they needed Lee's interpretation of the Indian sign language. Chernov guessed that I had figured out the puzzle or was about to. So he came out to see what I was up to. Susan told him about the photograph of me standing in front of shaman's cave holding a gold cross. The cross was small and crude and that it possibly could have been made by sand casting. I showed Susan the Spanish reals my grandfather had found, or rather that Chance's father and his workmen. Susan told me that they were minted in the 1730s to throw me off the trail. I didn't believe her, so I checked them out with a dealer in old coins when I was in Santa Barbara. They sell a lot of mission era coins over there. The Spanish stopped minting the silver reals with a cross on the obverse in the 1540s. The first coin ever used in the Americas was the Spanish Mill Dollar. My coins are *cobb's*, that's short for Cobo de Boro. They look like a crude piece of silver because they are hand struck, semi-circular and slightly rectangular. Marcos de Niza was authorized by the Viceroy to mint his own coins. On the reverse, he had a cross and the Greek words *chi-rho* stamped on the reverse. The same mark he made on the rock. That particular coin had been used to pay the garrisons in Mexico and Peru. They didn't begin pressing circular coins until the 1730s. So, once again, Susan and Mike were fluffing me off."

"So the reals had to have been left here by Marcos de Niza soldiers," Wes interjected.

"Yes. The Spanish kings didn't trust their viceroys or the officials. Gold objects found in Mexico were melted down and recast into bars. Later they did the same to the gold that was mined," Jack said. "The gold was sent home but the Spaniards paid off everyone in silver. If an official returned to Mexico with gold dust, or gold ingots, he had a lot of explaining to do. At the time the Inquisition was practicing 'tough love' for heretics and embezzlers."

Alex snickered. "That's a good one, Jack. I'll use it in my column."

"That's when you bought the metal detector," Kris said.

"Yep. It was more than a hunch. I remembered Mollie's story about the sheriff chasing the bandits out here someplace where one of them supposedly hid the loot under an ironwood tree. Actually the Yaquis were mining turquoise and actually found some gold in the deposit. They took some to town, spent it on a spree, and the banditos followed them back to the cave, murdered them and took the rest for themselves."

"Like a jack-ass, I had Dave dig up half the ironwood trees in this valley."

"Chance tipped me off, Mollie, at the reunion. Chance's uncle told him what the thief really said: 'Bury me under an ironwood tree.'"

"I'll fix you for that, Chance Clark," Mollie shook her fist at Chance who stepped backwards and pretended to hide behind Wes.

"I didn't want to spoil your fun, Mollie."

"You just wait…"

"That's a good one, Chance," Curly Bill hooted and everyone started laughing.

"Well, I guess the laugh's on me," Mollie said.

When the laughter subsided, Jack continued. "The Pimas ambushed a Mormon wagon train on its way home from the California gold fields and hid the gold in the old mine shaft. That was the gold dust the Yaquis found. Mormon documents verify that the survivors made their way back to Yuma Crossing."

"Let me guess," Kris said. "Someone named Chernov wrote a monograph on the Mormon Massacre!"

"No, Susan wrote that paper and gave it to him to critique."

"Chernov fooled everyone," Kris said, "but so did Susan." The Rat Pack looked at each other uneasily.

Wes studied his feet. "She used us."

"You fellows wanted to show up the archeologists," Star said. "Well, you have and Jack helped you do it."

"To tell the truth, I suspected Chernov. But I thought maybe Susan was in on it with him," Jack said.

Cierra smiled. "So you invited her to clean up at the house, checked her pack…"

"…and left her alone with the photo album and Virginia's diary," Jack grinned. "You told me to look for a woman, remember?"

"Meaning what?" Wes asked.

"If Susan saw the photo of me holding that golden cross and had taken the gun-sight glyph, sooner or later she or Mike would have turned up at the cave," Jack said.

"Then Jack took the icons and gold cross to Trisha," Cierra said.

"Another fishing expedition?" Wes asked.

"In a way," Jack replied. "I remembered Lee's explanation about signs. A symbol for 'bountiful' might be a basket of fruit or a tree full of fruit; it's the same concept, but each artisan would see it in a different way."

"That red blanket on the wall!" Lee exclaimed.

"What red blanket?" Wes asked impatiently. Jack fished a photo out of his pocket and handed it to Wes. Kris looked over his shoulder.

"That's San Xavier," Kris said. "And that one is the Tubac Mission. The one on the bottom is Morning Blue's Ruins at Casa Grande. There's a tree loaded with fruit and an owl beside it. And the water sign…"

"Hidden water," Lee pointed out.

"I got the idea for the symbols on the red blanket. Those symbols on the bottom were taken from Indian sign language. Whoever made the blanket wove in the symbols for water and for fruit trees beside each mission. But, beside the mission at St. John's is a different symbol – an inverted cross. On one side is the symbol for chi and on the other is the symbol for *rho*. The same mark that Marcos de Niza used on his coins on that he put on the boulder at South Mountain Park. Whoever made the blanket incorporated this symbol and placed it beside the mission at St. Johns."

"It's a new sign," Lee said, "and it's a local one. No wonder I couldn't figure it out."

"I tapped the symbols onto the icon with the gold cross that Jack brought me. I used a mallet to tap the gold leaf. They looked just like the ones the old shaman made," Trisha said. "I mentioned the icon to Owens like Jack asked me to. And he told Susan and she told Chernov what I had done."

"But it was a fake," Wes said.

"A very authentic fake," Trisha replied.

"And it worked because Jack had you copy the symbols from the blanket," Lee said.

"I found the symbols for the cross on the Indian blanket. I found a couple in Ryder's collection of photographs and there was one on the Marcos de Niza rock. They were all just indicators that I had seen. So I had Trisha put them on the icon as well as a triangle for turquoise or blue and the sign for hidden."

"Chernov swallowed the bait," Cierra said. "His curiosity got the better of him. He couldn't figure out why Jack wanted a fake icon with gold leaf. So he followed us to the mineshaft. Jack actually had Trisha replicate one of the icons the shaman had made and he had the other icon that Trisha made for him. Chernov couldn't figure out what Jack was up to."

"Why did you do that?" Wes asked.

"Remember I was working backwards. We had all the pieces; I just projected what the missing link would look like. Remember when Lee told us there were some missing glyphs while he was unraveling the HA-AK story. So, I had an exact replica of the stolen icon and on the blank one Trisha incised the symbols from the blanket. This made Chernov think I was up to something. The symbols on the icons really didn't have anything to do with the location of the treasure. The symbol on the blanket was just an indication that the Papagos knew the Spanish had been here and that they had left something behind. And that something was hidden in the ground or in a cave. That same message was on the backside of the stolen petroglyph."

"I'm still not sure how you figured out where the treasure was hidden," Wes said.

"Well, you have to think like a shaman," Jack said.

"He sure did," Cierra said. "I saw him do it. He prayed and then he breathed into the icons and then he set them up and prayed again. It was like magic, well not exactly like pulling rabbits out of a hat."

"That night at the campfire, Lee explained how white men see the world as having one four directions: north, south, east, and west," Jack said, "while Native Americans see their world as having six directions – up and down are the other two – the Sky and the Earth. The shaman left the human icons in his cave. They breathe the shaman's spirit into the stones and pray for good fortune or for a vision to guide them."

"I just put myself in the shaman's place. I pointed the stones in the four directions and put the two icons in the center facing up and down for sky and earth."

"Did it work?" Wes asked.

"Well, in a way it did. Chernov and most white men, myself included, would have looked in any one of the four directions. The shaman was telling us to look up or to look down. There were two sets of eyes in the cave, one pointing up, and the other down. I should have gone up, but went down instead and found I'itoi's maze. But all along the way we found all kinds of arrows and directional signs and we ended up in the kiva. I misinterpreted the spiral…"

"…and the signs in the cave led to water and to the treasure!" Lee said.

"Yes, that's right. But if we had started out in the cave across the wash, the signs and arrows would have led us through the maze and back to the shaman's cave. He must have used both routes. Possibly so he could seem to appear or disappear 'magically' for time to time."

"An old shaman trick," Wes said.

"As old as the Oracles at Delphi," Felix said.

"When we got out of the maze, Chernov was waiting for us. You know the rest," Jack finished.

"Why would a successful man like Chernov risk his life and reputation just to get his hands on some gold relics?" Mollie asked.

"Chernov was an angry and very frustrated man, Mollie. One big discovery, and he could have moved up a notch, maybe to a Los Angeles or a Chicago museum. I think he realized that other board members were beginning to catch on to him as Carver had. So, he was ready to move on. A moving target is hard to hit," Jack paused. "I don't think it was easy for a man like him. He watched others get rich robbing Indian graves. Then envy and greed caught up with him. He used his connections to concoct a series of shady deals. He used the Mallorys, Arnold, and others to dispose of rare kachinas, baskets, and pots from the museum. They split their profit with him, and they supplied him with false appraisals for the fairly worthless artifacts they had exchanged for the rare materials that he then sold to clients like the Baxters."

"A lot of people were involved and they were doing what the Baxters were doing," Cierra said. "The Baxters, in turn, would donate them to an obscure collection like the one at ASU and claim a huge tax write-off, but Arnold and the Baxters were also trafficking in drugs. The FBI have ten investigators checking out Obregon, Carver, Colucci, and a dozen other dubious donors. Chernov cooperated with them," Cierra said. "He decided not to go down alone, especially if the kidnapping charge, which was 'ify', was dropped. The paper trail he created was very complex, sometimes involving five or six transactions. The agents couldn't have unraveled the maze without his help."

"Chernov panicked when the Mallorys drowned with a couple of pots full of drugs. He wanted to distance himself from Carver. He thought Lazar had died in the Land Rover with the Mallorys. He knew they were shipping drugs to some of their mutual clients," Jack said. "In the beginning, he used the money from the deals to improve the museum, but the temptation was too much for him and he began pocketing the cash. Carver, who was on the museum board, caught on and began squeezing Chernov and Susan. Later on, he supplied Susan with cocaine in exchange for false documentation on the archeological sites. Chernov tried to turn the tables and, at the same time, protect himself and Susan."

"I always said that those damn archeologists and curators are all thieves, with the exception of you, Fred, and maybe a few others," Curly Bill said.

"I appreciate that, and so will all the other honest archeologists and anthropologists in the world. And most of them are honest, Curly."

"Tell that to the Indians, Fred. There're skulls and skeletons in the Smithsonian and now the archeologists want to pull up everything they can from shipwrecks on the ocean floor. Ask them why, and all they can say is that we need to bring it up and look at it. What are they looking for? Clues to human history? No. Just loot – anything they can market or put in a museum, draw a crowd, sell tickets and souvenirs. Same old story. They should leave the dead alone."

"Murder? Suicide? Drugs? Aliens? Thieves? Forgeries? Tax scams? Crooked art dealers? What's the world coming to?" Mollie sighed.

"Chernov, Lazar, the Mallorys and that poor Mexican family are all dead. What an ugly business," Star said.

"I don't understand how two capable men could drive their vehicle into a canal and sit tight and drown," Lee asked.

"They didn't." Cierra said. "Carver flashed his lights and blinded the driver. He didn't see the turn in the road and he skidded into the canal. Or it was a flash of lightning? We'll never know for sure. Carver isn't going to tell us. "

"What happened to the Mormon gold the bandits stole?" Mollie asked.

"We didn't find any in the caves. Maybe it's still out there under an ironwood tree."

Jack winked at Chance Clark. He handed her a copy of Chernov's monograph. "It's all in here, Mollie. Good hunting!"

Mollie shaded her eyes and scanned the horizon. "There must be ten thousand ironwood trees out there, Jack."

"But not many real old ones, Mollie. It's a good thing you have five strong boys."

"I think I'll stick to the dairy business, Jack."

"Thank God!" Dave said.

"What about the Spanish relics? What will become of them?"

"They are going to the Pacific Rim Institute, Mollie. They'll be put on exhibition there and then tour other southwestern museums," Felix said.

"I still don't get it," Buck said. "Is the Legend of the Blue Owl really real?"

"Yes, Buck, there is a Legend of the Blue Owl. It lives and will live forever," Felix answered. "A thousand years from now, Buck, maybe ten thousand, as long as the Pimas and the Papagos live. No Blue Owl? You might as well say there is no Santa Claus. Suspend your disbelief Buck. The legend is real. So are the petroglyphs and unfortunately, so are the corrupt land developers and art dealers and other thieves of time."

"So the legend of HA-AK, the Blue Owl, is real and so is the curse," Kris said. "If you have an evil heart, the Blue Owl or I'itoi will cause you a lot of trouble. Don't mess with their spirits."

"We're about there," Dave yelled. The Rat Pack moved closer to the cave entrance. Mollie held Jack back.

"Well, you found your water, Jack," Mollie said. "Out here, that's liquid gold. You can develop your land anyway you have a mind to. But to my way of thinking, the real treasure is Cierra Rose."

"I've thought of that."

"I wouldn't waste any time if I was you," Mollie added.

"I won't, Mollie."

"Almost ready," Dave said. "One more rock will do it." The Rat Pack surrounded the entrance and Jack inserted a plastic bag containing the shaman's amulet, owl feathers, and the gold cross into the slot. Dave finished sealing the hole.

"The fetishes and the old shaman's bones are back where they belong," Lee said. "May they rest in peace for another five hundred years."

"A time capsule? Perfect," Wes said. "It's our secret." The Rat Pack bowed their heads.

Lee began singing the Blue Owl's song:

> *"Tcutcunoni ko'kovoli sis'vunuka-a*
> *Apu tuvavki wunanita*
> *The Blue Owl is bright*
> *And happy when we leave her home alone."*

EPILOGUE

Jack sat on the porch of the darkened adobe quietly sipping a glass of wine and watching the stars. Orange Cat was curled up on a leather stool. Mama skunk, her bushy black-and-white tail arched over her back, led a parade of five kits, their tails waving from side to side, across the yard. Jack and O.C. watched until they rounded the corner of the stable and disappeared into the dark shadows of the citrus grove. "Good-bye Mrs. Hindsquirt. Good luck out there."

Overhead, Altair and Vega were marching across the sky, followed by the Pleiades. Cassiopeia, its lazy W, hung low in the corner of the sky over the Estrellas. A gibbous moon floated ghost-like over the San Tan Mountains. The sage and the desert floor glowed with a silver sheen.

A wraith-like figure wrapped in a soft Kaftan and carrying a kerosene lamp appeared in the doorway. The light flickered and accentuated Cierra's slim figure, round hips, dark hair, blue eyes, and high cheekbones.

"You once asked me if I believe in God, Cierra. There're billions suns out there, and it's all mystery. If God is mystery, then I believe in God. All my life I've wondered where I belong. Now I know. I belong here. I really love this place."

Cierra plucked a crimson blossom off an ocotillo near the porch. She squeezed the base of the bloom, held it to her nostrils, and then drew the pistil down her cheeks creating phosphorescent yellow streaks that glowed in the lantern light. Cierra smiled and said, "I've always wanted to do that."

"It must be your Yaqui blood. You are a Yaqui maiden."

"I brought a lamp just in case either of us wanted to set the house on fire."

"I'm ready to light a fire, but I'm not planning on burning down the adobe." Cierra laughed softly as Jack bent to blow out the lamp. "Your hair smells like rain." He took her in his arms.

"That's the creosote bushes."

An owl hooted in the distance.

"A tecolate. That's good luck."

"Cierra, I thought you said that a tecolate was bad luck."

"Not if it's a blue one."

THE END

ACKNOWLEDGEMENTS

I wish to thank Dr. Frederick Dockstader, director of the Heya Institute in NYC, deceased. He was my friend, mentor, and guide and gave me wonderful advice regarding my unpublished manuscript *Sons of the Tropics* and for his insightful suggestions that led to the development and ultimate publication of *Blue Owl.* Rest in peace.

Phil Garn, former president of the Western Petroglyph Society, did a laborious and meticulous job editing my first draft and my final manuscript. His knowledge and passion for all things western and of petroglyphs was invaluable. If there are errors of interpretation, they are due to me, not Phil, and to my occasional use of "artistic license."

Le Van Martineau whose explanations of rock writing have opened a whole new world of understanding of prehistoric man for me and countless others. I am especially indebted to him for the interpretation and unraveling of the mystery of the Blue Owl petroglyphs, the Pima Legend Stones.

Boma Johnson in my mind is not the only the seminal author on the subject of the Colorado River, intaglios and geomorphs, but also an archeologist who been the foremost advocate for their preservation. We need more men and women like Boma Johnson who believe the traces and memories of past cultures have value and are worth preserving.
I am singularly honored to have men like these as my friends. Thank you.

I also wish to thank all the members of the "Rat Pack." You know who you are and I know what great good you all do, each in your own way have made unique and substantial contributions to the protection and preservation of everything from artifacts to the Bill of Rights.

My thanks to John Prince, Steve Villalobos, Vance Strickland, and Alex and Patti Apostolides for believing and for keeping the faith.

To Dale Garner, a friend for life, who promised that writing would be my salvation. It was and is. Muchas gracias.

To the De Grazia Gallery in the Sun for permission to use Ted De Grazia's painting, HA-AK the Witch, for the cover of this novel and for their enthusiastic support.

To Rocky De Llamas of De Llamas Design and Graphics for the attractive and colorful cover design.

To the volunteers who serve in the Maricopa and Yavapai County Sheriff Posses. They cannot be praised enough for the time, energy, and assistance they render, often at great risk, to the people of Arizona.

Most of all, I wish to thank my wife for the prodigious unswerving efforts and devotion she gave me throughout the development and endlessly time-consuming revisions. Most of all for loving me throughout the web and wheels of our lives and for sharing her sunshine with this moonchild.

AUTHOR'S NOTES

For those readers interested in the Legends of HA-AK, also commonly called Ho'ok, the Blue Owl, I would recommend the following books: Frank Russell's report of his encounter with the last of the Pima shamans; *The Pima Indians*, Bernard L. Fontana's *Of Earth and Little Rain;* Anna Moore Shaw's *Pima Indian Legends;* and George Webb's *A Pima Remembers.* Although the accounts differ slightly in interpretation, the legend remains essentially the same. The Papagos claim HA-AK's cave is located in the Baboquivari Mountains, south east of Sells, Arizona. The Pimas and some Papagos believe her cave was hidden in what today is the South Mountain Park in Phoenix, Arizona. There is considerable evidence to support both theories. It is important to note that some members of both tribes still carry on the celebration, usually in early July following the saguaro blossom harvest. The Papagos are still propitiating HA-AK. There is a cave near Sasabe on the border of Arizona and Mexico where coins are still left in bowls. The Papagos there still ask her for protection for their children.

If the reader is interested in rock writing, I highly recommend Le Van Martineau's *When the Rocks Begin to Speak,* now in its eleventh edition. Garrick Mallery's (1877) early work on pictographs and petroglyphs and Indian sign language *Picture Writing of the American Indians* is excellent. Carol Patterson's *On the Trail of the Spider Woman* is an interesting in that it links myths with petroglyphs and pictographs of the Southwest. Finally, Alex Patterson's *A Field Guide to Rock Art Symbols* is also extremely useful.

For information on intaglios and geomorphs, see the seminal works by Boma Johnson, chief archeologist at the Yuma BLM Southwest District, *Earth Figures of the Lower Colorado and Gila River Deserts: A Functional Analysis.*

Ted De Grazia in *De Grazia Paints the Papago Indian Legends* has brilliantly and beautifully illustrated the HA-AK legend in this entertaining and inspiring work. The permanence of his personality, the presence of the artist, is forever enshrined at The Gallery in the Sun, in Tucson, AZ, in his books, and in his art, but most of all, in the hearts of those whose lives have been made brighter and less burdensome through the generosity of Ted De Grazia. For many years De Grazia, himself of Italian and Indian parentage, maintained a friendship with the Native Americans of the Southwest. During this time, he was especially interested in the Papago Indian legends. With his usual sensitivity to the mystical and the mysterious, he has painted these myths in oils, watercolors, and black-and-white sketches. To these paintings he has added his own word pictures. The reader will notice many similarities to certain Pima Indian legends, such as Ha-ak the Witch. Through his eyes we are enabled to watch the creation of the world. We can observe the dreadful giantess in action. We can watch her transformation from smoke to becoming the Blue Owl. We can view the world from the cave that was her home. We are privileged to meet I'itoi who somehow suddenly becomes a reality to us. Reality? Who can say what constitutes reality? Where is that faint dividing line between so-called reality and mythological representation when it appears on a painting by De Grazi or on a petroglyphs incised by I'itoi? As we view them, a new, strange and subtle reality begins to speak silently to us.

Sons of the Tropics is now Available from Morro Press

Sons of the Tropics, another novel by Wayne Parrish, is set in the 1930s in the unexplored territory of the island of New Guinea, the last unknown in a world that had almost run out of mystery. The exploration of the "Roof of the World" remained the last great challenge. During the economic decline following World War I, the Australians perceived Papua New Guinea as their Pax Africa; a place to step into the international arena. The Canberra government made a decision to pacify the region. The primary task was to civilize hostile tribes and prepare them to live and survive in the modern world. The chief instrument was the creation of a cadre of patrol officers to explore the territory, map the terrain, determine potential economic resources, and prepare the local tribes for the inevitable exploitation of the region by white men. The successful patrol officers became justifiably renowned as "Outside Men."

Patrol Officer Jack Reed is secunded to explore the unknown territory by his mentor Judge Murray. Jack is a rarity, the son of an expatriate Australian couple, reared in Port Moresby where he met the adventurers, the shopkeepers, the missionaries, the colonial officials, the village fishermen, and the nearby hillmen. In this environment, Jack develops a taste for adventure and exploration. He enjoys the companionship of people, but is wary of social institutions. Nature – the forest is his domain.

Jack is chosen over more senior officers to command the expedition to discover an inland route up the Fly River, cross the highlands, and come down the Purari River to the coast; a journey into the "Never Never," the unknown territory. When pressed to explain his choice, Judge Murray replies that Jack possesses the qualities of perseverance and restraint and that he will bring the men home. Furthermore, he won't shoot first and create another

30-year war with the natives. But most of all, it is because the constabulary men trust Jack and are loyal to him.

The second in command is P.O. Tim O'Rourke, a giant good-natured Irishman from Queensland who is well versed in bushcraft and long in patience. Sgt. Manu, a veteran of a hundred patrols, is the NCO in charge of the native constabulary. Somatu, the colorful and complex orderly, is often a thorn in everyone's side, an irrepressible mischief-maker, a morale-lifter, part-conscience, and often the glue that holds the party together.

The carriers, constabulary and supplies are assembled in Port Moresby and the expedition sets out for the Daru peninsula at the mouth of the Fly, the jumping off spot into the lush and foreboding interior. Along the way, they encounter majestic forest, the flora, the fauna, and the mystery of the enchanting river. They trade with tribes, are ambushed by headhunters, are cursed by sorcerers, and discover the Happy Valley, a paradise inhabited by peaceful warriors. Jack has a mystical encounter with the Great Mother, who guides him in the quest to discover the meaning and purpose of his life.

Patrol Officer Jack Reed and his men are marked by their heroic quest and the future courses of their lives are altered forever. Each man, in his own way, becomes a true son of the tropics.